MOB 11/13

17. JAN 14.

17. AUG 16.

08 DEC 16.

MAY 17.

APR

MAY 17

22. OCT 17

15. MAY 14.

JUN 16

07. JAN 15.

24. MAR 15.

APR 15

07. SEP 15.

28. OCT 15

15.

Please return/renew this item by the last date shown

BATH & NORTH EAST SOMERSET

THE COLD EYE OF HEAVEN

THE COLD EYE
OF HEAVEN

Christine Dwyer Hickey

ATLANTIC BOOKS

LONDON

First published in hardback and trade paperback in
Great Britain in 2011 by Atlantic Books, an imprint of
Atlantic Books Ltd.

1 3 5 7 9 10 8 6 4 2

A CIP catalogue record for this book is available
from the British Library.

Hardback ISBN: 978 0857890306
Trade paperback ISBN: 978 1843549895

Printed in Great Britain by
TJ International Ltd, Padstow, Cornwall

Atlantic Books
An Imprint of Atlantic Books Ltd
Ormond House
26–27 Boswell Street
London WC1N 3JZ

www.atlantic-books.co.uk

For Desmond, with love

The mind blanks at the glare. Not in remorse
– The good not done, the love not given, time
Torn off unused – nor wretchedly because
An only life can take so long to climb

Philip Larkin, 'Aubade'

Tak, tak. Zaden, zaden.

15 January 2010

FARLEY IS AWARE OF a blur in his right eye. A bauble of light in the darkness. It fills up, then drains off. Every few minutes it does this – as if he has his own little cistern inside his head. A recurring blur. He chances a couple of words: *hello*, then *blur*. He tries them again – nothing. And so he begins to take stock. It's the middle of the night, he's in the jacks – one side of his face shoved into the linoleum, right shoulder pressed into the radiator. His nose is a few inches from the pedestal of the toilet, and his body, in an awkward curl, lies in the space around it like a dog that's outgrown its kennel. He may have fallen and broken something – that could be it. But there's no pain. There is no feeling at all. He remembers the dark space of a dreamless sleep. Otherwise nothing. It's as if he was born here, with his face nuzzled into the bowl of this jacks.

The thing to do now would be relax. Just relax. Not to go thinking the worst. Get the mind steady before thinking at all. That would be the thing to do now. Like that time years ago, when he fell off the boat into the Shannon. Young then, not that long after he'd started working for Slowey, in fact. The middle of winter, a sparkling cold day, he'd been dressed in thick jumper and boots. Not much of a splash when he fell overboard, down between the side of the boat and the slimy dock wall. The sensation

1

of the water suckling on him. Nobody had been able to believe their eyes when he bobbed back up, un-fucking-drowned, as they had all kept saying later in the pub – *unfuckingdrowned!* And why was that? Because he'd refused to panic. He had surrendered to the water, let it pull him all the way down. And then, as if it had just got fed up with him, it had spat him right back up again. Slowey had often mentioned it after; at the Christmas do or other speechy occasions: 'And from that moment on,' he'd say, 'I knew our man Farley was a *survivor*. Not even the Shannon could keep the bastard down!'

Farley takes in a deep breath. That's it – *relax.* He has a feeling he has to be somewhere tomorrow, or – depending on what time it is now – that could be today. Somewhere important. He seems to remember collecting his suit from the cleaner's anyhow, soft in its cellophane wrapper. And the girl behind the counter with the eyes like a goat. The heat and hiss from the machines behind her. The little moustache of sweat on her lip and how it had crossed his mind that he'd love to lean across the counter and lick it clean. And how shot through that thought had been smaller threads, like was it normal for a man of his age to be thinking that way? And if it was, should he be proud of himself or ashamed? He can remember all that now. But the reason for needing a clean suit?

The dark. The dark still holding the room. Through it he can smell the toilet; layers of old piss-splashes around it. His splashes – it would have to be – no one else had used this toilet in years. It consoles him to know this – he never could bear the stench of the herd. As far as he recalls, the last time a stranger would have used this room was the day of Martina's funeral. Thirty odd years ago that would have been. A queue halfway down the stairs then. Men only. Ladies had to go to the house next door. A sign on the gate had told them so: 'Ladies This Way' with an arrow pointing at the house of – whatever this her name was. Brown eyes she had in anyway. She'd made the sign herself, knocking in first thing to show him. 'Martina would have preferred ladies to have their *own* facilities,' was how she had put it. And Farley, on the morning of his wife's funeral with rolled-up shirtsleeves, one hand tucked into one half-polished shoe and a blot of tissue on his chin where he'd cut himself shaving and a grin in his eyes from something he'd been listening to on the radio, had opened the door without thinking. For a few long seconds he'd stood gawking at the sign, wondering what he was expected to say. Until Mrs Brown-eyes had finally prompted, 'Ah, you know what she was like.' And Farley then duly responded, 'O God, yes I do.'

By the end of the night the sign for the Ladies had fallen on the ground. Slowey's big brown brogue stamped on it as he stood with Bren Conroy waving a sombre goodbye. As if they weren't going to sprint down to the County Bar for last orders, the second they got round the corner. Nowadays people don't hang about at funerals. Nowadays, they say their piece and scurry back to work. Except those with nothing better to do; old folks or garglers glad of the excuse. You'd even see some dressed in tracksuits and trainers. Conroy's son, for example, a few months ago. Turning up to his own father's funeral with his junkie pals in tow. The bony hand when you shook it, the old woman's voice when he accepted condolences, the swivel eye. Better no son than the likes of that.

Farley regrets. What? He isn't quite certain. It could be that he hadn't thought to turn on the light before stepping up to the toilet. It could be something more distant. But he can see all he wants to see for the moment by the light of a lamp post outside; looking in at him like the cold eye of heaven.

The outline of the bathroom around him; the hump of his dirty laundry; the dressing gown, ghoulish on the back of the door. The murky long mirror. And what good would a full 60-watt be to him now? What could it show him? Ancient bottles of shampoo and other squirty stuff that's been lying there for years? His reflection in the bottom of the mirror? A wall of white tiles like a cul-de-sac to the imagination? At least the dark allows him to wander.

His headache resumes. He feels it like a red-hot bulge in the corner of his head. His thoughts return to Mrs Brown-eyes. He wonders why. Why he should keep thinking about the oulone next door? A woman he hasn't seen these years. Not dead though, not so far as he knows. But in a nursing home someplace. The house let out by her grown-up children, to foreigners. He realizes then, it's not the woman he's been thinking of, but the house she lived in. The house next door. Ah right.

For a moment Farley can see her kids. Three of them; standing on his doorstep with cards in their hands, looking to be sponsored for something or other. Plain, timid, little things, rigid in their clothes, always looked like they were coming from Sunday Mass. He'd had a few jars on him, tried being friendly, saying the sort of things he thought you were supposed to say to kids. About school and Santy and how old are you now?

Pardon? They'd said pardon a lot.

Martina used to love buying them presents. Pencil cases in September, masks at Halloween, selection boxes at Christmas. Seasonal stuff. She seemed to get a kick out of doing that. He'd never say but he'd often felt it made her look a bit needy.

He tries to remember the man next door. The father of the three little stiffs. The husband of Mrs Brown-eyes herself. A little chap. Tight arse running for the 79a bus, holding the button of his jacket into his belly. He can see the most of him, the knob of his elbow, his little shoes rising and falling as he trots along, his little grey suit even. But the face?

His own father comes into his mind then. Face unfortunately clear. Died of a stroke, or six months after a stroke, though the stroke was the cause of it. A surly bastard anyway, who hadn't time or a word for anyone. A snarler. He'd snarl at his newspaper, snarl at the radio, snarl if you spoke to him while he was having his dinner. Yet anything like the crowd at his funeral. Standing room only. People his mother had never seen or even heard of before. Later back in the house one of them had made a speech, clipping his whiskey glass for order! Order! Farley and his brother left looking at each other. It was like he was talking about a man they had never met – a raconteur. A wit. A great family man. An honour to have known. A pleasure to have worked with. A fly-fisher.

Farley listens to the beat of his heart. The only thing of movement or sound in the bathroom. A good strong beat, not too fast, maybe a bit on the slow side. The headache has subsided again. Not gone, just taking a little breather. He pictures it like a big thick tongue, hanging over a rock, heaving.

His father had worked as some sort of court clerk, a runner for a judge or a barrister maybe. Farley never knew much about his job, beyond the fact that he'd hated it. And he only knew that because any chance his father got, he reminded them of the fact. No matter what childish gripe you'd come up with; going to school in the rain, or out to the shed in the dark for the coal, he'd come right back at you with his – and what about *me*? How do you think *I* feel? Do you not think *I'd* rather be elsewhere, doing elsewhat? Instead of going into that kip every day. I hate that bloody job. Hate it! Hate it! But then his father had hated most things. Except for fly-fishing. 'The love of his life,' his mother used to call it, with a look on her face Farley had never quite been able to read.

He'd be gone for the day. Sometimes a weekend. Loading up his fishing gear first, wrapping up sandwiches he'd made himself, while Farley looked on and tried his best not to whinge; 'Ah Da, you promised me, you did.'

Farley sees his young self for a moment, clutching the bars of the garden gate, with his brown hair and sticky-out ears, like a little monkey in short pants, bawling his brains out. The sound of the old Morris tittering off up the road, rods sticking out the rear windows, wobbling goodbye. And his mother waiting with a biscuit in one hand and the corner of her pinny in the other, ready to wipe his eyes. 'Ah, he'll bring you, another time. Didn't he promise, he would? There, there now, you'll be grand.'

5

Back in the house, she would sigh into the kitchen, a warm sunny sound, pressing her hands down on the draining board.

The love of his life.

His brother had been indifferent to it all; what do you care where he goes or what he fishes? And he didn't care, not really. He'd just wanted to see what his father was like, happy. And the sandwiches of course. He was curious to see what sort of sandwiches a man like his father might make. By the time he was eleven he'd stopped asking to go. By the time he was twelve the promise had slipped from everyone's mind. Soon enough after came the stroke.

Farley decides to stop thinking about his father. To concentrate instead on a plan. A strategy – that's what he needs. He knows he can't move. That every bone, every inch of his flesh is locked into the floor and that he'll have to rely on his voice. He's confident that there's plenty still in there. It just needs a bit of a rest, that's all. The thing to do would be to wait. Allow the energy to recharge of its own accord. Let it gather and thicken. That would be the thing to do now. When it gets bright, or almost bright. When the youngone from the house next door goes to take her bike out of the shed. That's when he'll let it go. *Then.*

The house next door. The youngone living there now. The tenant. That's right. An early riser, thankfully. A busy, early girl. Off every morning to work in the fish market except Sunday and Monday. He often wonders how she survives down there with her pointy face and dainty ways, in among all those targers. Sonya – was that her name? Sonya or Sofia maybe. Silvia, that was it. From Poland anyhow, or one of those places.

The minute he hears her. Whatever strength he will have managed to save up by then, he'll muster it up, give her a roar. He wonders how many times he'll need to call out? A few times, probably. He'll have to ration himself so, not throw it all out first go.

He imagines her now, unclenching her bike from the other bikes in the shed, and drawing it towards her. Then pushing it a little way up the garden path, a strip of white polyester from her overalls showing under the hem of her green tweed coat. Her wellies in the basket, the Fagan-style gloves on her hands with her little pink fingers poking out. He imagines her stopping just before the side entrance. Cocking up a delicate ear – *what? what was that?* – reversing her steps and the wheels of the bike. She'll frown. Then listen again. She might think she's imagined it. In which case she'll have to call on her housemates for verification. Three Polish blokes coming out to the garden then; tall, high-arsed, fairish. A touch of the Luftwaffe about them. 'What?' they'll say. 'What?' (or whatever the Polish equivalent would be). 'Where? Up there? I can't hear no thing. Are you sure? Are you certain?'

He'd have to be ready for round two then, just at that precise moment to collect, aim, and fire: 'Help…'

And she'd go, 'Now – hear it *now?*'

'Ah wait now – yes. Yes, yes.'

'*Tak,*' they might say. (He thinks that could be Polish for yes.) He seems to remember she told him one day across the back garden wall. *Tak* is for yes, *zaden* – was it? *Zaden* means no. Or maybe it was the other way round.

Farley knows that it must be freezing. A sugary frost on the window-pane, a scrap of old snow on the cill. He should be freezing all over. He should be able to feel the radiator like a block of ice behind him. But he can't. Only on his left side can he feel anything, where the cold is lifting the skin from his flesh. The right side doesn't even notice. It's as if half of him has been cut away and moved to another room. More than anything else – the headache switching on and off; the recurring blur in his eye; the refusal of his voice to come out of its box – it's this uneven distribution of cold that gets to him.

He brings himself back to the matter on hand. The Polish bird – yes. She leaves around six. Unless it's a Sunday or Monday when the fish market is shut. But it can't be Monday if he collected the suit yesterday because the cleaner's doesn't open on Sunday. But it could be Sunday, in which case he's fucked. But he won't think about that, it could be any day as far as he's concerned, except Sunday or Monday. So – she'll leave around six. And she'll hear his call and she'll bring the Luftwaffe out to the garden. The Polish blokes, being blokes, will be reluctant to intrude. They'll have to stand in a circle and have a discussion. They'll probably have to have a cigarette to help the discussion along. *Tak, tak. Zaden, zaden.* Should they call the police? Should they kick the door in? Get a ladder and look in the window? They won't want to involve the police. One of them might ask if she has a key to his house. Then she'll have to explain herself. At this point he could try sending down another shout.

Tumbling ashes. Soft grey light hatching out of the darkness. Farley notes the sudden rush of wind outside, the swish of the trees. He listens for sounds of traffic from the Kylemore Road. A squawk of a near-empty bus, the infrequent snore of a car, a motorbike's buzz. In between, the long silence. For a minute he thinks he's in his grandmother's house, the house where he spent so much of his childhood. Bang up against the wall of the Phoenix Park. When he was a boy the silence never seemed complete. You'd always hear something. Owls or other nocturnals, horses neighing from the army barracks up the way. Even the night sounds from the animals in the zoo. A lonely sound that. It used to make him fret, the thought of an animal howling alone in a cage, no one to heed or help it. He used to have to go to sleep with his pillow over his ears. But he's in a different house now. The house of his adulthood. Another area altogether. For all he knows they're still howling in their cages.

His headache is back, in full form now, pushing to break its own record. Farley feels the bulge rise and expand, rise and expand. A little stronger each time, a little hotter. Lava.

*

He opens his eyes, the light has lifted again, and he thinks he may have passed out for a while and if so, wonders where to and how long he's been gone. Then he wonders about the state of his pyjamas. Whatever way he has fallen, the top has risen and rolled under his arm. He knows this. But he can't remember when he last changed the bottoms and hopes the brown streak up the inside is a memory from a different pair, on a different occasion.

A day last summer comes back to him. The Polish girl hunkered down in the garden, hacking something out of the ground. He'd been busying himself in the shed, keeping an eye on her through the little window. Her dress had been flowery, her shoes made of rubber and he'd been thinking to himself how old-fashioned these people were, with their vegetables in the back garden and their cycling everywhere and their knitting and their second-hand shops where they buy their flowery frocks. Nothing wasted. Like people you'd see years ago. Or people during the war. When he came out of the shed, she had looked up and smiled at him. Then stood and came over to the wall for a chat. She was going later to have a picnic in the Park, near the Furry Glen. And that had seemed so old-fashioned too, a picnic in the Park, something he hadn't seen anyone doing in years. She'd been picking radishes to bring. 'Look,' she had said, holding the bunch up, fresh clay dribbling out of it. 'Everybody, they bring something. I have also a bread I make this morning and chocolate I buy in the new Aldi store.'

He had liked that she told him all that.

Then she had asked if he had plans for the weekend himself and for some reason the question had embarrassed him. 'Ah you know,' he had shrugged, 'just the usual.' And she had cocked her head at him as if she expected more. As if she expected him to explain what 'the usual' meant.

'Well, good luck now, enjoy the picnic,' he had said and began to walk off, afraid that she might think he expected, or even hoped, to be asked in for a taste of her bread.

She had called after him. 'I just wanted to say, if you want you could. You know, give me a key, in case maybe there is ever—'

'Sorry?'

'In case you have. Or you need. If I have your key then I can? In my country is usual when an old person is a neigbour…'

For some reason the suggestion had winded him. He hadn't been able to think of a way to respond, so he just looked at her. And then began to step back.

'Does that mean you don't want to give me the key?' she asked, her face colouring up.

He turned his back to her and kept walking until he was inside the house again, the door closed behind him. He'd been offended. But more than that – he'd been hurt. Hurt and even humiliated. Why though?

Because he had looked over the wall at an old-fashioned girl and liked what he'd seen? Because the truth was he'd had a little smack for her? Not that he would have expected or even wanted anything to happen. He had just liked having the possibility there on the air over the wall, between the two houses. Not that it had made him feel any younger, just a little less old.

Almost light. He can see more clearly now, the rusty bolt that fixes the toilet to the floor, and the white porcelain rise of the bowl's exterior, like a dowager's throat. He can see the pallor of the tiles on the wall, the faded beige folds of his dead wife's dressing gown on the back of the door. And the architecture of himself in the bottom of the full-length mirror on the wall beside it. He follows the curves and angles; the sole of his foot to the cap of his knee, above it a length of thigh. The bottom of his pyjamas are slightly down, flap wide open. It takes him a moment to understand the grey fleshy bloom lolling over his groin and inner thigh. He draws his eye upwards, sees an elbow, a part of a grubby vest, the tip of one shoulder. The jaw then, which looks broken and twisted off to one side. The view from the mirror shows one eye. It blinks at him, then blinks again.

Farley listens. There's a click from the side gate of the house next door. Footsteps. Then the thud of the shed door. The rattle of a bicycle being pulled from the tangle. And Sofia, or Sonya or Silvia down there, unravelling the lock from her bike, standing in a moment to wheel it down the path towards the gate. In a few moments she could be standing right here, in this room. Standing above him, looking down. At him curled like a dog around the toilet, bollix hanging out of his dirty pyjamas. Drooling gob twisted off to the side. One weeping eye.

He opens his mouth, then closes it. It seems uneven, the lips not quite meeting. He goes to open it again then changes his mind. For some reason the dry-cleaned suit comes into his head. He searches for the colour, the texture of cloth. The pinstripe navy? The charcoal grey? Or was it the black – funeral black?

The Suit

14 January 2010

EVERY DAY HAS ITS purpose; a structure on which to pin up his hours. Thursday – the pension; Wednesday – his visit to Jack. On Tuesday he feeds Mrs Waugh's cat while she visits her sister in Skerries. Friday he goes into Thomas Street; buys his few messages, has his weekly ration of pints. And Saturday; Saturday is his day for the garden. Sunday and Monday are a bit loose for his liking. At least, whenever he's looked back on a time to regret, it always seems to have fallen on one of those days. Boredom, he supposes. Other factors too that he doesn't care to put a name on. Before he so much as opens his eyes he rummages for the day and the date. Then he draws up a map of the hours in his head. It's a habit left over from his working days – scheduling was what Slowey used to call it – the ticking off of a list, the margin at the side for the where, what and when of it all. But he knows there's a touch of his mother there too, preferring one thing to belong to one specific day, from Monday a stew day, to Sunday a roast; week in week out, month after month, all the years of her housewifey life.

Today is unique; a day of preparation. He'll be run off his feet. For a start the clothes brush will have to be located, ditto his black overcoat. And in case he decides to go up to the altar, he'll have to check on the soles of his black leather shoes. The two white shirts he left steeping last night will need to be rinsed out and hung up to dry – one for the removal tomorrow evening, the other for the Mass the following morning. That's the thing about funerals, they derail the whole week, giving rise to an entirely different batch of errands; a Mass card, the clothes brush, the shoes, and flowers – he'd better see about getting a few flowers. A wreath or maybe one of those oval-shaped jobs? He'd leave it to the girl in the shop to decide.

Farley stands in the hall, the suit rolled into a bag at his feet, his fists inserted into his good black shoes, turned upside down for inspection. The first safe day after snow. Nothing in the house but cornflakes and butter. He'd better get a few messages while he's at it. A list; maybe he should have considered making a list. He studies the shoes. Just as he thought – a hole in the right foot, the shape of an eye. The left one is perfect. Would he get away with just bringing the one shoe in to be soled, or would that seem like he was just trying to save a few bob? Should he bring both in then, just to prove he's not? He weighs the shoes, stepping them up and down on the air. But what sort of a fool would only get one shoe soled anyway unless only one shoe needed it? He tilts the shoes now to see what they'd look like on feet attached to legs in the kneeling position. The eye still glaring out. He feels a bit agitated, sort of itchy all over, but on the inside of his skin where it can't be scratched. And the light of snow is making his eyes a bit wonky. A short flare of anger warms up his chest. So what if they think he's a skinflint? They either want his business or not. And come to think of it – why is he even considering going up to the altar in the first place? It's not as if he's believed in *that* fucking eejit for more than forty years.

Farley pulls in a long breath and looks at himself in the mirror. Even under his good tweed hat and over the knot of his maroon cashmere scarf, his face has a greyish hue. A small round stain of resentment on each cheek. Cabin fever. Cabin fever on top of a bad's night sleep plus a lack of nourishment. That's all that's wrong with him. Nothing a bit of air, a decent bit of grub wouldn't sort out. He plonks the right shoe into the bag on top of the suit and drops the left shoe onto the floor. And as for going up to the altar? Why wouldn't he go, if he feels like it? What or who's stopping him? It's not a question of believing anyhow, it's a question of belonging. He gives himself a nod in the mirror and repeats the phrase in his head. A question of belonging. Then he tucks the bag under his arm and releases the first chain on the door.

He notices the bag comes from Clery's then and can't imagine why, because to the best of his memory, he hasn't been there these years. A woman was with him last time – maybe as far back as his first suit for work. In which case it wasn't a woman as such; it was his mother.

The phone catches his eye, sitting up there on its crescent-shaped table. He reminds himself that in the past twenty minutes, he's checked it twice already for messages. Once after he'd been upstairs having a shave, in case, just in case. And again when he'd come back in from doing the rounds of his snow-injured garden. No point in checking again. He sets to work on the door bolts, shoving and grinding until, reluctant as old bones, they eventually give and he draws them back; one, two and three. Then, as if to catch himself off guard, he skips back to the table and snatches the receiver from the phone. The earpiece cold on his ear. He listens for the broken signal that means a message is waiting. But all he can hear is the relentless *eeeehhhhhhh* jeering down into his earhole. He replaces the receiver and pulls on his gloves. You'd think one of them, even *one* of them, would have bothered their arses to pick up a phone.

Outside the cold air grabs a hold of his face. His hand, clumsy in its glove, stays on the doorknob. Maybe they left him a note? He toes the corner of the doormat back – nothing but a light skim of ice. Then he checks the letter box from the outside in, in case – alright, a very small note – had somehow got jammed there. But all he can see is a clear view of the hall he's just left, the curly iron legs on the hall table, the shoe on the floor, the smug, silent phone. The mirror.

A dark blue car comes around the corner, a quiff of old snow on its roof. An Audi it looks like, a good car in anyway; something one of the

Sloweys would drive. Farley feels his heart reach out to it. That could be one of them now, come to break the news to him in person. The car slips by, a stranger's face at the wheel. No. No, of course not. He'd had to hear it from Mrs Waugh last night. And she'd only phoned because the cat had gone missing: 'I can't stop thinking the worst,' she had said. 'I mean, every time I open the back door, I keep expecting to find him frozen stiff on the step, like that poor man in Wexford found at his own back door – imagine.'

He hadn't liked to point out that it was hardly the same thing; a man, a cat. And that anyway a cat would be far more likely to survive with its pelt of fur and its natural slyness, than some poor snow-bewildered fool who'd probably just locked himself out of his house by mistake.

'Ah, he'll be back, Mrs Waugh,' he'd said, 'don't you worry, he's just gone off on a ramble, cats are like that, you know.'

'He's been neutered,' she'd sniffed, like he'd been trying to insult the cat's character. And then just as she'd been about to ring off, like an afterthought she could just as easily have forgotten: 'Ah, comere you'll never guess who's after dyin!?'

The way she had said it. Detached but affectionate – the way people are when an old actor or television personality pops off. A distant death anyhow. For some reason Bruce Forsyth had come dancing into his head.

'Who would that be, Mrs Waugh?' he had asked, wondering how much longer he was going to have to stand freezing his balls off in the hall.

'Ah, you know, your man, what's his name? Always drove the big car – even when no one else had a car. Ah God, what's this his name was?'

An alarm went off in his head – the car.

Mrs Waugh cackled, 'Ah, what am I talkin about – sure you probably know all about this already – didn't you used work for him?'

Silence. He couldn't think of the smallest word to break out of his silence. He was sure she would notice and wonder.

'Slowey!' she squealed, all delighted with herself for remembering. 'That's right, Mister Slowey. Of course, I didn't know him meself, just to see, like in passing, he might give a wave out the car and that. Fine-looking man but. They had the house with all the extensions on it – that's right. A few kids – hadn't they? Two boys and a girl? No, three boys. One of the boys emigrated – am I right? '

'Yes,' he'd said. 'No, yes. I mean, no.'

'How old would he have been – in his seventies anyway, I suppose – was he?'

'Seventy-seven last week.'

'Go away! Well, he didn't look that now. Not a bit. Harriet got the impression the removal was Friday, which struck me as a bit funny because you'd think it'd be tomorrow. Like if he died this morning? The snow maybe, delayed matters.'

'Harriet…?'

'Ah, you know Harriet?'

'O, of course,' he had lied, just to avoid a big long explanation of whoever Harriet and all belonging to her might be.

'She heard it in Centra. Anyway. There you go! Another one gone! Which one of us will be next, I ask! So listen – won'tin you not forget now to give us a ring if Shifty turns up?'

'Who?'

'Shifty, the *cat*. If he turns up. And meanwhile if he comes home I'll be sure to let you know straight away.'

'O, please do,' he'd said, as if he gave a fuck about her or her stupid cat.

Farley looks into the snowy estate and slowly lets go of the front door knob – there will be nothing to hold onto for the ten steps or so that it will take to get him from here to the gate. He looks up at the sky, a fragile blue curve above the dark houses that puts him in mind of a china bowl from a long-ago sideboard; his mother's or maybe his grandmother's. Then he pulls his hand through the loop of the bag, settling it in at his elbow. Martina hadn't thought much of Clery's – a dear hole, was what she always called it.

He won't fall, he won't fall. He imagines what he must look like now,

16

dithering along the garden path like a half-pissed tightrope walker, testing each step as he goes. He wonders should he keep his foot light, in case he needs to regain his balance, or should he put the weight down on it, to secure his position? He thinks of the two boy scouts who called to the door during the last big snow in the eighties and tries to remember what's this they'd said was the trick to keeping the balance? Something about turning the toes of one foot inwards or was that outwards? A picture comes into his head then; an upright skier padding along in the snow. He turns in his right foot and proceeds.

At the gate Farley pauses, holding on to it for a moment while he peers up and down the endless road. A mile and a half long – someone once told him. He sees others who have ventured out, moving at intervals, gingerly along, keeping close to the railings. Even the younger ones seem a bit wary, although most of the snow has skulked off during the night. Only a few grey humps remain, along the shaded side of the road, caught against a wall or tucked into a kerb, like mounds of dirty underwear waiting to be brought to the laundry.

You'd think they would have sent *someone*. A grandchild, a neighbour, a lackey even. Or had the Sloweys run out of lackeys by now?

He moves off. Gaining a bit more confidence as he goes, he loosens his stride and firms up his footfall. The lukewarmness of a fizzy sun on his face. No boy scouts this time to see how the old folk are faring. Conroy would have said that's on account of all the child molesters that's going these days. Kiddie fiddlers, Conroy used call them; a term Farley always found a bit hard to stomach. Years ago they'd say a child was interfered with. But then again, that's probably not strong enough either. He straightens his toe, his two feet realign – he won't fall, he won't fall.

His eye grazes ahead, pausing on houses where he knows old people live on their own. People he might never have even spoken to, beyond an occasional nod or a 'not a bad day after' in passing. But he watches out for them just the same, the way he knows they watch out for him. Older people are like that, he reckons. A combination of concern and competitiveness. Who gets through a cold spell, who perishes. Who's been unlucky, who's been a fool. It keeps them going. That touch of glee in Mrs Waugh's voice last night when she broke the news about Frank, for example. Or the way you'd see some fellas in the pub hop on the obituaries in the paper before they'd so much as read another word. Often it would be the fellas in the worst shape who'd be keenest to read, like they were half-expecting to find their own names in there. There was a time you could rely on the house itself to keep you informed. A wisp of smoke from the chimney; a bottle of milk not lifted from the doorstep. Now bar banging down a door and sticking your nose right in, it's near impossible to guess who's in and who's out. Who's lying on their own at the bottom of the stairs. Who's turning into a human iceberg right outside their own back door.

He leaves the estate for the main road where he waits at the kerb for a pause in the traffic. Farley knows he could stand here all day waiting like Moses for the Red Sea to cut him a passage. Or he could walk on down the road to the pedestrian crossing maybe fifty yards or so away. But he feels tired, a bit weak even, and fifty yards just seems way too far. All the sudden fresh air, he supposes. One tingling cheek, like a dentist's anaesthetic beginning to wane. He's as happy to have the traffic as an excuse to stay put. His eye relaxes into the blur of moving cars, his ear is lulled by the dull arrhythmia of passing sounds. He thinks about snow; man's strange relationship with it, almost romantic. The way it lures you into a false sense of serenity with its beauty and silence, and yet would do you, given half the chance.

A few days ago, enchanted as a child, he had stood at the window, watching its dainty arrival. Twilight, and as the light had diminished, the snow had gained momentum. And a sort of yearning had come over him that it would stick to the ground, stay and expand until all the houses and gardens in the estate were swollen with snow. It had grown dark, but he hadn't turned on the light. He wanted to stay gawking out, without the neighbours seeing him. Even though all over the estate, grinning like simpletons out from dark houses, there were probably others just like him; Mr Kerins around the corner, Mrs Waugh in the house backing onto his; the youngone next door. By morning it had already started to turn vicious, devouring his garden, killing his little plants, freezing the blood in his body. Laying siege to him too, making him afraid, making him worry. About food and fuel and the fact that he'd no candles if the electricity went. About the fact that boy scouts don't call any more. Nobody did, nobody would. Not even the girl next door. And yet for all that? He had stood out in the back garden mour ng all that had perished, while at the same time he'd been filled with an inexplicable belief in life, feeding the birds with bits of fruit pulled out of the back of the fridge – stupid fuckin tears in his eyes! He had said out loud, 'I don't want to leave this; I don't want this to be my last snow.' Wherever that morbid thought had come from! Of course, he hadn't known about your man in Wexford at that stage or he probably wouldn't have chanced going out in the first place. Garden or no garden. Birds or not. Elderly, the news had said the man was. Sixty-five years old? Since when did sixty-five become *elderly*?

Behind him a bus screeches and stops. From the corner of his eye the shapes of passengers alighting, tiny and blurred, spilling out of his eyes like tears. He blinks and his vision almost settles. Two youngones, school bags to bosoms, step up beside him, faces turned to the traffic, knees slightly bent as if waiting to jump into the turn of a skipping rope. He decides to take the lead from their young eyesight, placing one foot off the kerb onto the road. But the youngones are too quick for him, and are across the road before he can think, in the careless half-run, half-walk of limbs that don't have to worry about falling. Two men come up behind him, yoddling to each other in foreign voices. Farley wonders if maybe they're his neighbours, the housemates of the little gnome next door. They step around and stand right in front of him as if he just isn't there. Big brawny lumps smelling of baby talc. They don't even break their stride as they cross over, in fact one car has to slow down to facilitate them. Finally, there's a father holding his daughter's hand, patiently listening with a tilted ear. The child breathless to report every inch of her story which they take between them across the wide busy road. Leaving Farley alone.

He looks up the road. Traffic herding over a crest in the distance. There's definitely something the matter with his eyes. The cold maybe? Because it feels like he's looking through a skin of ice. Shapes tumbling into one another, breaking into pieces, then re-forming again. He closes his eyes and shakes his head. When he opens them again, one side of his vision is completely blotted out. A speck of dirt maybe. He pulls his right eyelid to one side, stretching it out, until bit by bit the darkness disperses. He steps back up onto the kerb and passes over the grass verge towards the pavement that leads to the pedestrian crossing fifty yards or so down the road. Yet another thing he knows he will never do again – is stand at that particular section of the kerb, taking his chances, cheating the traffic. He walks slowly under the lean winter trees.

By the time he notices the Hardimans, it's too late to backtrack.

They are standing at the crossing, linking each other; short and sturdy, both dressed in monkey hats and puffed-up coats. Mr Hardiman isn't a bad sort; does a bit of gardening and in the summer evenings they might stop by each other's gate for an exchange of gardenish talk. He wouldn't be too keen on the wife. One of those community types. Always pushing things through the letter box; leaflets about drop-in centres and cake sales or envelopes looking for church donations. Stops him now and then about old-folksy things; a tea dance one time, another time a meals-on-wheels deal. As if he wouldn't prefer to eat his own vomit.

Farley hangs back and hopes for the best as the green man hops up and begins to beep. The Hardimans waddle off. He lets three people go ahead of him and then dips in behind, trying to measure the distance – enough so as to keep out of their sight, but not so much that the lights turn red before he's crossed over. At the same time he has to be prepared to zip off in the opposite direction of whatever direction the Hardimans take. He almost gets away with it, but for the wife, at the last second, lifting her head, like a dog that senses someone behind her. When he gets to the far bank they are standing there waiting like a pair of talking immersion heaters – 'O hello there' from one, and 'There you are' from the other.

'Ah!' Farley says.

'We were awful sorry to hear the news,' Mrs Hardiman begins.

'O, we were,' her husband confirms and for a second Farley doesn't know what they are talking about.

'What happened him at all?' she asks. 'Was he not well or what?'

'Well, I—'

'Did he slip in the snow maybe? Would that have been it? Because the way I heard, it happened in the street.'

Her face is bulged from the cold and there's a jellied, goitred look about her eyes that Farley finds distracting. He looks at the husband. If she wasn't here they could have a conversation. He could ask his opinion on the garden, how best to get it over the cold snap. And he could tell him too, about feeding the birds in the snow with the strawberries the drunken dealer had given him Christmas Eve in Meath Street. He could describe the various reactions; the way the thrush had milled into the strawberries and the blackbird, although a bit more cautious, had tucked in too. And how the one that probably needed it most, the little sparrow, wouldn't go near them: the strangeness of the fruit maybe or the seeds just wrong for its gullet. He could see what Hardiman had to say about that. Bring it up all casual like, so he wouldn't think him soft. If the wife wasn't there, gagging for information, that's what he'd do.

'Well, I better be...' Farley says. 'You know yourself—'

'His heart – wasn't it?' the wife is saying now.

'That's right,' Farley agrees, not that he knows for certain. But with Slowey it was always going to be the heart.

'And the arrangements?' she asks.

'Why, you thinking of going yourself?' Farley says, pleased to see that, although he hadn't intended it, the question has embarrassed her.

'Well, I don't know really...' she falters. 'I mean, we are neighbours, I suppose. At the same time, I wouldn't like to intrude. Although we didn't really. I mean, I might just go to the Mass, and that. It depends really, on the snow situation.'

The snow is gone, Farley feels like shouting in her face. Gone, gone, what is it about you oulones blaming everything on the snow?

21

'Well, right so,' he says, turning away. She puts out her hand to stop him. 'Will the son, the one who's abroad – will he be coming back? Where's this he is again?'

'India, last I heard,' Farley says.

'India!' she goes. 'God, what would possess you to go to a place like that?' Then she puts her mittened hand over her mouth and lets out a horrified laugh.

'I better be…' Farley takes a step backwards.

'Of course,' Mr Hardiman says. 'Anyway, our condolences.'

Farley wants to tell him that he neither wants nor needs his condolences, that any grieving he did for Slowey, he did ten years ago.

'Thanks for that,' Frank says and turns to the wife. 'Goodbye, Mrs Cardigan.'

He hears his own mistake, stands blinking at it for a moment, but doesn't seem to know how to correct it. Cardigan?

'I mean, Mrs, Mrs…'

He sees husband and wife exchange a glance.

'Are you going up to the house?' she asks

'Eh no. Not yet. Later maybe. A Mass card and that; flowers.'

'Still, it'll be nice for the family to have you there.'

'What?'

'I said it'll be nice—'

'Yea. O yea,' Farley says, turning away into a spume of his own icy breath.

The owner of the dry-cleaner's calls him 'a senior' – a title that always makes him feel like he's back in primary school. If she's serving someone else when he comes into the shop, she'll hurl over her shoulder, 'There's a senior needs serving out here!' And the girl with the goat's eyes will come out from the back, with the separate book they keep for seniors snuggled between one floppy tit and a plump upper arm. In the senior book they don't write down your name; they give you a number instead.

Today, the owner is on the phone, fingers lightly tossing the top layer of hair the colour of margarine. Beside her, a pile of clothes waiting to be sorted: trousers, skirts, a red satin dress. Farley waits at the counter, staring into the stains of other people's Christmases. The owner puts down the phone and looks at him. 'You know now that today is not a senior day – you are aware of that? And what that means now is that I'm going to have to charge you full price – is that alright with you? Because if you prefer like, you can come back next senior day which is Tuesday?'

She talks down her nose, voice like a bagpipe's drone. She speaks slowly and louder than necessary and he responds in a put-on telephone voice. Farley isn't quite sure why he does this, except that she's one of those culchies with notions about themselves who love looking down their noses on a Dublin accent.

'I'm aware of that, yes, thank you, ma'am.'

'Well, so long now as you know.'

'I was wondering if I might possibly have it for this afternoon?'

'Well now, you can forget *that* for a start!'

'O.'

'We're out the door here between the post-Christmas rush and I've two inside off with the so-called flu.'

'Well, what about tomorrow morning then – if that would be convenient?'

'Are you joking me now or what?'

'It's for a funeral,' he says and for some reason feels ashamed for mentioning it.

The phone rings and she reaches out for it, leaving one hand behind splayed on the counter. He cranes to see into the back room, wondering if the girl with the goat's eyes is in there. His sight is still a bit wobbly but he notices this is only when he lifts his eyes to the middle distance. Little bursts of minute crystals, rotating on the air. He peers under this display and his sight begins to clear again. There now, he can see her in the back, the rise and fall of her ample arm, pushing the presser on and off a stretch of steaming cloth. He feels a rush of warmth in his veins; his arms, his legs, his groin. He doesn't know why he fancies her nor does he know how he possibly could. In fact, every time he sees her he gets a small shock at how, not so much ugly she is – he wouldn't like to say that exactly – but certainly, peculiar looking. And yet anything like the dirty dreams he has about her! By times he can barely look her in the face he's so ashamed of them. The dreams are always set here, in this shop; the pair of them hard at it – in the back room with steam pumping all around them; on the counter sliding and slipping off each other's sweat; even standing up against that big drying machine there gyrating in tune with the big drum inside it. Any and every way; backwards, forwards, sidewards, him well able for it, and she loving every minute. And really, the poor girl has nothing going for her at all, no figure, no face, certainly no personality – except maybe that in all the years she's been working here, she never seems to have aged. Skin like a pig's, if the truth is told – all the heat he supposes. Makes her lazy too; even the way she speaks, the effort it seems to cost, like she's talking with her mouth full of oats. And as for the mad-looking eyes. But for all that, he fancies the arse off her and has done so for years.

The owner's hand lifts from the counter, fingers click and begin to beckon the Clery's bag as if it has a mind of its own. He slides it across the counter to her. Farley looks at her; she thinks she's so posh, the state of her, with the fancy tailored suit as if she's running a big international company instead of a poxy little dry-cleaner's. And the face plastered in so much greasy brown shite you can hardly see her nose. And the skinny lips like a pink elastic band. She catches his eye, he gives her a nod and a small half-smile.

The heat is making him dozy, the churn of background machinery; the fumes and the tumble of clothes in the machine. The owner, still yapping, lifts her hand again; this time it begins pulling the suit out of the bag. The shoe comes along with it, toppling off the counter and onto the floor by her feet. She's looking at him, an irritated glint in her eye. She puts her hand over the mouthpiece of the phone and goes, 'I *said*, would it get away with a pressing – do you think?'

Farley looks at her, puzzled.

Her hand idly turns the jacket of his suit, turning the cuffs, lifting the sleeves. Then it starts on his trousers, passing up a leg, brushing an inner thigh, patting and pulling at the mickey area – '… right so, right, right, and the same to you, happy New Year – o, I'm sure, I'm sure. Goodbye to you so and best to herself.' She slams down the phone and looks at him. 'Ah no, a pressing would be *useless*,' she says, as if it was all his idea, ''tis a good cleaning this lad needs.'

Farley tries to cover his embarrassment, wrapping it up in a joke. 'When you get to my age, the only suit seems to get any wear is the black one. Probably I could do with a new one but like – is it worth the expense at this stage of the game, I ask myself?'

'Indeed,' she says, the joke slipping by her.

She thinks it's his only suit, probably. He wants to put her right. To tell her about the other suits; five of them hanging up in his wardrobe, two still in cellophane, cleaned in this very shop. He wants to describe them; the navy pinstripe, Italian cloth. And the charcoal grey that he bought for business – a Savile Row label on the inside. And the summer linen he bought three summers ago and never wore once because he's still waiting on a decent summer's day to coincide with a worthy outing. And what about the tweed job that he's wearing this minute? He wants to open back his overcoat like a flasher and show it to her: 'Here, take a look at that, missus!' And then there's his tux. Granted, he bought it years ago from the hire place at a reduction – but she doesn't need to know that.

'Unless I start wearing me tux to funerals,' he says, with a half-wink so that this time she knows for sure that he's joking.

'Ah now, I wouldn't go doing that if I were you,' the owner says, pulling the docket book to her, 'there's fellas been locked away for less.'

She opens the book, then closes it again and looks into his eyes. Pity, he sees or an attempt at pity. Because for some reason he doesn't believe it's genuine.

'Tell you what,' she says, 'seeing as it's a funeral, we'll let you have the senior rate.' She roars back over her shoulder, 'Will you bring the senior book out here to me a minute?' Then she comes back to Farley pointing her pen at him. 'Just this once, mind, and come here to me now, don't you go telling the other seniors. Or I'll have you hanged and quartered.' The owner looks satisfied, relieved even, to have got her good deed for the year out of the way.

The goat's eyes pass behind the owner, the senior book tucked into its enviable position. He remembers one time in the County Bar, years ago now; Slowey, himself, Conroy, Brophy. Slowey opening the paper to a photograph of Boris Yeltsin. 'Jaysus,' he said, 'wouldn't you think he was related to your woman in the cleaner's?'

'O yea,' Conroy added, 'if Yeltsin married a pig and they had a baby.'

He should have stuck up for her. He'd wanted to. But of course if he did, the rest of them would have sensed something; given him a slagging that he'd never hear the end of.

He speaks to the owner. 'Well, thanks all the same but to be honest, I don't mind paying full whack, I don't mind in the least. So long as I can be certain of having the suit for tomorrow, you know?'

She looks at him again and the pity is gone. The pink elastic band tightens. 'Suit yourself. But it'll have to be tomorrow *afternoon*, mind. That's the absolute best I can do for you now. Full price so.'

In the heat of the shop, Farley feels something gather inside him. The sound of the machinery, the heap of stained clothes, the hard blue eyes freed from their pity, the senior book with the numbers instead of names. And he feels an urge to click his heels and give her a Nazi salute. To call her a jumped-up fuckin Nazi bitch.

She hands the pen to the girl with the goat's eyes and flounces off into the back of the shop.

The girl lowers her voice to him across the counter and one by one the words crawl out. 'Come back abou' half five and I'll have it for you.'

Farley looks into the back room. 'What about the boss?'

'Ah, don't worry about that oul fuck, she'll be gone for the afternoon.'

She gives a small sweet grunt as she bends to retrieve his shoe from the floor which she then hands to him, sole facing out, hole looking up at him.

She's put on even more weight over the Christmas, rolls of fat pressing against her lime green jumper, diddies floppier than ever, legs poured into those black trouser things that look more like tights. He wants to lean over the counter and lick her face, then ask her to marry him right on the spot. He nods and takes the shoe, turning for the door.

She calls after him, 'Here?'

'Yes?'

'Your Clery's bag.'

She takes the shoe back from him, places it inside the bag and pushes it across the counter.

'The wife,' he hears himself say then, 'the wife, you see, wasn't that keen on Clery's.'

'Yea?'

'A dear hole, is what she called it.'

She lifts an eyebrow. 'Righ'…' she says, her voice full of doubt.

On the pavement outside the dry-cleaner's, Farley stands, one eye involuntarily winking; his right one, leaking again. He pats it with the back of his gloved hand. Cars parked all around him. The rear of a stationary bus farting out a long bloom of fumes. Farley stares at it for a while and wonders – what's he doing here? What does he want? He looks around; behind him is a row of shops. That's right, the shoe.

He heads into the newsagent's and immediately has to step back out to check the name above the door along with its position in the row of other shops. Both as they should be – yet inside the shop is all wrong. It's too small for a start. And the L-shaped counter has been replaced by a single short one blocking the entrance to the side corridor that should hold the barber, the shoemaker, the fella who cuts keys, a few others too, each at their own little higgledy station. Where's the speckled floor, the drifts of damp sawdust? The litter of sweet papers and lolly wrappers all over it? There should be things hanging out of the ceiling or thumbtacked all over the walls: fishing nets, plastic dolls, ropes of chewing gums like shrunken golfballs. And how come, instead of the usual sour-faced oulones serving behind the counter, an Indian chap is smiling?

He stays in the doorway trying to locate himself. The Indian nods encouragingly.

'You've changed the shop around?' Farley asks.

'Excuse me?'

'The shop, have you, you know, got rid of half of it?'

The Indian glances quickly behind him. 'Em, no, sir. I don't believe so.'

Farley thinks for a moment. 'Well, are you not doing the shoe repairs any more?' He pulls the shoe out of the bag and holds it up to show.

'O, we don't do anything like that.'

A woman's voice behind him. 'Can I get by you there?' and Farley quicksteps out of the doorway into the shop to make way for her. He shows the Indian the shoe again, pointing to the hole in the sole in case the chap's command of English mightn't be the best.

'See, I'm looking to have it repaired,' he explains.

The woman says, 'Ah now, you're goin back a bit, aren't you? It must be years since the shoemaker was in this shop – ah ah, showin your age there, you are.'

Farley looks at the woman; not all that young herself, if it comes to it but her eyes are smiley and he sees that she's speaking to him as an equal, as if to say 'we all have our vacant moments'. She's holding a small fat child by the hand. The boy staring at the shoe. Farley feels like giving him a wallop with it on the back of his head. He struggles with the bag, trying to get it to take the shoe back as quickly as possible. His hands are shaking.

'Well, have you a Mass card then at least?' he barks at the Indian.

Outside, the ground tilts as if it's moving away from him. And it feels as if he's slipping in slow motion – a patch of ice maybe? But when he looks down his feet are steady to the ground. He feels a bit lost. Like he's fallen asleep on the bus with a few jars on him and gotten off at the wrong stop. Everything is different and yet he knows it's still the same. The roundabout is missing; that's it. The roundabout that should be there in front of him, in the middle of that crossroads, right there – is gone. And the pub across the road is all changed; painted a sickly colour for a start with a stupid-looking clock tower stuck on one side. His left arm feels numb – he swaps the bag over to the other hand – still numb. Out of nowhere the Berlin Wall comes into his head and he has to wonder now about the state of his mind, all the things muddling around inside it: shop counters, roundabouts and now – for fuck sake – the Berlin Wall. He sees the woman from the shop standing looking at him, the youngfella behind her, gloves flapping from his wrists as he plunges his hand in and out of a bag of popcorn.

'Are you alright there, love?' the woman asks.

'I've an awful headache,' he says, 'sudden like.'

'Do you want me to phone someone for you?' she says.

'Who?' Farley asks.

'Well, I don't know – a relative, a neighbour maybe.' He can see by her face she's beginning to regret that she stopped at all. The youngfella, munching on the popcorn, staring up like he's at the pictures.

'Ah no. I'll be grand. It's going now anyway. Just came on sudden and now – that's it, gone.'

'Ah, it's this bloody weather. What you should do now, is go into the pub over there and get yourself a nice hot whiskey – put a bit of heat into you.'

'I don't drink whiskey. Not any more. I drink two pints a week – would you believe that? On Friday, usually. The same thing this years and years. In fact, I didn't drink at all for a long time – bar the odd breakout.'

'Well, a cup of tea then,' she says.

'I will,' he agrees, because he knows she only wants to leave some sort of a solution behind her. 'I've a few things to do first but then, a cup of tea.'

'Well, if you're sure you're—'

'The roundabout's gone,' he says.

'What? O yea, that's gone this good while.'

'O yea, yea, of course I *know* that. I just saying like. And the pub's different.'

'That's right. They done it all up.'

'They did yea. Nowhere for the men to stand though on Sunday after Mass.'

'Ah no, that day is gone. Do you remember? Droves of them with their tongues hangin out.'

'Yes!' Farley smiles. 'The Berlin Wall, we used call it. Where they used to stand. The Berlin Wall – that's right! That's right.'

She gives a little laugh. 'Me mother used go mad.'

'"May I never lack the dignity" as a friend of mine always said,' Farley says. 'He thought it was a shameful thing to do – I suppose.'

She nods her head a few times at him. 'Well, I better be gettin this fella home.'

'Ah yea, a grand little fella there, eatin his... Eatin his... His...'

She begins to walk off, dragging the boy behind her.

Farley calls after her, 'Excuse me, you wouldn't know where I'd get a new sole?'

'A new...?'

'For me shoe.'

'O, for your *shoe*,' she laughs. 'Town I'd say would be your best bet.'

'Thomas Street?'

'O yea, Thomas Street should do it.'

'Right. Thanks so. Good luck to you now.'

Farley watches her walk to the corner, the youngfella straining at the end of her arm to look back at him. He'd love to give him the two fingers, but he'd be afraid she might catch him. His eyes again; the halo of lights. He waits for it to subside. Better now. A bit on the weak side but nothing to worry about. He'd just slipped back into a past moment there for a while. And now he's back. Popcorn. That was the word he was after.

*

There's no answer from the priest's house. He thinks he can hear someone moving around in there and so presses the bell again, this time adding a double bang from the door knocker for good measure. Then he peers through the ridged glass panels on the side of the hall door. Inside the priest's coat is hanging on a rack, the housekeeper's red anorak beside it, her welly boots on a mat on the floor. On a long shelf by the wall a few letters and holy Joe pamphlets. There's a full-sized statue of the Virgin leaning against the opposite wall, taking up half of the hall in fact – a statue, if he's not mistaken, that used to be outside in the garden. On the shelf there's a smaller version of the Virgin, and another on the cill of a window halfway up the stairs, although he only has a restricted view of this one; feet standing on a bed of plaster roses. A shadow scurries over a door at the back of the hall that he presumes leads into the kitchen. Quickly he presses the heel of his hand on the bell, gives the door another sharp knock. Then he bends to the letter box and sends his voice in. He wants to say – *Hey you, I'm not blind, you know, unless I'm supposed to think it's them statues is moving?* But instead he says, 'Eh hell-o-oo, sorry to disturb you, but I was just looking for the priest, to sign a Mass card for me.'

He listens. A door closes. A hoover begins to howl. Farley feels a ping of rage in his right temple.

He comes round to the church. The door is locked, the gates chained together. 'Ah, for fuck sake,' he says aloud, holding onto the bars and staring in. 'I mean, Jaysus, what if someone actually *needs* a priest?' A man comes up beside him, pushing a bike with one hand.

'Alright there, Farl?'

'Yea,' Farley says, 'I was just looking for the priest, you know.'

'I'm Timmo's son,' the man says as if he can read Farley's thoughts, 'you remember Timmo?'

'O yea, Timmo,' Farley says.

'I work in the hospital.'

'O yea, sure I know. I know that. Timmo's son. The hospital.'

'I look after Jackie.'

'Of course you do.'

'How are you keepin in anyway – alright?' the man says.

'Ah, you know. Not too bad. Bit of a headache earlier, but that's gone. And the oul eyes have been giving me a bit of trouble, other than that – not a bother.'

'The headache's probably on account of the eyes. Better get them checked out, Farley, you need your oul eyes. Do you not wear glasses?'

'Just for reading and the telly and driving and that. Well, when I used to drive. So just for reading and the telly now.'

'Better get them checked anyway.'

'Ah I will, I will. But I'm too busy now. Maybe next week.'

'Bad bit of news that, about Frank Slowey.'

'Yea, it was alright.'

'An interesting character. Very intelligent, I always found.'

'O, he was. He was that, alright yea.'

The man blows down into his fist. 'You shouldn't be standing around in the cold, Farley. The next couple days'll be tough enough on you. Anyway, listen I'll see you at the funeral – right? I'm working tonight so I won't be going up to the house.'

'The house.'

'You know he's reposing at home?'

'What?'

'He's reposing at home, there's no removal.'

'O, I know that, of course I do. So the funeral's…?'

'Tomorrow. Ten o'clock Mass.'

'Tomorrow, that's right. I wasn't sure if they said ten or half, you see.'

'Well, now you know.'

'I do. Anyway, I better be, I've a load of things to do. Up to me eyeballs.'

'Ah, take your time, nothin is that important.'

'That's all very well to say. But see, I have to get the Mass card signed. And like they won't even answer the door around there. And then. And

32

then, I've to go down to Thomas Street for a new sole and that, and come back and collect me suit and your woman, the housekeeper that oul bitch is pretending not to be in and like I can hear the hoover and all. As if I'm a fool or something. These people. Who do they think they are? Just who? They should be trying to win people over, not the opposite – am I right? I mean, they'd take a statue in out of the cold before they'd give a fuck about another human being.'

Farley stands gulping at the shock of his own little speech.

The man puts a hand on his arm. 'Relax, Farl. He's not the only priest in the world – is he? There's a church in Thomas Street, you know. Churches all over the city.'

'Sorry, sorry. It's just... I didn't mean to sound disrespectful but you know?'

'You're upset, Farl. Don't worry. It's understandable; you've just lost your pal. Look, do whatever it is you have to do, but try get a little rest – wha? God knows you worked for the man long enough.'

'I was a partner in that firm, you know.'

'That right?'

'Yea, I was made a partner. I didn't just work for the man, you know. You don't believe me?'

'I do, of course. I just never heard that before.'

'Well, it's true. A partner. For years. And not one of them. Not one of them would bother. Well. Never mind all that.'

'Look, when you're finished in town, get yourself home and have a snooze by the fire. I'll tell Jackie you were asking for him and see you at the funeral – right?'

'Yea. O, bye now. And tell Timmo I was, you know, asking for him too.'

The man looks at him funny, then gives him a half salute and pushes off with his bicycle. Farley watches till he's out of sight.

He crosses the road, heads towards the bus stop and wonders – whoever Timmo's son is, he must be well in with the Sloweys all the same, if he was thinking of going up to the house. But at the same time he couldn't be *that* well in, if he didn't know about the falling out. Timmo? Timmo's son? And who's this Jackie is again?

The bus is jammers. He's sitting upstairs, as he always does because he likes looking down on other people's gardens, giving them marks out of ten for appearance. He's sitting upstairs in the solid, stuffy air, the windows fogged with the breath of strangers and some little bollix down the back smoking a cigarette – but who's going to say a word to him? One vacant seat on the right, two thirds of the way down. Farley goes to it, then settles himself in by the window, Clery's bag on his lap; the shape of the shoe, the corner of the Mass card – everything in order. Grand. Around him people are talking into mobile phones. Mobile phones are beeping at people. One girl roaring at the top of her voice: 'So I just said to him, yea? Is that righ'-is-it? Because if you fucken tink I'm puttin up with that you can go and fuck right off and you and your scabby bleedin oulone.'

Farley tries to remember when this started to happen – people shouting on the bus, letting everyone know their business; turning their minds inside out, broadcasting every thought in their heads.

Near the front of the bus, two large African women, startlingly dressed, sit across the aisle from each other. As they speak, huge hats like big paper bags plonked on top of their heads, nod softly to each other; flax yellow to scarlet red. That's how it should be. A quiet conversation, a little bit shy, a little bit open; let people eavesdrop because they want to, and not because they've no choice.

He stretches up to open a window, glancing around as he does so, as if he should be asking someone's permission. A squirt of clean, sharp air quenches his face. The woman sitting in front runs her hand over the back of her neck, gives a little shudder and tuts. Farley pretends not to notice. He sits down again, rubs a viewing screen into the steam on the window and looks out. He wants the bus to slow down a bit so he can look at the gardens. But the bus, too full to stop, is barrelling along. All he can see is rows of houses jigging loosely by, like old-fashioned freight trains; flat green, dirty white, brown.

In the seat just behind him, a man and a woman are talking, voices pitched secretively low: 'Look at them, just look at them,' the woman is saying, 'make you sick, it would. There must be a shipment in or something – I mean, you can just feel the buzz in the air. Make you sick they would.'

And that's when it comes to him – the pension – did he collect it or not? He just can't remember. He has an image of himself standing in the post office queue, surrounded by people lumpy in winter clothes, shuffling one by one to the top. He has a memory of the recurrent thump of a rubber stamp, and he can remember too, turning around to see a woman fresh in from the cold, going, 'O Jaysus, I'm blinded,' as her glasses clouded up from the sudden heat. But he doesn't know was that today or another winter's day? Last week, the week before? Years ago, even? He takes off his gloves and puts them in the Clery's bag, then slips his hand into his inside pocket. He can feel the pension book there, the wallet stuck in behind it. At least he wasn't dipped. At least, that much. He's getting ready to pull them out to have a look, when he hears the pair behind him again.

She says, 'Scumbags is all they are. Look at them, rob the hair out of your head for a hit, they would.'

Farley looks around and sees what she means – junkies all over the bus. Better wait till he's somewhere safe before he goes opening his wallet. There's one squirming in his seat across the way; another with a twitchy face further down the aisle. Two more of them are whingeing to each other with their underdog eyes, like everyone else is to blame for their great misfortune. Ghosts, that's what they're like. Ghosts in purgatory. He feels nervous now – worse than nervous – afraid. Of being on this bus full of ghosts. He has the sense that if he doesn't get off quick, he might not get off at all. That he'll snuff it here on this very seat. He raises himself, begins to gather his bag and gloves. Then he sees a woman's head appearing at the top of the stairwell. A big heap rising slow and full like a genie coming out of a bottle. He sees her eye wandering down the aisle and stop at the space beside him. Farley sits back.

It's alright, it's alright. Everything is going to be alright. Hasn't his headache gone, his eyesight cleared? Hasn't he enough money left over from last week's pension, thanks to the snow and no opportunity to spend it? Enough to keep him going till tomorrow because that's when he'll really need it, that's when he'll want to haul out his wallet, open it up for all to see – 'No, no, this one's mine now, I insist, I insist' – stuffed with you-can-all-go-fuck-right-off money. Everything is grand. No headache, clear vision, money in wallet. And a big fat woman squeezing down the aisle towards his seat to protect him from all the ghosts. He flattens himself in against the window.

Downstairs, the bus driver is as black as Foley. Farley asks him if he knows of a shoemaker's shop in Thomas Street. He doesn't. 'Not even when you'd be driving by, like?' he asks and the man gives an apologetic shrug. Farley stays near the door, keeping an eye out for his stop. The traffic is brutal, budging for a couple of seconds then halting for ages. He wonders who Foley was; where the expression came from, and if it's a racist one. Because as far as he can tell, the only way not to be racist is to pretend you don't notice if a chap is black. Or pretend you don't notice him at all. Coloured people – that used be the polite way to describe it, but now, as a woman at the bus stop recently told him, that's the height of racism. The height of racism? Surely there must be worse than that. His mother used to have a coat she called nigger brown. And a barman in the Four Courts Inn had a dog one time called Nig-nog. You could call that racist alright. Or what about that Spencer and his mates, giving out stink about 'them blackies stealing our jobs'?

'What jobs?' Farley had said to him. 'Sure you haven't worked since you were twenty.' Spencer, not a bit pleased, had kept a coolness between them ever since.

He glances at the driver; skin like a soft black chamois leather, beautiful really. All the different faces you'd see now around the place: Asian, Chinese, African – like this chap. Takes the pasty look off the general population. Foley now was probably a coalman. Someone is watching him. Farley tightens himself up, pulling his coat in closer to his chest so he can feel his pension book and wallet, tucking the bag further under his arm, turning his body towards the driver. He feels a tap on the arm. It's a man with a face he knows from the Thomas House pub, also waiting to get off the bus. But he doesn't know his name. This doesn't bother him because he knows he never knew his name in the first place. He's just one of those blokes who presume a friendship.

'Just on the way back from the hospital,' the man says.

'Is that right?'

He takes out his tablets and starts to show Farley. 'This is for the water-works, this is for the blood pressure, them yellow there's for the arthuritis, and these here, you see, is for *before* all the rest of them, to protect the stomach – are you with me now?'

Farley nods politely at each brown plastic bottle. 'Would you know if there's a shoemaker's near abouts?' he asks.

'Nah.' The man shakes his head. 'No shoemaker's, no bootmender's, no any kind of shops in the Liberties any more except those all-night jobs selling overpriced rubbish, rubbish, rubbish. That's Baker's pub gone – remember Baker's? Yea gone. And Roger's, that was a grand pub, for a quiet pint like when you'd wouldn't want to run into anyone. And of course Frawley's. Did we ever think we'd see *that* day? And what are we left with now – kips like that one across the road.' The man ducks to look at a pub on the far side of the street and Farley follows his example. 'A venue – it's called. Or so I was told when I went in to chance a pint there. Do you know what that is – a venue?'

'Emm?' Farley says.

'Well, I'll tell you. It's where you go to listen to people singing who can't sing and eejits tell jokes that aren't funny and for fools that'll pay to hear them doing it. And as for them three yokes on the path out the front of it – would you mind telling me now what they are?' He says this with a tone of accusation. Farley frowns out the window at three big multi-coloured sculptures.

'Would they be puppets, maybe?' he finally suggests.

The man's eyes open wider: '*Puppets* – is that what you call them now? I see. Is that it now?'

The man's voice is raised; angry. Farley looks away in case people think he's responsible for the puppets. He looks at his watch, then pretends to root for something in his bag. The man takes a step nearer to him, lowering his voice and tapping him on the arm, speaking confidentially. 'Your best bet now would be stay on the bus right into town and be the back of Clery's shop near Cassidy's pub – if that's still there of course. You'll find a little place'll do the job for you.'

'The job for me?'

'On your shoes like.'

Farley gets off in Westmoreland Street; dank, cold and greasy. Junkies to the left and right of him, slithering off the bus, slipping around corners, melting into the inner shadows of this already shadowy street. The clash and wallop of noise; Irish-flavoured music from gaudy interiors of souvenir shops; buses wheezing and squawking like wounded animals. Motor cars. His head starts hopping again. Two foreign gypsies, long skirts and shawls, come sidling up to him, whimpering a begging prayer. A long thin hand comes out of a doorway asking for change. Another gypsy is changing a child's shitty nappy on the step of an office. She folds it over and just fucks it there on the ground before hauling the child back up on her hip and moving away. He reaches the corner where yet another junkie, hood pulled over his head, is whining into a mobile phone. Farley stands a few feet away from him. From the side of the hood, an eye surveys him. Farley moves further away. Twenty years ago he'd have planted the bastard. Ten years ago he might have even tried.

He puts his head down and keeps his walk brisk until, in a step that passes from shadow to light, he finds himself in the centre of the bridge.

The sky clear and broad, the river air cold and sweet, the light sitting on water like cut glass. The ghosts all departed now, Farley sighs through his teeth and squares back his shoulders; stronger now, renewed. He has walked through his fear. He's alright.

It just goes to show you, Farley says to himself as he comes out of the shoemaker's with an hour to kill. It just goes to show you, he says it again, while he tries to shape and capture the end of the sentence into whatever it is that it just goes to show you. Ah yes – the way you'd be worrying. Worrying about things like the business with the shoe and being thought of as a skinflint and after all that, there was no need to explain himself or make up a story about a one-legged brother. 'Can you fix that shoe?' he'd asked and been told then to come back in an hour. Bang, deal done and no more about it The shame of poverty, Farley wonders, does it ever really leave us, no matter how distant or dim?

An hour to kill, that's all he needs to remember. An hour. He looks at his watch, just gone eleven. Across the street a large group of men are standing at the wall smoking and talking; a look about them, slightly run-down, a shimmer of danger; eyes watching his every move. On this side of the road, just outside the pub, a girl in a red coat is smoking, hands mauve with the cold.

'What's going on over there?' he asks her.

She gulps on her cigarette smoke. 'Taxi men.'

'On strike?'

'Ah no. Just waiting.'

'For what?'

'Customers, I suppose.' She bites down on another blast of smoke.

Farley only notices then all the taxis parked along the road from top to bottom. A rush of yellow comes into his eye. He pats it with his glove, the yellow curdles, then disappears.

'I used to know a taxi man owned a racehorse,' he says.

'Yea?'

'Yea. Are you not freezin standing there?' he asks.

'Sure, what can I do?'

'I gave them up meself, years ago.'

'Still miss them?' she asks, not unfriendly.

'Ah, not really, I was never much of a smoker. Did it more for show than anything else.'

'I tried to give up a few times,' the girl says, 'but I missed the company of them like?'

'Why, do they talk to you or somethin?'

The girl smiles. 'Going in for a drink?' she says, tilting her head towards the pub door,

'I'm not much of a drinker either.'

'Don't smoke. Don't drink, Jesus what must that be like in this country?'

Farley shrugs. 'I tell you what it's like. It's like being a foreigner. It's like you don't belong here. Like everyone secretly hopes you'll shag off back to wherever it is you've come from. That's what it's like. Anyway, I'm off, mind yourself now, good girl.'

'Girl! What age do you think I am in anyway?'

'Ah, you're all girls to me,' Farley says and walks away.

There was a time he would have thought she was making a pass. A time, not that long ago, he would have been flattered by it. And a time, long before that, he would have been insulted that she'd think a bloke like him would be interested in someone like her. Now he knows she's just being nice.

He finds himself crossing back over O'Connell Street and turning onto the quays. Retracing the steps he would have taken every day, from the office to the Four Courts; forty years' worth, that's a lot of steps, a lot of miles. When he started he could do it in eight minutes flat. The week he retired it took ten. What would it be now? Not fair to challenge himself on a day like today, he decides, with the ground so uncertain and him not feeling the best. Next time. Maybe then.

He's halfway up the quay when he remembers that Slowey's son had finally got his way and relocated. Somewhere in Capel Street, a whole floor of offices in a brand-new block; barristers and solicitors below and above, only have to reach out your hand to get a bit of business. Suffering now though in the slump and even solicitors getting the boot every day. 'I'd say now the Sloweys is feelin the pinch.' He can hear the voice in his head that said that; one of those voices that takes pleasure in a recession, but he can't find a matching face.

Farley stands for a moment on the first of the four granite steps. The railings, the door, the windows at the side – all the same. The brass plate is gone, leaving a bald square patch surrounded by dirtier brick. The company name is still etched in gold leaf on the ground-floor and first-floor windows. He remembers the day it was painted, the office not long opened. A lad from the West slowly explaining the process and Farley torn between watching the liquid gold unfurl on the glass and attending to the screaming chorus of black phones behind him. Later, that evening they had come out onto the street to admire it; the painter, Slowey, himself, Brophy, that little blondie one who used to do the secretarial. They had crossed the road to stand at the quay wall; a warm dusky evening, the hum from the river. Slowey in shirtsleeves, the girl with her frock stuck to her legs. 'Now,' Slowey had said, nodding his approval. 'Now, what do you all think of that!' His voice had been shaky and for a minute Farley had thought he'd seen tears, actual tears, in his eyes. But then Slowey had turned round and started messing, pucking them on the arm, slapping them on the back of the head. Lifting the youngone up and swinging her around, her screaming like a seagull, while at the same time trying to hold down the hem of her dress. 'Ah Mister Slow-eeey, Jaysus, Mister Slow-ee-eeey, will you stopit!'

Farley looks up and over the windows; the house appears to be empty now. In his time he'd seen every room of it occupied over and over; a mixed bag of oddballs through the years. A struck-off solicitor, nose the shape of a little red arse, sniffing around for a few crumbs. The tailor, of course. The dress-hire woman. And there was an architect that only came

41

in for an hour a day, sandwiches tucked under his jumper, like he was ashamed of them. A dodgy enterprise or two, usually called something with the word 'Export' in the title.

Slowey & Co. had been the longest tenants; bit by bit taking over most of the rooms. Except of course for the top-floor flat where the sisters had lived. Three spinsters and one widow. The widow had lasted the longest: Jane, the youngest. Even into her seventies you could tell she'd been a looker, not because she still was, but by the way she behaved and the way she treated men, taking their attention for granted.

Farley climbs the steps and stands at the door. There's a planning permission sign on the wall beside it. He is leaning in to read it when the door jumps open, frightening the life out of him. A man standing there. 'Alright?' he says.

'Yea, I'm grand. Ta. I was just. I used to work here, you see and. For years, I did.'

The man has a bunch of letters in his hand, holding the door back with his foot while he racks through them. Behind him, the hall as dark as a cave. The same lino on the floor, old letters in a box on a table.

'Were you looking for anyone in particular?' he asks.

'Unless meself?' Farley says, then turns and comes back down the steps.

He stands on the street for a moment, a face in the flow of passing faces. The cold shudders through him. Tea. He was supposed to be getting a cup of tea.

Now in a shopping centre; blast of white light, a screeching baby. Too late he remembers the Mass card, after passing right by the church on the quays. Other churches pop up and down in his head – Marlborough Street; Whitefriars; John's; Adam's and Eve. Churches from all over the city. All very well, but which is the nearest because he hasn't a clue where he is now? One shopping centre bleeding into another; lights, glass, bawling children. He needs a little rest, a sup of tea, sugar. Maybe a bun. And a newspaper to hide behind, he could check on the death notice, make sure Frank really is dead. He looks for a cafe. But all he can see is a place with no front wall, opening directly out onto the aisle of the shopping centre; plastic tables, plastic trays, paper mugs of tea that you have to go up and get yourself and then stand like a thick looking around till you see a table and then climb over yourself to get to it, so you can drink your tea from your paper cup while the world goes by and gawks in at you sitting there in your plastic grotto. It doesn't even look as if there's a jacks in there and he'd be looking to have a piss soon enough. Is it too much to ask – a bit of comfort? Someone to serve him, maybe say a few words? Solid things all around his hands like a cup and a saucer, a stainless steel pot, milk in a jug – handles to hold on to – is *that* too much? Now if Bewley's was still going. But no point thinking about that.

He sits down on a bench in the centre of the aisle. Plastic fronds from an imitation palm tree behind him. On one side a woman sending a text. On the other side a schoolgirl staring into space. On the mitch, he'd say. Can't be much fun mitching on your own. A plain little one, face dotted with freckles. Lonely, he'd say. Something going on at home maybe. He'd like to talk to her, but already he can see she's wondering should she get up and leave because an oulfella has sat down on the bench beside her.

He watches for a while, shapes waddling by. The amount of fat people. Everywhere. Men, women, kids, even babies. The size of people these days. Years ago there might be one or two puddners in the whole school, or a fatso living around the corner. But now? Now the only skinny ones you see is the junkies. Or people who look as if they're just out of the cancer hospital or on the way in. His eyes feel tired; he closes them for a few seconds; vague sounds around him; a man mumbling somewhere close by, coincidentally about Bewley's; the chatter of footsteps; blurts of passing conversation. When he opens his eyes the youngone has gone, wandering down through the centre, he sees her little copper head. The woman still there, staring at him. She looks away and something about the way she does this makes Farley realize that the voice he's been hearing mumbling in the background, was his own. The light starts beating again. His head. A long skewer pierces through, then pulls out again. There's a rush of pinpricks in his arm, a smaller one in his face. More unpleasant than painful. Peculiar. It lasts a few seconds. Then all clear again.

He keeps losing moments. It's like they're falling out of a hole in his pocket. The Clery's bag is back under his arm, the shape of a shoe through its skin. He pulls the shoe out, the unblemished surface of a new blank sole looks up at him, lightly tan in colour, a perfect archway of minute and pristine nails. Yet he can't for the life of him remember collecting it. Was the girl in the red coat outside the pub then or before? Were the taxi men eyeing him hungrily? Did someone ask him if was he alright? And when did he remember that Jackie was his brother?

And now here he is, standing in the island in O'Connell Street, looking up at the the glint of a giant needle that used to be Nelson's Pillar. And thinking about the junkies again and trying to pull the two ends of the same idea together; the junkies and the giant needle. And staring up at the needle and imagining himself on the bus, the wall of the Park on one side, the scrag-end of the Liffey on the other. And the next thing is, he *is* on the bus, and crossing the river to turn into Parkgate Street, wondering how he got from staring up at the needle. To here. Splinters of light in his eyes again and a huge cruise ship rises before him. It takes a moment to grasp it – that's right, the new criminal courts building. A big bellyful of glass. The falling sun spitting all over it; barristers outside flapping like crows on its steps.

Outside the Slowey house the headlights of cars catch on the walls; doors clip into the darkness. Farley, from the side lane, watches the parade of condolence bringers. His arms are full – the suit in its cellophane wrapper, the few last-minute messages he bought in Centra, the Clery's bag with the newspaper inside it, page turned out that says Francis Slowey is reposing at home. Reposing at home? That'd be a first.

He lays everything down at his feet before fishing the Mass card out of the bag, then he moves into a cone of street light. Farley pulls a pen out of his inside pocket, opens the Mass card, lifts one knee and leans the card on it. He scribbles a name that comes out as approximately Father Clearihan – a mixture of Father Cleary that used to be, and that other bollix who taught him catechism when he was a boy. He puts the card back into its envelope, prints 'The Slowey Family' across it, and slips it into his pocket. Then he steps back into the shadows.

The house of mourning is completely blinkered. Only when the front door opens to admit newcomers or let others out, can he see by a vertical strip of hall light, that a black wreath is pinned to the front door and that the door has been painted a different colour since the last time he was here. For some reason this bothers him, as if they've sneaked behind his back to have it done, as if somehow he should have been consulted. But he reminds himself that it's been well over ten years since he's crossed that door and the Sloweys were always a house-proud lot. Once he knew this house better than his own. He knew the structure and little secrets of each room. The press in the kitchen where the good biscuits were kept and the corner where Slowey kept his single malt whiskey. He knew the way down the back garden in the dark, to the den that Slowey had built for the boys on the bit of land he'd bought from the Corpo. He knew the downstairs toilet with the dodgy plumbing and the jacks upstairs with the walk-in shower. He knew where the Christmas decorations were kept in the attic, the spare fuses, the box with the kids' old school reports in it. He knew the beds, the wallpapers, the family photos going up the stairs. The safe in the hot press. He knew all that and more.

Farley retrieves his bundle and hoists it into his arms. In the street light he can see the frost honing; the pavements already glittering hard. A cold, cold January night. In the garden a group of people are smoking; the group changes formation every now and then, somebody leaves, somebody new comes along. Here and there he recognizes, or thinks he recognizes, a figure from the past; the sound of a voice, a profile smeared in the light from the hall. Relatives of Slowey, work colleagues, pub friends, court acquaintances. He knows that each one, at some point in the evening, will turn to another one, and, after checking first that no member of the immediate family is within earshot, ask, 'So what's the story with Farley then?'

He turns away from the house and walks up the back lane. A soft light shows in the den, the cast of another light across the back garden from an upstairs window. He wonders where Slowey is laid out and if he's lying on a bed or already in a coffin on top of a table. And he imagines the shape of him lying there like some sort of a chieftain; long and large and quiet at last, and he wonders too what suit he'll be wearing and if he makes for a handsome corpse.

Farley takes the Mass card out of his pocket, holds it in his hand for a moment, then corner down, sticks it like a flag into the top of the back garden hedge.

He opens his front door. The silence sucks him in. He heels the door shut, unrolls the dry-cleaned suit and hangs it on the end of the stairs. Then he turns on the light and comes back to the door to bolt himself into his house. He opens the Clery's bag and removes the resoled shoe, then picks up its match from the floor and turns the shoes upside down. The two soles are a completely different colour. The new with its bright tan colour, the old a dark worn grey. After all that trouble. After all that day.

In the dim light of the hall he stands at the table before the smug, surly telephone. His reflection hangs above it in a gilt-edged frame. An old man, in a dark mirror. At what point, he wonders, does it become about fear? Fear of being caught talking to yourself, of pissing in your trousers, of pretending to remember a name, a place, a face you once knew well. Fear of getting done over by everyone out there; junkies, taxi men, youngfellas, kids. Fear of your own face in the mirror.

A clatter comes from the kitchen and now, instead of thinking about fear, he's feeling it. It tears through his heart then burns all the way out to the ends of his fingers and toes. His bladder. A burglar – he must have left the little window open again. He glances at the front door and wonders if he has time to unchain and unbolt his way out. But he finds now it's no longer a question of time, it's a question of movement. And he can't move at all. The skewer goes through his head again, deftly inserting itself in as if it's testing a joint of meat. Then twists and pulls out again, leaving a halo of blinding scintilla around his head.

So this is it. Farley closes his eyes and waits. Another sound, like a voice. And yet not a voice. He opens his eyes. The sound again and this time he recognizes the coy, needy miaow of a cat. Around the door a fat black body appears. One paw stretches, then another. The cat gives him a deep green blink. Then he sashays into the hall and stops at his feet. Farley leans on the table and waits for his heart to resume beating. Slowly he stoops and lifts the cat up in his arms before painfully bringing himself back into a standing position. He feels warmth, strength, frailty, life. The cat miaows again. He hugs it closer to him, nuzzling his nose into its fur. His eyes fill up, his heart gives a little. 'O Shifty,' he says.

The Party

April 2000

FARLEY HANGS HIS COAT on the rack, smoothes down his suit, settles the bag of presents he's bought by the wall. First to arrive. It occurs to him that this could well be the first time he's ever been completely alone, if not in the office, then certainly in this building. Even those times when he'd worked into the night or come back after the pub had closed because he couldn't bear the thoughts of going home – there'd always been someone. In a room somewhere. The sisters in the top-floor flat. The mad tailor. The parrot. Or that time with young Slowey.

He feels a bit spooked. The silent, dusky house around him. The long hallway. A sense of something or other prowling the empty rooms of the flat upstairs. He half expects to see Jane's painted face rise like a Venetian mask over the bannister: 'O there you are, Mister Slowey, I wonder if I might inveigle upon you…?' No insult that she called him Slowey – whether fixing a plug or shifting a piece of furniture – they were all Mister Sloweys to Jane. He thinks now of the day she retired – how old she'd seemed to him then – a drama teacher in a secondary school. Her two elder sisters already dead and Chrissy in a home down in Meath. The loneliness of Jane after. You could see it trailing up the stairs behind her, hear it in the way she pounced on the phone the minute it rang. For a while she'd taken to giving elocution classes to kids after school. The bored chant on winter afternoons through the floorboards: ub awb eeb; how *now* brown cow.

He opens his jacket and snuffles each armpit, worried now that it may have been a mistake to walk into work, what with the long day ahead, the retirement party after – by which time he could be stinking. But he'd enjoyed these past few days, walking into work, even though he'd never have done it but for the bus strike. And he'd enjoyed too the fact that he was fit enough to do it; fitter than most of them in here, young Slowey included. And the further fact, that after all the giving out about the carry-on of the taxi men on New Year's Eve, all the swearing to give the greedy bastards no more business, he'd been the one, the *only* one, to stick to his guns. All that aside. Walking the route he had so mindlessly made, first by car, later by bus, for near on to forty years, it had been sort of like doing it all in a slow-motion rewind, so that he'd remembered all sorts of odd things, like the names of shops that used to be, or the colour of doors on houses that once stood on this or that pile of rubble. People too; the old man in the dust coat who used sit on the bench at Wolfe Tone Park shooting at birds with his invisible rifle. Or the youngfella in the bright yellow sou'wester who used to sell newspapers at Sarah's Bridge – whatever happened to him? What he'd liked best though was the moment he came onto the quays and the first sight of the river, sturdy and dirty and looking at it, *really* looking at it, the way he used to do when he was a boy; noticing things. Like the blind-eyed river heads or the loose scabs of algae hanging off the walls. And the feeling then as he got further along, of being pulled into the machine of a city just as it was about to take off. Footsteps and purpose all around him. And the skyline all the way down to the sea where skeletons of cranes and half-constructed buildings rose up, reminding him of an exhibition in the Natural History Museum.

He stands in the doorway of the main office, looking through. The cleaners have been – wax polish over the dry, musted aroma of paper. Above all that a taint of lavender. The lavender not real of course, but from one of Noreen's plug-in contraptions: Ocean Breeze, Highland Heather,

Malaysian Mist or some such. She'll often make him guess and he'll play along to please her – although they all stink the same to him. He likes this vantage point – one room blending into the next; the feeling of space and possibility. The opposite to his own little house – like living in a snackbox, as he overheard some snide bitch say the day of Martina's funeral. It appeals to him too, the sense of past lives that have been lived in here; first as reception room for a family of merchants. Later a tenement flat for God knows how many. Later again a series of come-and-go offices before Slowey & Co., Legal & Town Agents, finally came to roost here. Chrissy once told him that these two rooms were a ballet school in the twenties and that she could remember, when she was a child, the girls doing their bar exercises along the walls and the walls themselves lined with mirrors so that just a few could make it look like a full company of ballerinas. He had just loved the idea of that. Slowey, of course, had knocked it on the head: 'Do you not think now, there'd be traces, the mark of a nail, a Rawl-plug – something?' he'd asked, stroking a large dismissive hand over the walls. And he'd been sorry after that he'd mentioned it at all.

He comes into the office and stops in the centre. He could happily live here in these two rooms. Not now maybe, but a couple of years down the road. After he came back from his big trip, gotten used to his new life, his new money. Money made anything possible. What he'd do now is this – turn the back office into his bedroom, maybe knock a door in the side wall to give direct access to the kitchen, the jacks too of course, stick in a shower while he's at it; something decent like you'd see in a hotel. The front room here meanwhile could be his living area – sofa by that wall near the window, desk (he'd have to keep the desk) at an angle over there. And the two fireplaces of course; Italian marble. He'd have them opened up. In winter he could light a fire in the bedroom – the luxury of that! Lying in bed watching firelight pat up the walls. And to be living right in the centre of town – it could open up your whole life. Better than walking the streets of a housing estate day after day like some bewildered oulone, up and down to the shops, stopping at gossipy corners. Or else fluting around in the front garden, hoping someone would drop an hello over the railing. The suburbs is no place for a man. Not unless he's a dedicated drinker. Nothing to inspire, nowhere to go. Where do they go? A few of the retired men on his road joined the gym in the new hotel up near the Naas Road. He'd considered it, for about half a minute. The thoughts of the changing rooms had put him off; oulfellas standing around in the nip, hands on hips, waggling their nudgers at each other, while they pontificated on the issues of the day; issues that were really no longer any of their business. A city would be different but. A city could make you feel part of itself. He could join something; a film society, a chess club. Learn how to play chess first of course. He could go to the theatre, broaden his range, start reading the *Guardian* maybe, like Jackie – give himself something to talk about. You'd never see Jackie short of a topic. He could make new friends, invite them round for a drink. 'You know,' he'd say, resting a careless arm across the back of his new leather sofa, 'in the twenties this used to be a ballet school.'

He passes through the front office, into the back. The rack is filled with job sheets hanging like bunting, corner to corner; jobs for today, jobs for tomorrow, jobs for next week. He is leaving the business in good fettle; it both pleases and saddens him to know this. In the middle of the room, a big square table is topped with telephones. On one wall pigeonholes climb towards the ceiling. A counter runs the length of the other two walls. The fax machine, the photocopier over to the side. In between, the nap of the carpet worn down like footpaths in grass. The turn and return of clerical footsteps. How many have worked in this room? Must be near to a hundred clerks clocked up by now. Unusual names may drift into his head now and then: Titley, Wheatley, Carabini, Quirke. Or faces maybe of some who, for one reason or another, left a mark. That Easton bloke that he'd had to sack one time. Or the ginger messenger boy from Longford who threw all the deliveries in the Liffey and pretended he'd been robbed. But the truth is, once gone, usually forgotten. Alright in ones or twos, for a drink at the bar or a bit of company walking up to the courts, but an annoying bunch of fuckers, by and large – much as he was himself at that age. The stupid jokes and young man's swagger; Monday morning farts and the stink of cheap aftershave; the countless umbrages and senseless cruelties; the know-alls and the know-fuck-alls – will he miss any of that? he wonders.

Farley comes back to his own office and stands at the window. Outside on the quay, a shoal of passers-by. Across the road, a foreign-looking youngfella is huddled by the river wall, begging. It used only be the tinkers you'd see; Paddy the knacker, women with children shawled into tartan rugs – a little some-hin for the babbee, God'll give you great luck – he will in his bollix, he often felt like saying. But you only ever see foreigners begging now. He doesn't know why this should make him feel proud, but it does.

Noreen, he will miss. He'd interviewed her himself, God knows how many years ago. A smiley little thing in a pink fluffy jumper, scratching her forearm. Just out of secretarial college and O so eager to please. Slowey had slagged him at the time about keeping his hands to himself. 'Youngones love a bit tragedy,' he had said, referring to the fact that he was a young widower, 'so you keep your eyes *and* your hands on the job.' But he'd known she'd be no distraction – not with the woman he had on his mind then, filling every inch and corner of it. A silent screeching siren, only he could hear.

He looks down at Noreen's desk, adorned with the toys of a middle-aged clerical typist: baubles and dangly toys, pictures. A framed photo of Clinton with her own face superimposed on it, so that it looks like her head is lying on his shoulder. A holiday postcard from her mother, now dead. A photo of her husband before he went gaga, a pitch-and-putt trophy in his hand. And hanging overhead the birdcage of course, a planted pot standing in place of the tailor's parrot. Back in the hallway he throws a glance up the stairs. The tailor topped himself up there, on the second-floor landing. A Saturday afternoon, some time in the seventies. Summertime, because he can remember the sisters were away on holiday, and down here in the office they'd been getting the accounts in order for an audit; Slowey, Noreen, himself. It was the squawks of the parrot brought them upstairs. Slowey had cut the tailor down. Noreen rang for the police. It had been clear from the room that the tailor had been living there. A filthy sleeping bag rolled into the corner. Scraps of cloth on a long table; fractions of unsewn suits all over the floor; a small primus stove on the window ledge; a bottle of curdled milk. When the guards left they went over to the Abbey Mooney for a drink; somewhere quiet, Slowey had said, where they wouldn't run into anyone and have to make conversation. Best keep this to ourselves, they'd agreed, huddled together in a corner like abandoned children.

The violence of the death had been what really upset Noreen. The fact that he should choose to die that way when he'd left no one behind him. 'Why didn't he just slip quietly away,' she had said, 'take sleeping tablets or something – you know? It's like he was trying to punish someone. But who?'

'Himself maybe?' Farley had suggested. And Noreen had covered her face in her hands.

'Or the parrot?' Slowey said. And Noreen had taken her hands away. They'd looked at each other, shocked for a second and then suddenly they couldn't seem to stop laughing.

Farley looks across the hallway; two doors to two offices. The one on the right belongs to Frank. The other one was, at one time, intended for Farley. They had taken over the two rooms after the dress-hire woman had packed it in, leaving a right bang behind her – old perfume and dead women's sweat – that no amount of airing or Noreen's Highland Heather could subdue. For a few years they'd used the space for storage, then, when Farley became a partner, it had been decided to turn them into offices. One for Frank, the other for himself. About which time young Tony Slowey decided to honour the company with his presence. And so Farley had let him have the office. Partly because he knew that the others wouldn't work well for Tony out in the main room, and partly because Frank, without quite asking, had asked.

He turns the doorknob of Tony's office – locked, of course. The cute bastard, no doubt has something to hide.

53

The door to Frank's office opens with a tell-tale-tattler's whine; the neatness inside betrays the fact that Frank hasn't so much as stuck his nose in for the past few weeks. Because between one thing and another and Cheltenham included, he's been sticking it elsewhere. 'Time for us oul fellas to start taking a step back,' he'd said, a few years after Tony had come in. What he'd really meant was, time for you to stay where you are, and for me to spend more time racing. Not that he'd minded – the truth was he'd rather have been here than anywhere else. And besides, someone had to keep an eye on young Slowey.

At the desk now he pulls out a drawer. Old notebooks and legal forms that have recently become obsolete. A confetti of ancient bookie dockets. A stainless steel comb. At the back the baby bottle of brandy that Frank always keeps for bad news and accidents. He opens the second drawer: an array of unused gifts from various staff members over the years; lighters still in their boxes; cartons of old cigars; pen and pencil sets, or pens on their own – like nobody ever noticed that Frank, apart from the very odd cigar, had given up smoking and that due to some obscure little superstition, has always preferred to write in an ordinary green-inked biro. In the last drawer Farley finds an old-fashioned hardbacked ledger – Slowey & Co.; 1960 – their very first job book. He flicks through the pages, plenty of them blank. The end of June 1960 records forty-nine jobs for the month. By December the number has increased to 102. Slowey's green comment at the bottom of the pages: 'A hundred jobs in one month. Did we ever think we'd see the day!!!!' Farley claps the book shut; a hundred jobs in a month? They'd see that in one day now, and the rest of it.

Replacing the job book he notices the silver corner of a photograph frame. Cracked glass at one corner. The frame nearly comes apart in his hand. He lays it carefully on the desk, puts on his specs and the Slowey family shift into focus. Michael's first communion day; taken about twenty years ago, judging by the age of the kids. There's Tony, like a beanpole, the big mop of hair on him, of which not one blade remains. Miriam next, a teenager dressed up like a little oulone. And young Jamesie looking down at his feet, as if he's ashamed to be part of the family photo. At one end of the group sits Slowey, his hand on little Michael's shoulder; steadying him up. And Kathleen on the far end, in a ladylike perch on the edge of the photographer's sofa. He remembers that dress – green leaves with flecks of orange, although time and the camera have dulled its colours. He remembers the matching shoes and bag too. The dress was made of a silky material. Farley returns the frame to the bottom of the drawer, then changes his mind. He takes it back out, pulls it apart and releases the photograph, then lifting the wastepaper basket to the corner of the desk, scoops bits of wood, glass and sly little nails, into its open mouth.

He lifts the photograph, folds it once, then twice, then eases it like a letter into an envelope which he slips into his inside pocket. He notices then a shiny red seed of blood on the inside of his trigger finger. Closing the door behind him, he sucks it.

Back in his own office Farley sits at his desk; his own little territory. His field of land. He has always loved the old-fashioned sense of importance about it, the insert of green baize, the weight of the drawers in his hand. They got it at an auction somewhere off the South Circular road – the Office of Public Works giving the stuff away, in their hurry to modernize the civil service. A relic from a non-disposable past – himself and Frank had nearly broken their backs getting it up the steps.

Farley lifts his head and looks into the room, a lurch in his stomach that feels a bit like homesickness. He comes back to the stack of letters waiting for his signature; reports on summonses served, or failed to be served; files that need a final update before he passes them on to dopey Brendan who'll frown at them for a while before thumping his stamp on them and passing the buck back over to Noreen. His eye catches on the last paragraph of the top letter... 'let me just add that's it's been a pleasure doing business with your company over the years and that I retire safe in the knowledge that Slowey & Co. will continue to serve...'

He throws his signature across the bottom of two letters but he can't seem to sit still or concentrate for more than a few seconds. It's like all this energy is squeezing through his veins and he'll burst if he doesn't get rid of it quick. After the long walk into work and the lack of sleep in an endless last night, he'd thought he'd be at least glad of a sit-down. A mixture of dread and excitement had kept him awake, like a kid at Christmas who knows where his ma has hidden the presents but still can't help worrying that Santy won't come. He stands again, arches his back, begins pacing the floor. At what point should he start giving out his own little presents that he's bought for the staff? Cufflinks for the blokes, bracelets for the girls. Before the party? Or maybe just leave them here for them to open themselves when he's already gone? A day from his childhood comes to him; the day after his first communion when he'd spent all his money on sweets for the boys in his class because he'd been the only Catholic in their little school and had felt bad for getting a day off and a new suit of clothes and the few bob of course, on top of everything else. And he remembers going around, the fat, holy face on him, handing out the sweets with a sanctimonious air, and then later getting battered by Jimmy Ball for his trouble and then getting another wallop from his mother when he got home because there'd been blood from his nose all over his good new suit. He glances at the bag of presents, the small individual cards he's written, the messages and little jokes inside each one, that he'd tried to make personal. The cards no doubt that would be turfed into the bin in a day or two and he worries now that the presents will make him seem like some sort of a sap. He's struggling with the notion of maybe hiding them away somewhere, not giving them out at all, when he hears Noreen pushing on the front door: a quarter to nine. Bang on the second. He listens to her fiddling around with the locks and knows he should go out and open it for her, because it'll take a few goes before she realizes that somebody has already opened the door and that she's in the process of locking herself back out again. But he's too nervous suddenly; shy even. He stands at the window and watches the jig of her elbow, her clenched shoulders, the slight lopsided pull to her right shoulder. Her face. Even in profile it has the strain of her husband written all over it. The front door gives; Noreen steps into the hall.

She nearly jumps out her skin when she sees him. 'Jesus Mary and fucken Joseph,' she cries out, slamming two crossed hands on her chest and gasping at him, 'you frightened the life of me yafuckabastardya.'

'O, that's lovely language for a lady, I must say!'

Noreen gives him a slap in the arm as she passes. 'I can't wait for you to leave,' she says, 'you oul bastard, I'm sick of the sight of you.'

She takes off her coat and hangs it outside in the hall, alongside his. He notices she isn't dressed up and hasn't the hair done either. Their eyes catch, then look away. Noreen stretches her back and rubs one shoulder.

'Go out and stick on the kettle there,' she says to him. 'Go on. It's the least you could do for me on your last day.'

When he comes back in with the steaming kettle in his hand, she has the mugs out and ready, two napkins laid out on her desk, a small fat bun sitting in the centre of each one. 'Special occasion,' she says. 'You're early. Don't tell me you walked into work again?'

'I did.'

'The bus strike is over – you do know that? So it's not as if you would have had to get a taxi or anything,' she says this with a glinty eye.

He plays along, 'Don't start me. Hungry shower of bastards. The more I think of…'

They smile at each other. 'Ah, I felt like the walk,' he says, accepting the mug of tea from her hand. He waits a moment before asking, 'How's himself doin?'

'You don't want to know.'

'O. Well, will you be alright later like, for the little do, and that?'

'What do you mean *little* do? I heard half the city is coming. A few strippers, Catherine Nevin jumping out of a cake. That's what I heard in anyway.'

'O yea, right.'

'I'll have to go home first. I've asked his sister to keep an eye on him but well – I wouldn't bank on it, Farley. She's not the most reliable.'

'No?'

'That's the worst about having no family of your own. If we'd had a few kids at least *one* of them would be bound to be alright. I mean they couldn't all be selfish shitheads – could they?'

'Some families have them in litters.'

Noreen nods. 'So, any more about Jackie? How's he doing?'

'One minute he's grand. The next he's… Well, I don't know what he is really. They'll be running a few tests on him in the next couple of weeks. They're talking as if, as if it's you know, the same thing as your fella, but I don't know. He seems a bit young for that – like he's younger than me. And a schoolteacher too, Jaysus, you'd expect them to, you know? He's coming tonight. I think. Maybe. I hope. Well, I do and I don't. What do you think? You know, after going through it with Jim, what do you—?'

'Shut up and eat your bun,' Noreen says.

Farley picks the bun up and holds it in the palm of his hand. Then closing his fingers around it, bites down; a dry bulge in his throat. He throws a wallop of tea in after it and gulps. 'Sorry, Noreen. I shouldn't have brought it up.'

She shrugs, takes a sip of her tea, then begins plucking the bun apart with her fingers. 'Not today, Farley.'

Farley watches her. She probably knows him better than anyone else – since Martina died anyway. Things he would have told her, other things she would have just picked up by herself. If he was to be honest she could well be the best friend he has. And yet, after today he might never see her again, or at least seldom see her. 'We'll keep in touch, Noreen,' he says.

'What are you on about? Of course we will. So – tell us, have you decided about your trip yet? Come on, details, I want details.' She claps her hand off the desk, her eyes suddenly bright.

'What sort of details?'

'For a start, *when* are you going?'

'I better hang on a few weeks – you know, till everything's settled here.'

'You mean till the dosh is safely in the bank?'

'Exactly. The meeting is today so, we'll see how that goes.'

'Right. Who'll be at the meeting?'

'Frank, Tony, the accountants, I presume.'

'O God, Farley, you'll be loaded – why didn't I ever ask you to marry me? Make a pass at you, even.'

'Would it be because you have taste?' he asks, even though he could just as easily have said – Actually you did make a pass, several times when you'd a few on you.

'O, that's right, I forgot about my taste.' She rolls her eyeballs at him and he wonders if she's relieved or vexed that he appears to have forgotten.

He leans forward. 'Anyway. What I've decided to do is this – when everything is settled this end I'm off to London. Stay a week or two and book the rest of the trip from there. They say you get a better deal in London and you know what – I've never been there in me life – have you?'

'Once. Just a couple of days.'

He waits, but she's dipped her face behind her mug.

'Right. Well, that's the plan so far,' he says.

'How long will you be gone?'

'Depends. After London – America. I've always wanted to see America. I might even chance a tour round the world. You see they do these flights and you can go one way round the world and back another – sort of like a spiral. The thing is, once I started reading the brochures and looking at the options. Well, do you know what it is, Noreen? The world is a terrible big bloody place.'

She laughs. 'You'll probably never come back.'

'Course I will. I can't leave Jackie. And I've the house to worry about. But do you know, do you know what I'd really love to be able to do? Rent the house out for maybe two or three years. And not come back at all during that time. Do the lot, you know? Lay a map of the world out on the table and look at all these places and names I used to read about when I was a kid and just say fuckit and *go*. Places like Malaysia. Or Bombay. You know, I always swore one day I'd do the lot. But of course, I never did. Because that's the way it is, isn't it? One thing leads to another, one year the next, and you postpone things and then postpone them again. Till you simply forget all about whatever it was you always wanted to do and, and by then it's too bloody late anyway.'

'You could still do it, Farley.'

He stares into the carpet, turning the idea over in his head. 'Ah. I don't think so. I'll be happy with a few European capitals, Paris, Rome and that. And of course America. New York. San Francisco. Vegas maybe. That'd be enough for me. More than I ever thought I'd have, let's just say.'

Noreen stands up, flicks the bun crumbs off her blue jumper. 'You'll probably forget all about us in here.'

'What's this your name is again?' He looks at her, waiting for the joke to be turned back to him.

But Noreen is saying nothing; her mouth twisted, tears stand up in her eyes. He nearly dies when he sees them. 'Noreen – what is it?' Farley puts his hand out to touch her, but she's turned from him and is walking away into the back room. He hears the front door open into the hall then and the hall fill up with the sound of young men's voices talking young men's shite. Behind him a telephone starts to sing, another one follows. From the back office, a fax machine clucks.

He still calls him young Slowey, although he turned forty last year and getting to look more like a slug every day – the smooth, clammy head on him, the thick neck. Farley pats his palm on his own greying hedge, more salt than pepper these days, but still there at least. He wonders about younger men nowadays and why, the minute they start losing their hair, it's out with the razor? An act of defiance maybe? An all or nothing bravado? Because surely they can't think it makes them look any better?

Young Slowey. He wears an earring which annoys Farley as much as it makes him ashamed – on behalf of the Slowey family or on behalf of the company, he couldn't say which. Bad enough if it were the same earring, like he put it in there when he was fifteen or sixteen and just forgot all about it, but the fact that he has a selection which he changes on a regular basis: a little gold cross, a silver stud, a small gypsy's hoop – for fuck sake, and of course worst of the lot, the diamond he is wearing today – that's the one that really gets on Farley's wick.

He has tried with Tony. But the truth is he never really took to him, not even when he was a kid; a spoilt little whiner then with far too much to say for himself – in other words a smaller version of the man he would grow up to be. All bluff and blow with his 'projections' and his 'thinking outside the box' and his stupid waste of time monthly management meetings. Along with the rest of the arseology he brought with him from the so-called business college his oulfella had to pay for, because he couldn't even muster up two honours in his leaving cert to get himself into UCD. 'Number crunching,' that's another one. Or his 'I'll be swinging by the courts on the way to the office'. That's another – as if he was a monkey. Or what about last month's special? 'What I'm about here is injecting a younger image into the company.' And Farley had felt like saying, 'But you're not young any more, Tony. Forty is *not* young.'

He glances out to the hall, young Slowey, phone set stuck to his earhole, deep in conversation. Of course, he couldn't just take the call in the privacy of his office, he had to do it on full parade, up and down the hall, in and out of the rooms, now back in the hall again, moving as if a camera is following him. Young Slowey looks up, catches him watching. Farley gives an upward nod, a sketchy smile which is returned with something similar.

In fairness, Tony has never liked him either. The only one in the family who has never called him 'uncle' as Miriam with a few jars on her had highlighted last Christmas. 'Ah, we all love our Uncle Farley with his cute little sticky-up hair – don't we, Tony? Don't we love Uncle Farley?'

'He's not my uncle – is he?' Tony had said.

Farley sticks his nose back into a file. He sees the hulk of Tony's shadow loom from the hall into his office and now here he is standing at the edge of the desk. He looks up, tries to arrange an air of mild surprise on his face.

'Ah Tony.'

'And how is our soon-to-be man of leisure?'

'Not bad now. Not bad. Yourself?'

'Great yea, great. So – what time suits you for this meeting?'

'Whatever time suits everyone else, I suppose.'

'Actually, there'll just be you and me.'

'O? I thought—'

'What?'

'I thought your da, the accountants and that.'

'No use dragging the accountants in till we've everything settled – wha'? Time enough then. And Da's only back from Spain this afternoon.'

'I didn't know he was in Spain.'

'Just a few days, a bit of business. That apartment block – did he not tell you?'

'O yea, that's right,' Farley says. 'I forgot.'

'Anyway, he's back this afternoon. Wouldn't miss your party now would he?'

'No. I suppose.'

'I was up with Ma on the way in this morning, she wants him to have a bit of a rest before tonight. He's probably been tearing the arse out of things over there without her to keep an eye on him, you know what he's like and with his blood pressure and that.'

'Your ma wasn't with him then?'

Tony scratches the side of his nose. 'Anyway, I thought we – you and me – could have a prelim.'

'A prelim?'

'A preliminary – you know?'

'Jaysus, you make it sound like an exam or something.'

Tony smirks. 'A chat then. Will we say after five? When things die down here?'

'Yea, grand. After five. Whatever you want.'

'No, no. It's whatever *you* want, Farley, whatever suits you.'

'After five, then.'

'Great.' Tony gives his desk three short pats. 'We'll crunch a few numbers anyway – righ'?'

Farley watches him cross over the room. He'd love to shout after him, 'The only numbers I'd like to crunch is the two little balls between your legs.'

Young Slowey stops at Brendan's deak; skimpy Brenner, invisible behind him. He can hear the mumble of office talk between them. And he remembers again, the night a few years ago when he hadn't been able to sleep for worry about the poxy VAT man and had decided to come back into the office to have another look at the returns. And there was young Slowey, hard at it, trousers looped around his shins and his big white arse rutting away at some young one who was sitting up on the desk; the legs on her like two bendy sticks wrapped around his thick hips. Only three days before his wedding.

Farley bites down on his pen. It annoys him that he continues to remember this because it's not a sight he wants to keep in his head, nor does he care what Tony does or doesn't get up to. And yet every time he looks into Tony's eyes, it's like it only happened yesterday. It dawns on him now that this could well be because it's never left Tony's head. It's there like a condensed photograph in his eyes. An accusation, even. Like it was Farley was the one who did something wrong. And Tony was the one who couldn't forgive it.

Tony moves away from Brendan's desk, leaving an exposed Brendan blinking in the light.

'Later, Farley – righ'?' Tony says.

Eleven o'clock. Something's not right. His skin feels too tight; the back of his hands, under his collar, his scalp. And there's a small anxious lump heating up in his gut. Like someone is sticking pins in him. Needled, that's it. He feels needled. Farley continues to play the morning; pulling letters off the pile, throwing his signature across the bottom of them, taking or making the odd joke over his shoulder.

Every few minutes he lifts the phone to his ear. The punters friendlier than they'd usually be; lingering. Word has obviously got around. Sometimes he's even called to a phone on another desk – Just wanted to say. Good luck to you now. Well for some. God I'd tell you, what I wouldn't give.

He hears himself talking about his trip. 'Well, you see, I've decided to organize it from London.' And regrets not having something more definite to say, something that sounds a bit less pie-in-the-sky. Maybe along the lines of, 'After the States, I'll be heading to Hong Kong and then on to Australia, you see, in time for the Melbourne Cup.'

Each time he puts down the phone he has a moment of calm; the doubts disappear, his skin eases. And he stops worrying about Tony and his meeting this evening, the fact that Frank won't be there, the absence of accountants. It's only a chat, after all. Probably just to make Tony feel a part of the process. In fact, it could well be a ploy to get him out of the way while the rest of the staff organize a little something before the party; balloons, drinks, all that jazz. But as the minutes tick on, his skin starts to tighten again, the lump expands in his stomach and a dread starts to take shape and blazes into a fully formed notion. That fucker, he thinks, that fucker is going to do me.

He has to get out for a while. Have a stroll up the quays, maybe wander in through the courts or up to the Deeds, see who he might run into. He feels the need for some sort of diversion, or even acknowledgement on this, his last day. 'I'm going out for a bit,' he says to Brendan who gives him a watery look. Farley picks up a file as a mark of purpose and tucks it under his elbow.

He opens the front door and she's standing there. Even with the blinding belt of sunlight in his face, he still knows the shape of her.

'Kathleen?'

She nods a few times, like she's answering a question or agreeing with something he hasn't yet said. Then her hand goes up to her forehead. He sees her mouth open to speak but no words come out of it.

'What's the matter, Kathleen?' He stands back to allow her to step into the hall, but she remains frozen on the doorstep.

'Are you alright?'

She shakes her head, looks up at him now and he sees a few small tears squeeze out from the corners of her eyes. For a moment he thinks Slowey has died, there's been a plane crash, or that his jam tart has packed up on the way from the airport in the back of a taxi. He steps out, reaches down to her and, taking her elbow in the cup of his hand, draws her in.

In the subdued light of the hall he sees her face.

'I feel so… so stupid,' she begins.

'Why?' He keeps her elbow in his hand.

'They mugged me, Farley.'

'Ah Jaysus, no. That's terrible.'

'Just snatched the bag off me shoulder outside Arnott's. One of them started pulling at me. The other at the bag and—'

'They didn't hurt you, did they?'

'Farley, they were just kids. That's what's the worst of it, like children – that size.' She lifts out her hand to show a height of around four feet.

'But they didn't hit you or anything?'

'No, just frightened me. I feel so stupid. So.'

'Jesus, if I thought they hurt you,' Farley says.

She looks at him then reclaims her elbow, folding her arms.

'Look, come on into Frank's office and we'll sit you down. Get you a nip of brandy for the shock.'

'I don't want any—'

'Tea, then, I'll get you a cup of tea and after I'll take you home in a taxi.'

'No, really, I'll be alright,' she says but follows him through the open door anyway. Farley closes it behind them. She sits on one side of her husband's desk. Farley sits opposite her in Frank's chair. He picks up the internal phone and calls Noreen. 'You wouldn't do us a favour, Nor? Bring a cup of tea into Frank's office for Mrs Slowey, plenty of sugar. She's had a bit of a shock.'

He glances across and sees Kathleen's eyes filling up again, like she's remembering. He reaches into his pocket for a hanky but she's ahead of him, with a tissue pulled out of her own coat pocket.

'I'd love a smoke,' Kathleen says.

'Yea, of course. Go ahead. There should be an ashtray around somewhere.' He lifts his head to look.

'They're in me bag, Farley.'

'O Christ, yea, sorry.'

'Have a look there in Frank's drawer, he might have some old ones lying around.'

He can't say he's already had a look in Frank's drawer today and knows there's only cigars in there. 'Ah, they'd be stale, only make you sick. Hold on there, I'll get you one from one of the lads.' He's about to get up when the door opens and Tony comes in. 'Your mother…' Farley begins, 'she's—'

'Tony, I was mugged.'

Tony eyes pop. 'Christ, Ma, are you alright? Did you call the cops?'

'I told the garda on beat in Henry Street, yes. They took the whole bag, everything in it.'

'Did you cancel the cards?'

'Not yet.'

'That was the first thing you should have done, Ma. Right come on, I'll do it now.'

He stands beside Farley and waits for him to vacate his father's seat. Farley gets up and moves away from the desk.

'And Tony,' she continues, 'the cross and chain was in the side pocket, you know, from when I was a bridesmaid for—' She breaks down now. Farley takes a step towards her, then stops.

'Alright, Ma, alright. Just let me cancel the cards. The car is up in Jervis Street, I'll go up and get it, then drive you home.'

'I was just about to go out, get a taxi,' Farley says.

'I'm not havin her going home in a taxi on her own,' Tony says.

'Ah no, of course not. I'll go with her.'

'And why would you do that?'

'I only thought.'

'You only thought what, Farley?'

'Well, by the time you get your car out the car park and drive round in the traffic, we'd be halfway home.'

'Ah, stop it,' Kathleen says, 'stop fussin the pair of you. I'll be grand in the taxi on me own. Your da will be home shortly. I'll be fine.'

'That's right. Da'll be home. Da'll look after you.'

Noreen is standing at the door, mug of tea in her hand. 'Look, why don't I go with you, Mrs Slowey? I'll wait with you till Frank gets home.'

'Would you? O thanks, Noreen.'

She stands. He watches her tighten her coat around her, slip her hands in and out of her pockets, pull up her collar, roll it down again, fidget with a scarf. 'Me hands,' she says, 'I don't know where to be putting them.'

She moves past Noreen out to the hall. Noreen steps in, hands Farley the mug of tea. 'Here,' she says, 'stick your gob around that.'

He can't get near the courts, what with the cameras, the television vans, the amount of journalists hanging around. There's photographers perched along the Liffey wall and another standing on the roof of a van.

Between Catherine Nevin's trial and Gilligan's extradition, he knows this could go on all day. He decides to try the side entrance in Chancery Place. Into a squeeze of black cloaks and brief-clutching elbows, he tries getting up the steps and he feels like shouting into the shove and push of it, 'Ah, what do you have to do to get into this place, for fuck sake – murder someone?'

Farley gives up. He thinks about going round the back way, even walks as far as the corner, but sees the police have cordoned off the entrance. He could tell them he needs to go in for the purpose of work, but he doesn't feel like standing there explaining himself. And besides he's forgotten his file, so there's nothing really for him to do when he does get in. Except hang around and look like a spare waiting on someone to talk to him.

He stands on the street corner painted in shadow. Across the way, the two markets send out their own personal odours – fish gut and ammonia from one; the boozy smell of overripe fruit from the other. Down the way a young man splashed in sunshine loads the back of a lorry with sacks of spuds. A girl sits on the wall outside River House, leaning back on her hands, face tipped to the sun. But on this side of the street the chilled spring air passes through his clothes, then through his skin, before settling down on his bones. He doesn't want to go back to work. Not yet. But if he hasn't got work to go to, where has he got? Farley pulls himself away from this thought. His eye falls on Hughes's pub. And he imagines it inside; the soft glow of lamplight, the warm, quiet corners where the few lone drinkers at this time of day sit behind cover of newspapers. He crosses the road and pushes against the door. A belch of sullied air comes out to meet him: Bovril, cigarettes, porter, whiskey. He feels slightly elated. Something he hasn't done for years is go into a pub during the day for no other purpose than to drink.

He makes his way back to the office the long way round; from Hughes's to Slattery's, the Oval, the Bachelor: a pint in each one, till the afternoon has crumbled away and it's only by chance he happens to notice it's nearly time for his meeting with Tony. He can still hold his drink anyway, as he tells his pleased self in the mirror of the jacks of the Ormonde Hotel. And he can still remember all the old tricks, like plenty of grub to line the stomach and to keep the smell of gargle at bay; toasted cheese to stick to your gut; a ham sanger or two smeared with mustard; peanuts. And a few peppermints on the way back up the quays; sucked not chewed, because chewing makes the smell too obvious and also stings the fuck out of your tongue. He thinks of an oulfella, used to drink in around Queen Street, who kept a rotten orange in the cubbyhole of his car, and any time he was stopped by a garda checkpoint, he'd take a bite out of it so when he rolled down the window it smelled like he had the most God-awful halitosis and the garda, of course, would immediately back away and wave him on. Farley finds a chuckle bubbling in his throat at the thought of this, the orange, the oulfella, the recoiling garda. He bites down on his lip but the giddiness stays. He has to stop at an antique shop, pretend to be all interested in the statue of a Red Indian outside it while he takes out his hanky, blows his nose into it, pushing the laugh out along with the snots and then literally wiping the grin off his face.

On the way in he meets Noreen coming out. 'Jesus, where were you?'

'Ah now, if I can't go on the hop on me last day, Noreen.'

'Your man's waiting inside. I'm off to see if I can get Jim settled, I'll be back later. Now it mightn't be for too long, Farley – you'll under-stand?'

He nods and kisses her on the face. Noreen starts. 'Have you drink on you?' she laughs.

'Go on now, you loved it,' he says.

She goes down the steps.

'Noreen!' He says it a little too loudly.

'What? Jesus, what are you roarin for?'

'O sorry, I was just like wondering, how was Kathleen after?'

'Alright. A bit upset. Over the cross and chain, mostly.'

'Ah yea. She would be. She…'

'Farley?'

'What?'

'Take my advice now and shut up about Kathleen.'

'What are you on about? I was only askin.'

'O, never mind. Look, just go in and see Tony. And here, Farley, best maybe just listen to what he says. Say as little as you can get away with saying, if you know what I mean. And good luck.'

'But about Kathleen, I was only—'

'Farley – let me put it this way – have you ever discussed Kathleen with me?'

'No. No I haven't.'

'That's right, and you don't have to either. People aren't stupid, you know.' She pauses, puts her hand on his arm, 'Look, I know you'd never do anything.'

'No, no of course I wouldn't.'

'But still and all, Farley – you know?'

Then she looks at the sky and trots off up the quay.

But he can't seem to help saying it to Tony. 'Your ma? How was she after?'

'Yea, grand, yea, ta. Sit down, Farley, rest your legs there. Been out and about?'

'That's right.'

'Sure why not? Not as if we're goin sack you – wha'?' Tony throws him a wink, then inserts his little finger into the spine of a file and flips it open. The file has his name on it.

'You have a file on me?'

Tony looks up. 'Yea? Of course we have – why wouldn't we?'

Farley nods. 'No, I just, yea, grand. Go on.'

'Right,' Tony says, 'before we begin here, I want you to know this is just a bit of a chat about your retirement package. Nothing written in stone, you can go away, have a think about things, come back and we can talk again – right? Good stuff. Now, I've been looking at the figures. At your end there's the years of service to the company and all that and anyway, this is what I consider to be a fair amount.'

He writes something on a page, twists it around and slides it across the table.

Farley looks down. Then he puts on his reading glasses and blinks. 'What's this?'

'This is what I was thinking.'

'No, no, I mean what is it *for* exactly?'

'Well, obviously, it doesn't include your pension. Your pension is your own business from now on. We've paid it up to date since you started it. It's up to you to decide with the brokers what you want to do about that. It's a pity you didn't start it sooner though, Farley, but there you go.'

'The company couldn't afford it sooner.'

'Right. Anyway, that figure I've just given you is, well, I suppose, it's to say thanks for the years of service.'

'And that's it?'

'Well, yea.'

'I thought you were supposed to be buying me out?'

'What do you mean buying you out?'

'I am a partner in this company – remember? I own a quarter share.'

Tony joins his hands, begins tapping a knuckle off his chin. 'Look, I don't know where you're getting that from, Farley.'

'I bought into this company. I own a quarter share. Don't try and tell me you didn't know that.'

'Do you mean legally, like? Because so far as I'm aware there's no contract.' Tony rocks in his chair, shaking his head, vaguely bewildered.

'Hold on now here, just hold on now. The agreement was between me and your da.'

'But you've nothing in writing, Farley. No contract?'

'I didn't feel the need to drag solicitors into it. I felt our word was enough. Our... our trust.'

'I can only repeat – there is no legal agreement.'

'It was a *gentlemen's* agreement,' Farley says, his voice rising on the word gentlemen.

'Gentlemen? You pair. Don't make me laugh.'

'Are you calling me a liar?'

'Alright, alright, Jaysus will you calm down? I'm sure there was an agreement of some sort. All I'm saying to you now is that whatever agreement there was, it was never legal and the company is not obliged. However, in consideration of everything I'm willing to go—'

'Your da is obliged.'

'But not the company, Farley, not the company.'

Farley stands up. The drink curdling in his stomach, his tongue like a lump of sandpaper in his mouth. He needs to get out before he says too much. He needs to get to the door.

'Look, I'm not discussing any of this with you. I'll wait and talk to

Frank. None of this has anything got to do with you. None of it.'

'Da signed everything over to me, Farley.'

'That's impossible.'

'Everything.'

'Not everything he didn't. Not my quarter.'

Tony bites down on his lower lip. 'How many times do I have to say it, Farley, you don't own a quarter, you never did.'

'I gave your da money when he needed it to keep this company going. In return he promised me, *promised* me – do you understand?'

'O now, I might have known you'd fling that back in his face, Farley.'

'What?'

'In fact, I did know you would, which is why I'm also giving you back the money you loaned da.'

'I didn't loan it to him. I *bought* into the company. The deal was that when I retired we'd either sell up completely or he'd buy me out. That was the deal. And here's something else – twenty-five grand was worth a lot more then than it is now.'

'I will give you…' He brings the piece of paper back to him and scribbles something else on it, before twisting it back to Farley. 'Now, that includes interest as far as I'm concerned.'

'You must think I'm a fucking simpleton.'

'Farley, it's all the company can afford.'

'What are you on about?'

'It's not the business it was. The day of the handy number is gone. The computers have put paid to that. We need to expand, to start investing big time in modernizing this place, because believe you me, Farley, the whole legal world is changing. And we have to keep up. Business is just not what it used to be.'

'Don't give me that shite.'

'All I'm saying is…'

Farley stands up and leans over the desk. 'They're out there buying houses like they're fuckin sweets, Tony. I know that. You know that. Everybody fuckinwell knows that.'

'Keep your voice down, will you?'

He lowers his voice. 'I worked my bollix off for this company. Do you hear me? I was here right from the start.'

'It's a decent figure,' Tony says. 'I mean I don't know what else to say to you. You can always speak to a solicitor – if you want to go down that route, if you want to go upsetting everyone but, well, that's up to you.'

'I'll speak to your da,' Farley says, 'and meanwhile you can stick that up your hole.' He rolls the page in the heel of his hand and bounces it off the floor.

'It's nothing got to do with him, Farley, this is my company now. Mine.'

Both men are standing now. Both shaking.

'You see, Farley, I don't owe you a thing, but I would advise you to remember before you go whining to Da or anyone else for that matter, that I know. I know all about you.'

'You know what? What do you know?'

'Push me now and I'm warning you, you'll be sorry. Push me now!'

It crosses Farley's mind to reach over and grab the fucker, pull him in, slap the baldy head off him and rip the fucking earring out of his ear. But the front door heaves open, the sound of voices yapping excitedly in the hall. Then the door to Tony's office snaps open and Brendan pops a red face in. Noel and Paulie behind him. 'It's in,' Brenner says, 'the verdict is in.'

'The verdict?'

'The Nevin trial.' Brendan clenches his fists and lifts them over his head. 'Yes! O yes! I won the bet! Five days I said and five days it was.'

'Guilty?' asks Tony

'Guilty as fuck.'

He tries to enjoy the night; his night. The handshakes, the kisses, the spot-light following his every move. One minute he's downstairs at the bar with Brendan and Paulie, the next he's being herded along with a group of legs up the stairs to his party. Walls a familiar colour, trim on the stairs – that's right, the Bachelor Inn. He tries to forget about Tony, sometimes he manages; dipping in and out of half-drunken conversations, throwing his smile in with all the other smiles that are swimming around in the back-drop mirrors, laughing at jokes he doesn't always get, especially the ones he makes himself. He stands at the end of the counter for a while; drinks coming at him until the barman decides to maintain a bit of traffic control and starts telling well-wishers that he'll put the drink down for later because otherwise it'll go flat or worse, go to waste. The barman knows he's not a big drinker; not any more. A two-pint man, maybe three at Christmas or the occasional Friday night. Otherwise coffee, cheese and ham toasted, the odd time he might go mad and have crackers.

There's a small hill of presents on the seat by the door and Geraldine from accounts is shoving them into a big plastic bag. There's street lights outside on the quay, glaring in through the long windows. The river below puckered with neon light. Darkness. He'd forgotten that about the drink-ing life, the hide-and-seek trickery of public house time. It seems only five minutes since he had his first pint in Hughes's and at the same time it feels like five years ago. After Martina he had lost months and months, maybe up to a year. Somehow. A whole year. Bar one or two incidents. Bar many regrets. Farley blinks. Somebody hands him a greeting card. 'Go on, open it,' she says, then snatches it back and opens it herself, reads out the message, cackles. It's the exact same card, with the exact same joke, as two others he's been given earlier on.

'O yea, very good, very good,' he cackles back. He sits at this table, then that. But every time he gets settled someone else comes in and he has to stand up and greet them. Some of them he hasn't seen in years. One bloke – not Louis Grogan, is it? – is carried up the stairs, a folded wheelchair left at the door like a baby's pushchair.

'Leg amputated,' Louis says, with a twinkle and a theatrical flourish of one hand waving an unlit fag. 'Fucked basically – but hey, here I am! That's a large one, if you're asking. And here – anyone got a light?'

Objects keep moving. The bag of presents now behind the counter. His reading glasses. He loses them then, completely by chance, finds them again on the edge of a table he can't even remember sitting at. People disappear, reappear. He's looking at skimpy Brendan at the far end of the counter, stuffing triangle-shaped sandwiches three at a time into his gob, salad cream all over his fingertips. He looks away for a second and Brendan has turned into Una what's her name? And then Una is down the far end of the room talking to somebody else. A voice starts singing 'Low Lie the Fields'. Silence for the first few lines, before boredom sets in and bit by bit the chatter resumes and the singing voice is smothered.

There's solicitors and court clerks. Porters from the Registry of Deeds. There's two old school pals of Martina's that bring tears to his drunken eyes. He keeps saying, 'I can't believe you came, girls, I just can't believe it.' Then he can't think of anything else to say to them so he buys them a drink and slithers away. There's law searchers, clerks, for fuck sake a couple of barristers. There's some he'd know anywhere, and some he can't recognize at all. There's everyone and anyone, but there's still no sign of the Sloweys. He needs to settle. To stay in the same place. He finds a perch at the bar – somebody gives him their stool.

'Ah here,' he says, 'I'm not that old yet,' but he takes it anyway and gratefully.

A little blonde one is chatting to him and he half listens, spiking brown sausages with a cocktail stick. Like a tray of small dogs' turds, he's thinking to himself while at the same time he tries to work out who your woman beside him is and what the hell she's on about. Fortunately she repeats herself quite a bit so he's just about able to hold onto the jist, or at least to make the appropriate comment: 'Ah, go away?' he hears himself say. 'Isn't that terrible now?' 'O yea, yea, I know what you mean.' 'O God, there's always one – isn't there?'

She's drinking a pint as big as her head and after every couple of sentences she takes a good slug out of it. Whenever anyone comes up to say hello or wish him the best, when he turns back to his pint she's there waiting with the rest of her story: '… so in anyway, as I was saying…'

He thinks she's talking about the Nevin case, but then again she could be talking about her aunty too, who has a caravan down in Brittas. And there's some rigmarole involving a past injustice she never got over; a bitch in her class at national school. All he knows for sure is that this little five foot nothing has him trapped in a corner. He's about to make an excuse, slither off the stool and ditch her, but then he sees Tony Slowey come in, his sister, Miriam, close behind him.

Farley lowers his head, puts his elbow on the counter, his hand to his forehead and starts taking a sudden deep interest in what Blondie has to say. But he still has difficulty keeping up – whether this is because he's drunk or she's just thick, he can't say.

From the corner of his eye he watches the periscope of Miriam's head, hairdresser stiff, scanning the crowd for him and through the mirror he sees the broad pattern of Tony's poncy shirt brush through the party down to the back of the room.

Then he sees Jackie walk in and feels a gush of childish love. He wants to shout out, 'My brother! My little brother!' and run over and give him a hug the way he did when Jackie was four and went missing for hours and they all thought he was dead till the police brought him home. Farley clears his throat, stands his full height and waves at Jackie who spots him quickly enough but makes no effort to move. He can see that the crowd might be too much for him and that if he doesn't get over there quick, there's a good chance he'll leave. Blondie sticks her face in her pint again. 'Excuse me, love,' Farley says and makes his way through to his brother.

'I never expected anything like this crowd, Jackie, what?'

Jackie looks around.

'I mean – so many to turn up – who would have thought?'

'Yea,' Jackie says. 'So many.'

'Come on – I have a grand spot over here by the bar, let's get you a drink.' He puts his hand on Jackie's arm and feels it stiffen. 'Come on, Jack, it'll be alright.'

'Where were they all when you needed them?' he says.

Jackie turns and heads out the door. Farley tries to push after him but a woman from the Probate Office is throwing her arms around him, and somebody else is shaking his hand. A few seconds later Paulie comes up behind him and for once makes a pointless comment that happens to be useful. 'Just seen your brother there on the way back from the jacks, Farley.'

'The jacks? Thanks, Paulie.'

But he's not in the jacks. Farley goes downstairs and searches the bar, then hurries outside where he looks around both corners; first to the lane then to O'Connell Street. He peers across the bridge and up and down the quay but Jackie is gone. He decides to try the jacks again. Farley stands listening to the regurgitation of pissy water; the same stink in here as the jacks downstairs, as any pub jacks he's ever been in. The same shudder of revulsion at the back of his throat. Clamping his lips together he decides he might as well have a piss while he's here.

When he returns to the party he sees Jackie halfway down the room, this time with Frank Slowey's arm around his shoulder. They must have met on the stairs or down on the street. Slowey, dressed like a golfer, even though he doesn't play golf, is leading Jackie down the back to where Tony and Miriam Slowey have taken over a corner. He watches Slowey pause en route to shake a hand, kiss a cheek, slap the top of an arm. He always uses his right hand; his left hand stays on Jackie's shoulder. And then suddenly he can't see his brother any more, he's down beside Tony and his wife, Miriam and her husband, down in the Slowey nest. He wonders if Kathleen is there. Farley wants to push his way through, to go right down there and speak his mind – if he knew what it was his mind was trying to say. Alright then, to go right down there and demand his brother back. To say, to say—

Noreen's beside him. 'Come on, Farley, let's sit you down for a few minutes.'

'Jackie…' he begins

'He'll be grand with Frank for a while. They'll be talking horses – you'll only be bored. Don't worry, come on.' She turns him the opposite way and they bump into Blondie.

Farley attempts an introduction. 'Do you two know each other?' he begins.

'Mind me drink, will you?' the youngone says without looking at Noreen, 'I'm goin out to the jacks. And here, keep an eye on me smokes.'

'Jaysus, are you expecting to be robbed or something? I mean to say, you work with these people.'

'No, I don't.'

'Well, how come you're here then?' Noreen asks.

'I was downstairs and someone said an oulfella was having a retirement party and there'd be free drink and that.'

'Eh, excuse me. That oulfella,' Farley begins, 'that oulfella just so happens to be me.'

'O. Well, in anyway there wasn't.'

'Wasn't what?' Noreen asks.

'Free drink. I had to buy me own.'

'Yea, and you can mind your own and all,' Noreen says, pulling Farley over to a seat by the wall.

Faces above him zoom in and out. Sometimes they come down to his level which is better because it hurts his eyes having to look up, it makes it difficult for him to see straight. A jumble of voices:

'Here, Farley, I thought you didn't drink?'

'Well, like I take the odd pint.'

'Jaysus, you're well locked you are now. Here, look at Farley, he's langered he is.'

'Special. You know, special.'

'Occasion?'

'Circumstances. When I was younger I drank, of course I did. I drank a lot, too fuckin much in fact.'

'And what? Then you gave it up?'

'After me wife.'

'I never knew you had a wife – did you know he had a wife?'

'Ah years ago. Years. Where's Noreen?'

'At the bar. She's not your wife – is she?'

'No. No, amn't I tryin to tell you?'

'And what happened – she left you because of the drink?'

'Ah no. *No.* Do you know what it is? Me eyes are killing me. They're just.'

'Here, Jason, Farley is just tellin us about his wife.'

'You have a wife, Farley? Jaysus, you kept that quiet.'

'She died but. You fucken eejit. *Died.*'

'O fuck, sorry. Jaysus sorry, Farley.'

'No. No. No.Why would you lot be sorry? You were hardly even born. I didn't stop the drink because she, you know, *died* or anything. It took me about a year after and then I didn't touch it *atall* for ages. And now I just sort of *mind* meself like.'

'Mind yourself? O, you're minding yourself now – are you?' He hears Noreen's voice.

'You're back!' he says. 'Noreen's back,' he says to the chap sitting beside him.

'I see that, yea,' the chap says.

Noreen sits in beside him and pats his arm.

'Do you know what I want to tell you, Noreen. And you lads too, you lot should know this. Do you know what it is, this? This woman here. This Noreen woman here. Well, she's probably my best friend. *Ever* I mean. Now. I bet none of you knew that. Ah laugh, go on laugh. But it's true now. Yes, it's the truth. The truth, the truth. We never, you know. I mean I didn't, you know, nothing like that, and that's probably a pity, but then it's probably not.'

The weight of his eyelids. He clenches every muscle in his face then gives it an overall shudder. But the eyelids keep pulling it down. He hears Paulie's voice. 'Jaysus, he's falling asleep.'

'Ah let him,' Noreen says, 'just what he needs. Christ but, the weight of his head!'

*

Shuffling, shushing, hishing sounds. He's on a shingly beach. He's in his own little tongue-twister, selling seashells on the shore. Bag after bag, people can't seem to get enough of them, a queue all the way down the strand into the sea; the ones at the front pushing and shoving against his seashelly stall. Weary from all the serving, from all the shuffling of sea-shells into bags, he rests his head on a sea wall beside him. SHHHHH shhhhh SHH – will you? Order! Order!

The wall collapses; his head takes a tumble, something sharp digs into his ribs. 'Wha? Wha? Where?'

'Shut up will you – Slowey's making a speech.'

Farley looks around the table. Faces of clerks all turned in the same direc-tion like ugly flowers to the sun. The profiles and side views of people standing in the centre of the floor. Across the way Louis slumped in a chair with his head thrown back. Everyone looking at the back of the room, everyone still. Only the barman moves in his own sphere; busy hands searching, finding, sorting.

Slowey's voice presses down on the laughter: 'And that's when I knew – that's when I said to meself, Farley now is the man for us. Even the Shannon couldn't keep the fucker down!'

They open their mouths to let out the laughter. Hands clapping, a head turning here and there to glance at Farley. Noreen is giving him a glass of water; to clear his throat – obviously expects him to say a few words.

'Seriously though…' Slowey restarts and they all fall quiet again, 'on behalf of myself and Kathleen – who unfortunately couldn't be with us tonight but sends her very best – on behalf of the family and the company, which of course is really another branch of the family, I'd like to wish Farley all the best for the future and to thank him for his loyalty and friendship over the years. To Farley!'

'To Farley! To Farley, Farley. Good man Farley, sound man Farley, Farley, Farl. Faraway Farley.'

A parting in the crowd and he can see Miriam's hairstyle pushing through. Her father's voice follows her. 'This is a little something; a little token if you like from all the cast and crew to see you on the way.'

Miriam behind a large gift-wrapped box smiling away at him.

Farley clumsily gets to his feet. Silence.

She's smiling at him nervously. 'Uncle Farley,' she says, her eyes bright with drink or unshed tears. 'I hope you like it – it was Ma's idea. A sound system. Ma said now that you'll have more time to listen to your music, you might as well listen on something decent.'

'O,' he says, 'O, now.'

Speech! Speech!

He looks around the table at Paulie, Jason, skimpy Brenner. He looks back at Noreen, smiling encouragement. He looks down the room at Slowey standing in his golf jumper, and he sees the smooth naked crown of Tony's head by his elbow. Then he looks at Miriam, the parcel full of ribbons and bows that she probably put there herself.

'Speech! Speech! Speech!' An uproar of tinkling glasses and banging feet.

Farley nods and coughs down into his throat. Silence again.

'You can…' he begins, 'you can all…' He rubs his nose and looks down at his feet. Then he takes a breath. 'You can all. You can all probably tell I'm too drunk to make a speech. But thank you for coming; for the present, for the great night, and for getting me so locked I probably won't remember a bit of it. Thanks, Miriam, thank you, sweetheart.'

He gives her a kiss and she's telling him now that she's going to leave the present behind the bar for him.

'Jesus,' Noreen says when he sits back down. 'For a minute there I thought you were goin to say somethin else.'

Farley looks at her. Behind him someone is singing 'I left my heart in San Francisco'. 'I'll be back in a minute,' he says.

He crosses O'Connell Bridge, feels himself give a semi-stagger but manages to pull himself up just in time. When he gets to the other side he rests at the wall and looks back over the river. The leaves are barely up so he can see through the trees; the Bachelor's Inn, the light from its upstairs windows, the dark pattern of movement against it. He cannot imagine that, up to moments ago, he was part of that gathering, that someone else, someone he will never know, could well have been standing right here on Aston Quay just as he is now, looking across the river and watching through the window, wondering what was going on, and what sort of people were up there, and who was it all for anyway?

He turns and continues along the quays past darkened shops and rows of parked cars and cars rolling towards him out on the road. The further along he gets the fewer cars and the only people he passes now are stragglers at different levels of drunkenness, and a couple in a doorway sucking the faces off each other.

At the Four Courts bridge a man leaning over the balustrade attracts his attention; a fat little bloke dressed head to heel in red and white, scarf, monkey hat, jersey. The man looks up as Farley is about to pass by. 'Excuse me, mate?' he calls after him, 'would you have a cigarette please?'

'Sorry, don't smoke,' Farley says.

'Are you sure?' he asks in a pleasant sing-song accent, not Irish. 'Only I'd really love one – you know.'

'Sorry.' Farley looks at him. 'Are you not freezing with no coat on you?'

'Are you not?' the man answers.

Farley looks down and realizes he's forgotten his coat.

'I suppose I am,' he says. 'You don't mind me askin where are you from?'

'Cardiff.'

'Cardiff? What are you doin here anyway?'

'O, you know, over for the match like.'

'But the match was last week'

'Still trying to find my way home.'

They stand and look at each other for a few seconds.

'Well, night so,' the little bloke says and waddles away.

'Yea. Goodnight.'

*

Farley looks down over the bridge into the water. The river bristling away from the sea. He slips his hand into his inside pocket and is grateful for the small miracle he finds there: his glasses. He pulls out an envelope. He opens it and removes the folded photograph. Then he puts on his glasses and holds the picture under the light. The Sloweys on Michael's communion day. He returns the picture to the envelope, rests his hands over the parapet of the bridge for a moment and then begins to tear the envelope into shreds. Farley watches the confetti of paper bobbing on top of the dark oily water before bucking out of sight under the bridge, under his feet. He turns and staggers westwards along the quays towards home, bumping his arm at intervals as he passes beside the endless wall of Guinness's. It's darker up here, darker and colder than it is in town; the street lights are feeble. Across the road he can barely make out the outlines of parked-up trucks. A leftover brasser steps out of the shadow, throws him a look then dismisses him with another and turns away. He keeps going until two small moons of yellow light pop out of the darkness, a sign on the top blazing yellow. Farley steps out onto the road and raises his hand. 'Taxi!' he cries.

The Summons Server

June 1990

HE SETTLES HER INTO her little nest – duvet, pillows, shawl for her shoulders. She knit it herself, only a few months ago, when it was still safe enough to leave her with needles. The remote control is at her right hand; the phone, if she bothers to answer, a short stretch to her left. He tries to foresee the day through her eyes; all the small things she may need or later regret not having asked for – tissues, pencil case, copybook, a magazine showing more pictures than words.

'Tell me again,' she says.

'Tell you what again, Ma?'

'Tell me who? Who's coming?'

'Jackie. Jackie will be here around one.'

'I call him John.'

'Alright, John. John will be here around one o'clock.'

'Not the curly one?'

'Who's the curly one?' he asks, placing the small basket of treats on the table.

She smiles when she sees them. 'Club Milk, Jelly Tots, banana,' she says. Even if she never eats them, their presence at least seems to bring her some pleasure.

She comes back to the curly one. 'You know, her with the…' she lifts a crooked index finger and begins dotting it around her cheeks, 'the beans all over her face.'

The girl with the acne. 'Jeanna? No, she's taken the day off.'

'Good, because she makes me dinner *too* early and I don't like when it's *too* early.'

She lifts a lock of hair from her temple, smugly tacking it behind her ear and he can see in that girlish gesture that she's pleased with the sound of her sentence, the correct alignment of words, the musical use of the *too*.

'You see I don't be hungry.'

'I know.'

'Only babies eat their dinner at that time.'

'Right,' he says, going out to the scullery.

'The other one – the fatty?'

'Carol.'

'Yea, her. She makes it at the right time, but then she eats the half of it herself.'

'Carol won't be coming any more,' he shouts back to her.

'Why?'

'Well, it seems she doesn't like being called names.'

'Who calls her names?'

He comes back in with two tumblers; one of orange juice, the other water and he can see she's confused by the idea of Carol and the name-calling. She gives him a sheepish look.

'The orange juice is in the orange tumbler,' he says, lifting it first to show her, 'the white one is the water. Orange for orange. White for white.'

'O, that's very clever,' she says, 'who thought of that? The other one?'

'Do you mean John?'

'Who's John?'

'Jackie. No, he didn't think of it. I did.'

'Hah!' she says. 'As if!'

He checks the tightness of the lids, sees that the little beaks are facing the right way, then lays them on the table. Now at the window-cill he picks up his mug of tea and, standing with his back to the window, regards the infrastructure of her diminished world – the sofa where she lies; the foot-stool beside it; the bridge of the coffee table; the two little avenues of access at either end of it, for lifting her in and out of her nest. The sweet shop of medication on the shelf in the alcove. And the telly of course; all roads lead to the telly.

'Well, I better be going.'

'Why?'

'Because somebody has to work, seeing as the rest of the country seems to have the day off.'

'Why?'

'The match. Ireland play Romania today – remember I told you? The World Cup?'

'Ah no. Not that why.'

He waits while she throws out her driftnet and pulls in her catch of words. It's the questions, he notices, or the lead into them anyway; the whys, whats and whos, that cause the most trouble.

'Who? Who else? *Who* else will be here?'

'Nobody else.'

'No, I mean – who else will I *see*?' She bites her lip and glances over to the television.

'Ahhh, right. You mean what programmes? Do you want me to write them down for you?'

'Yes,' she says, then smiles and lifts her two thin arms up to him for a hug. He lowers his eyes and pretends not to see.

He might as well finish his tea. Coming back to the sofa he perches himself on the far end of it, places the mug on the floor by his feet, then opens the newspaper at the television page. Her arms are still open but at least they've veered towards the telly, now pleading a hug from a man on another sofa who's talking Ascot hats to a twinkling presenter.

'Ah no,' she says crossly, 'don't just mark it. Don't just do it the lazy-man's way.'

He looks up to see if she's speaking to him or the man on the telly.

'Lazy, lazy, always lazy. Write it proper out.'

'Pass me the copybook so,' he says.

She lowers her arms, lifts the copybook, kisses it, gives it a little rub, then opens it out on the last page, folding the cover back and passing it to him. 'Only that page,' she says.

'Right. Let's see now – this is breakfast television you're watching now. And that'll be over at half nine.'

'What time is it now?'

'Just half eight. You can see the time on the little clock on the bottom right corner of the telly.'

'I haven't got me glasses.'

'You're wearing them, Ma.'

'Ah, what are you talkin about now!' she shouts, startling him. 'If I get me hands on you, I'll give you such a, such a—'

He sighs. 'Do you want me to do this or not?'

'Yes.'

'Alright then, behave yourself. After this you can listen to the radio, if you like.'

'Who will it be – Gay?'

'No, he's not on at that time. Pat Kenny.'

'Ah, I'm not listening to him. He's as bad as yourself. Lazy. Stupid. Talking through his big backside.'

'Right. Don't bother with the radio so. Wait till this is over then change the telly to number three – see on the remote.'

'What colour is three?'

'Red, I've marked it red. So you can watch till *Home and Away* comes on and when it's over you'll know that Jackie will be here in a minute.'

'Give us a kiss,' she says, 'you oul puddin.'

'I have to go to work now.' He closes then folds the newspaper.

She picks up a cushion, cradles it in her arms and nuzzles it with her cheek. Now she is fluttering little kisses along the top of it and making mewling sounds as if it's a kitten. The mewling sounds turn into whispers, so it could be a baby either.

He hasn't told Jackie about this latest development, this talking to the objects she's chosen to love. Jackie is barely able to cope with the onslaught of affection as it is. 'Intolerable gush,' he called it last night on the phone before going off on a rant about how she never touched them when they were kids unless it was to hit them. And how she brought them up to feel that affection was some sort of failing.

Of course, Jackie blames her. For everything – his marriage break-up, his gambling, his having to come back from London. But most of all his failure to reach the lofty notions she put in his head when he was a kid.

'The trouble with Jackie,' Slowey often says, 'is that he's *too* fuckin intelligent. And that's why he makes a bollix of everything.'

Farley stands. 'I'm going now, Ma. You'll be alright?'

'Ah, don't go, don't leave me. I'll be good. Am I not good?'

'You are good. I'll only be gone a while. Jackie will be in soon.'

'I want to go home,' she says.

'You are home.'

'I want to go home. It's the wrong colour here.'

He thinks she could be talking about the wallpaper but then her hands begin stroking on the air and he recognizes the caress. She misses the long grass, the green of the Phoenix Park just outside her door. 'I'll get Jackie to bring you out to the garden, it looks great, all the flowers.'

Her bottom lip pops out. 'It's too small. There's no sky.'

'O Jesus, Ma. Come on now. I have to go to work.'

'I want to go home. I want to go home to the baby.'

'We're not babies any more, Ma.'

'Not you. *The baby.*'

'There's no baby.'

'The baby. Ah, you know her, the baby. Something beginning with, beginning with... B!'

'I'm goin. Now.'

She cocks up her nose. 'Ah shut up you, you big fool.'

'Right.'

'I want to go home. I want to go home.'

'This is your home now, Ma. You live here with me.'

'Where's your wife then?' she asks.

'She's dead, Ma, this long time.'

'What?' She puts her hand over her mouth and her eyes grow big with sorrow and shock.

'Ah no, I'm only joking.'

'You killed her, you bastard. You put a pillow over her face and squashed the air out.'

'She's gone to the shops.'

'But she'll be back on Sunday?'

He nods.

'At four or half four?'

'Four.'

'Will Mrs Kennedy be coming instead?'

'No.'

'Just a pop-in for a little cup of tea, even?'

'No, Ma, she won't.'

'A weenchy teenchy...?'

'No. Mrs Kennedy is not coming again.'

'O,' she says, 'O, O, O no,' shuttering her face with her hands, shaking her head from side to side.

He waits for her to forget. Because there is that at least; she always forgets. But he can feel his patience slipping away. The day already cut in half because of the match. The worry that she'll freak out now and that he won't be able to leave her. The amount of summonses he has to serve because they've fallen behind. He thinks he'll never get out that door. Away from this room, this woman, this unlucky house. A sour taste leaks into his mouth; a bile of resentment towards his brother; the thoughts of him, in his neat little teaching job finished at three every afternoon. His long holidays, his smug little flat, probably chosen for its lack of space; room for one only. One man and his misery.

He begins to gather up his documents, stuffing them down into his briefcase. Then he picks up his wallet and car keys.

She is glued to the telly again where a sinewy woman, poured into a shiny green leotard and matching tights is scissoring her legs and grinning like a maniac. Ma, grinning back, repeats the mantra, 'Point and flex, point and flex…'

She is his child now. The child he never had. Even the way she speaks, all sugar and spice, except for when she turns on him. Then her old voice takes over, cutting like glass through his head. Lazy. Stupid. Do you want a belt of this – do you? Stop hanging out of me for Christ's sake. We are not affectionate people.

He stands at the door and she turns and looks at him. 'I love you,' she says.

He nods and rattles his car keys.

He's still thinking about Jackie as he drives towards town; the memory he has, long and convoluted – all the shit it manages to hold on to, like he has another intestine inside his head. Figures and facts, politics, world history. Horses, horses, horses. And every minute from his own past. No wonder he suffers from headaches, having to lug all that lot around.

He thinks about Jackie's wife too, the sister-in-law he's never met nor so much as seen in a photo. Her name is Jasmeena, something like that.

'What is she – Indian or something?' Farley had asked one night in the Mullingar House shortly after Jackie had come back from London.

'Don't be so fuckin stupid,' was the reply. So she could be Indian. Or she could be a hippy maybe. Or she could be that oulone at the bus stop outside the tyre depot combing her hair. For all he knows.

The most Jackie had been prepared to say – and that was only because Slowey had put the screws on him – was that they'd met at Aintree, married in York, divorced in London, that she worked on the tote, that the marriage had lasted a few years and that somewhere in the middle of all the irreconcilable differences, they had managed to have a child. The kid would be about sixteen now. A photo of him as a toddler does exist but stays in Jackie's wallet unless he's really locked then he might take it out and look at it under the table. Only once did he show it – again, on Slowey's insistence – the picture so crumpled it had looked like the boy had one of those rapid ageing diseases. Turlough – that's what they called him, just in case there'd be any chance he wouldn't get slagged in his English school.

The traffic. When it does move, it moves in opportunistic little thrusts – every man for himself, every man in a hurry. A red van breaks the lights onto Con Colbert Road, comes tearing out from the Inichore side, so that he has to slap his foot down to stop himself from ploughing into the side of it. The driver loops out in front of him with an apologetic wave and a *you-know-yourself-the-day-that's-in-it* sort of a grimace.

'Yea, well we're all under pressure,' Farley shouts into the windscreen.

Before the second set of lights the traffic clogs up completely. And there's the van again, only two cars up, well and truly trapped – after all that trouble and risk.

He could be stuck here for at least ten minutes. He could be stuck with nothing to do only think. Think about her. Because it seems every time he gets a blank moment, in she slips. And he doesn't want that. He can think about work, Ma, Jackie, work again. But he will not allow himself to think about *her*.

He turns on the radio. A procession of women's voices; variations on a theme of selfish bastard husbands. 'He swore to me, *swore* like that he'd be back after Sicily and now he's off to that other place, that—'

'Genoa?' the presenter helpfully suggests.

'Yea there. Sleepin on the street like a tramp and askin me to send money. I mean to say – our *mortgage* money.'

'OK, stay there, Carmel. I want to bring Imelda in on this. Imelda, now tell us about your husband – he set off for two days, how long ago was that now?'

He switches to another station. A singer screaming blue murder; male, female, he couldn't say which but it's like getting your head kicked in from the inside out. He switches off the radio altogether and turns his thoughts on Jackie again. His brother is starting to wriggle. His brother wants out.

Of course, he takes it too personally, this whole business with Ma. This whole 'gaga carry-on' as calls it himself – as if she's doing it all for the fun of it. And the thing is, the *oddest* thing is Farley doesn't mind her that much at all. He'd prefer it not to be happening, of course. He'd prefer her not to be there at all. To be somewhere else, a nursing home maybe or even, if he's to be honest, in a plot in a graveyard that he could plonk a few flowers down on now and then. But she doesn't repulse him, not like she does Jackie. Other things get to him. The sense that death is waiting every time he puts the key in the door. But that's nothing to do with pity or love. That's all got to do with Martina. Martina's last months – that's what he hates. Whereas Jackie on the other hand just hates Ma.

He tries the radio again. More talk about the match. He's a pain in his hole listening about the match. He'll watch it, feel it, live and breathe it. He just won't listen to any more waffle from any more back-seat drivers. He lowers the radio, leaving a purr of voices to cover the silence. Then he flaps open his briefcase. Dipping his hand in, he fiddles about at the various papers until the rim of a yellow page shows – the schedule. He takes it out and rests it on the dial of the steering wheel. Five summonses that should have been served by now; solicitors threatening to go else-where if they don't get the finger out. He runs down the list. Two of them to be served in Fitzwilliam Square; a doctor and some poor fucker who thought he could make a living out of renting out fax machines. A woman who owns a boutique off Grafton Street. The doctor and the boutique owner – handy enough – bread-and-butter jobs, won't want a scene in front of customers. What next? A summons for St Michael's Estate – how had he missed that? He snaps the page with the back of his fingers. He could have gone there first, caught the punter unawares at this hour of the morning, missed all this traffic while he was at it. 'Ah fuck, fuck, and fuckit anyway,' he says.

He goes back to the list, the last name on it: Larry Phelan, a mainten-ance dodger – always a pain, usually have someone to cover for them too. 'He's not here, he was never here, O that's right I just remembered, he's dead.' Three unsuccessful attempts already made on Phelan. Farley turns the page and reads the report: 'No reply from the premises at blabla-baba. Two cars in the driveway, BMW and a Fiat Punto.' Second attempt: 'Only the BMW in drive. A man answered the door but never heard of anyone called Phelan.' Third time: 'Saturday morning only the Fiat, this time a woman answered, said the man called Phelan had moved to Australia.'

Of course, it would not have occurred to Easton to join up the dots. That's if he bothered doing anything more than driving past on one occasion.

He picks up the car phone and calls Noreen.

'Where are you callin from?'

'The car.'

'O yea, keep forgetting I'm working for James Bond now. What's up?'

'That summons – out in Rathfarnham, the maintenance dodger – was there a check run to see who owns those two cars, do you know?'

'Funny you should ask about that – Easton has just been on.'

'What's he want?'

'A reference.'

'Does he not realize he's been sacked? Does he not realize that when you write something down in a report it's supposed to be true? And does he not realize it's down to him that we could lose one of our best clients? And God knows what else he's made a balls of while he's been at it. This Phelan case for example.'

'I said I'd ask you anyway.'

'Yea, well you can tell him to go fuck himself.'

'Grand. Anyway, no, we didn't run a check on the cars. The solicitors said to keep the expense down. They don't hold much hope, but the wife, it seems, wants to take it to the bitter end.'

'Are there kids?'

'Think so. Three or four.'

'Right. I'll give it another go. Why do women put themselves through this, Noreen? Why don't they just forget about these bastards? No, actually I'll put it another way – why do they get married at all?'

'Because we – well, we're fuckin eejits, I suppose.'

He glances up, the traffic is moving again. 'Better go.'

'Hold on,' she says. 'Did Frank get you?'

'No.'

'He's been trying to phone you. From Italy.'

'He stayed on then?'

'Looks like it. He managed to get tickets anyway.'

A horn beeps behind him. 'I'll phone later,' he says, flinging the schedule onto the seat beside him.

Farley pulls into the left lane where the traffic is starting to move. He decides after all it might make more sense to double back and chance St Michael's Estate. As he turns his ear picks out a ripple of something small and soft; a flicker of sound. He turns up the volume and yes it is him, that big Italian bloke. The sound grows into the car and he feels the surge of music, the words that he can't understand, the story behind them, the richness in one man's voice. It oozes under his skin, into his blood, his heart, his balls. The car at last getting a good run at the road, flies up and over Sarah's Bridge as if the wheels haven't touched off the ground.

He didn't come back. He didn't come back.

He just might phone her. He promised he wouldn't, but he just might anyway. Only a few seconds – long enough to say, 'Look, I'll see you in Ma's house, after the match.' Then again, maybe he'll wait a while – see if she phones him first. What he'll do is this – if he gets lucky with this summons, he'll take it as a good sign and then he'll phone her. No, better still, if she doesn't phone him by midday he'll phone her then. But. It might be better to wait until he's finished work and available. Yes. That way, when he's no more than a quarter of an hour away from her, he can sort of spring it on her. The less time he gives her to think, the less time she'll have to change her mind.

*

He parks the car out on the main road, a short walk from the flats. Then he memorizes the details on the summons; the block and number of the flat in question; the name of the punter – Leonard Montgomery, which just goes to show you never can tell with names. A witness subpoena in an insurance case – at least it's not a criminal matter, so slightly less chance of getting battered. Farley rolls the summons into a scroll, sticks it down into his pocket and covers it with his elbow.

God he hates this desolate place; the block-built look of it, the speckled high-rise walls, the jumbled graffiti all over the landings and stairwells, the piss stink. Beirut, Slowey always calls it. 'Bay-fuckin-root minus the sunshine.' The last place anyone wants to serve a summons.

There's the skull of a burnt-out Volkswagen car on a scabby playing green behind the flats, and in the playground, the limb of a broken swing hangs from one hinge. He crosses the grey slabs of the courtyard, a crunch of broken glass under his feet. The yard deserted, apart from flutters of litter, a burst ball and a few buckled cans of last night's lager. At the west end a bright new Irish flag is hoisted to a pole. More Irish strips are draped over balconies; green, white and orange, all spanking clean against the general background of dingy grey and scribbled slogans – *Drugs Out. Up the Provos. Dolores sucks cocks. Fuck the Begrudgers.* The last two appear to be written by the same hand; he wonders if they could be connected.

At the end of the block he notices a pair of runners dangling on long laces from telephone wires: the merchant sign of a resident drug-dealer. He checks its proximity to the Montgomery residence. Good. At least whoever else he might be about to wake up – it won't be the drug-dealer.

It's more like a door to a meat safe in a butcher's shop than the door to somebody's gaff: reinforced steel, bolts all around it, one of those handles. No knocker, no bell. On the far side, a low sturdy growl. He gives the door a thump with the side of his fist and the growl combusts into a rage of barking; two maybe three dogs in there. He backs away and while he waits, leans on the balcony and looks out. Over the rooftops of Inchicore, past the coned spire of John's church, all the way across to the

Phoenix Park; a bush-covered skyscape and a slender glint from the pope's cross. All the same, what a view.

'Hey mister?'

He starts, then brings his eye back over the landscape down into the dirty-grey courtyard. A small girl, maybe four years old, standing outside a boarded-up flat. The youngone gawking up at him, mouth open, hair standing on end. She's dressed in a grubby night dress, wellington boots that come up to her knees, a scarf around her neck with the word Ireland written on it.

'Hey mister?' she says again.

Farley leans over the balcony. 'Yea?'

The child blinks a few times. 'Nuttin,' she says, but keeps looking up anyway.

Behind him, the rattle of chains. He turns and sees through the crack in the door, a nose, an eyebrow, the inky slur of a home-made tattoo on a large forearm. The dogs fling themselves off the door, begging to get out and get stuck into him. Farley shouts over the din, 'I'm looking for a Leonard Montgomery?'

'For wha?' a voice asks, rattling with phlegm.

'Well, it's personal,' he says, and the door moves to close.

'Alright, alright,' Farley shouts, 'it's only a witness summons in a road traffic case. No trouble, I promise. Just a summons and a cheque to cover expenses.'

A bit more face shows, hair blonde with long roots of black. It's only now Farley realizes that he's been talking to a woman. Sort of. Down at her knee a Staffordshire terrier is twisting his head to get out, his jaw like a vice grip dripping with ancient hunger. Behind him his twin is fighting for space, flat savage face ramming through now and then. The woman turns to the dogs. 'Shurrrrup youse,' she says through her teeth. 'Shuuruupp to fuck…' and the barking abruptly cuts off. He'd love to ask if her name is Dolores.

'How much is the cheque for?' she drawls.

'Eh, let me see now. I haven't got me glasses on – where is it now,

O yea,' he lifts the cheque to his face and squints into it, 'looks like two hundred and fifty quid here.'

The hand comes out. 'Righ' I'll make sure and he gets it.'

'Sorry, love, but. I have to give it to him personally.'

A sigh, a tut, a mumble. 'Hold on and I see if he's here.'

She closes the door and the two terriers completely lose it, until a yelp, probably the result of a kick, slides into silence. Now a man in his vest; a sour, sleep-battered face, just out of the scratcher.

'Yea?'

'Are you Leonard Montgomery?'

'Yea?'

'I have a summons here for you, cheque attached, details are on it.'

A hairy hand comes out, Farley puts the summons into it and quickly walks away.

He's halfway across the yard when he hears Montgomery's voice come over the balcony. 'Here you!'

Farley looks up, sees the cheque waving over the balcony.

'I thought you said this was for two hundred and fifty quid? It only says twenty-five here.'

Farley lifts his hand. 'O sorry, my mistake. Wasn't wearing me glasses.'

'Ah, you think you're fuckin smart – do you? You stupid bollix. You think you're so fuckin smart. I could be working that day, for all you know.'

'Get a letter from your boss so.'

'Ah yea, very fuckin funny. Bollix.'

He increases his pace, the little girl wide-eyed as he passes. 'Hey mister, he's after callin you a bollix.'

'Yea, I know,' he says, 'and I wouldn't blame him either.'

Farley drives through the tail end of the South Circular road. Blips of sunlight on a shaded street. He's forgotten how much he enjoys being out on the road, the sense of moving through a day, rather than having it come at you; locating the punters, planning the strategy, the little rush of success after. In the early years they worked as a team; Frank and himself, like Starsky and Hutch in their Ford Cortina. Every day was an escapade. The half-drunk blonde still in her nightdress at two in the afternoon who'd tried to get off with Slowey. The elegant wife of a businessman who'd ended up running after the car, bashing the bonnet with the lid of her dustbin. Or the time they walked in on a wake and had to pay their respects to the corpse before turning around to serve on his brother. There have been ones to regret, of course, summonses he'd rather not have served: some unfortunate bastard who got in over his head in a business venture; a doting mother going guarantor for her waster of a son; a domestic. But as Slowey says, what has to be done has to be done, if not by us then by some other fucker.

Under the sycamores a flock of girl guides wait for a bus, fidgety little tricolour flags in their hands. Like the car before him he gives them a beep and they raise their flags in response. On the far side of the road outside the garda club, two cops are having an animated conversation that could only be about football. A summer's day full of hope and glory.

He runs the jobs through his head again. One down, four to go.

The boutique turns out to be some sort of a bridal shop and the owner gives him no trouble. She turns puce of course the minute she sees him, putting two and two together – a man in her frilly shop and her up to her gills in unpaid loans. But she accepts the summons with a sweet shy smile and a slight genuflection, like he was a page delivering a love letter from her knight in shining armour.

The doctor is a much better actor. A quick glance around the waiting room to see who's watching and he takes the summons with a little 'Ah!' as if it contains some vital information that could save a patient's life, instead of news of a malpractice suit for making a hames of some poor bastard's gut. 'Thank you for that,' he says with just enough disdain for Farley alone to read.

'O, the pleasure is all mine, doc,' he returns in equal measure.

Farley comes back out through the carpet-padded hall, chandeliers winking overhead, and on the table a bowl of big-headed flowers. He crosses the granite threshold, closes the brass-badged door behind him and wonders if the grin he feels inside is showing on his face. He doesn't like doctors and the further up the scale they are, the more he doesn't like them. A fucker like that now, he hates.

He sits in his parked car under the leafy fringe of Fitzwilliam Square North, keeping one eye on the basement office of the fax rental man. Back in an hour, the jittery daughter/girlfriend/wife had said; pretending to be the secretary anyway, whoever she was. With the other eye he watches the drift of the day. So long as there's people to watch, lives to be guessed at, he never minds. That specky fella coming down the steps – a chartered accountant. That pretty little one in her late twenties – a typist who'll marry the first plonker who asks, just to give herself something to do. Those two youngfellas yapping at each other over a computer they're loading into a van, the one on the left is a benny, the other one senses something but isn't sure what. They'll come and they'll go and he'll watch and he'll wait. Workers and residents. Some trapped for the day in houses boxed into offices, others trapped for a lifetime in houses cut up into one-roomed flats. Like that old woman, a carefully dressed silver-blonde with her arm in a sling. Whippet thin. She takes each step as if she expects it to be landmined. She'll live in a room at the top or a room in the basement – nothing in between. Spinster. Not a bad-looking bird in her day. Just never met a man good enough. A dipso, he'd say – of the shabby genteel variety.

It's getting too warm in the car; the heat like a shell forming around him. He opens the door, puts his feet out on the ground. A man and a woman dressed in white shorts, tennis rackets tucked under oxters. Householders.

One bell on the front door and a gar-*adge* round the back. You wouldn't see that many of them nowadays. The man turns the key in the lock on the gate and they disappear into the garden of the private, residents-only-you-can-fuckoff-the-rest-of-you Fitzwilliam Square. By nightfall all that will have changed; it'll be flashes of white thigh from an open coat, cheap boots over the knee. Trickles of fag smoke under the street light. The glint of a slowing car. The thud of a deal-done door.

He stands for a minute, stretches, then gets back into the car. Dropping his arm through his legs he finds the handle under the seat, and jerks it back. His legs greet the sudden space, his arms go up, he pinches the leather and sponge of the ceiling; *stretch* and yawn, then watches a woman in a Toyota Starlet enter the parking spot next to his. One smooth, clean movement, bonnet first… aaand she's in. Across the way, a man is reversing his brown Opel into a space. His face contorted with the exertion of it all; puff, pant, hands this way and that, while out on the road two other cars are waiting for him to finish so they can get by. Nine times out of ten it happens this way; men reverse in, not giving a damn about how tricky it is or how much longer it's going to take, or who they hold up in the process – so long as they have a quick escape. Women on the other hand take the easy, fast way in and then worry about how they're going to get out later. Nine times out of ten. He wonders should he call her now, then he looks at his watch. The hour almost up, better wait so. He picks up the briefcase, begins rummaging through the pile for the fax man's summons, then notices something odd stuck in between all the documents. His mother's copybook. In his hurry to get away he must have bundled it in with the rest of the papers. She'll go on and on about it for the day and Jackie will do his nut. As soon as he finishes serving this he'll phone; maybe drop it in on his way to Rathfarnham. He opens the copybook. Her little drawings inside. He feels a slight ache in his chest. He remembers as a child, how proud he was of the fact that he had a mother who could draw. In those days women couldn't really do anything, unless it involved kids and the house. But his ma? His ma could lift things out of their location and put them on a page – the trees in the park, the horses from the barracks, the giraffe looking over the rails of the zoo. A child's face. She could put light and shade and life into them all with no more than a pencil. When she'd finish she'd ball up the picture and throw it in the fire, like it just didn't matter. He used to hate the way she'd do that; the slight violence in the gesture.

He turns the pages. Her hand is a little shaky but still good enough for him to recognize what or who has been in her little world over the past few days. This surprises him because he'd presumed the drawings would be like her thought process – full of scribbles and haphazard shapes. There's Barney and Betty Rubble from Friday's *Flintstones*. Flipper popping his head out of the water. A black fella at a piano – that's right, Nat King Cole. Your woman who reads the news. The girl on the sofa from breakfast telly. And notes too, she's written little memos to herself. 'The man says we're not allowed eat beef. Tell Charlie the cows are gone mad.' On the next page is a picture of Jackie on the telephone. At the end of that page is another note. 'Biscuits for Mrs Kennedy.'

He turns the page. 'Mrs K is dead. Mrs Kennedy is dead. Dead Dead Dead. No more Mrs Kennedy. Don't ever say her name again.' And he knows by the thickness in the ink that this was an angry note, a lucid moment when it all got on top of her; shame, anger, confusion. She often forgets Mrs Kennedy is dead.

He turns the page. 'But not Rose Kennedy. She's not dead. Yet.' Farley laughs.

There are two further pictures of Jackie on the phone and the telly in the background with a horse's head in the frame. He wonders if this is Ma's way of telling him that Jackie spends the afternoons watching the racing in between making calls to his bookie or Racefone or whatever the fuck it's called. He closes the copybook and begins to worry. What if she's recorded more than Jackie's carry-on? What if he were to flick through the pages and find a drawing of someone else? He thinks now of a careless moment in a careless afternoon a few weeks ago when Jackie hadn't been available to keep an eye on Ma. Ma was having her nap on the sofa when she'd arrived. They'd gone upstairs and when he was sneaking her back out again Ma opened her eyes – 'O, hello there, what are you doing here?'

He flicks over the pages, one after the other, looks for a trace of a handbag on the floor in the hall, a coat through the gap of the door hanging on the end of the stairs, a woman with black hair hurrying out the front door. Nothing. It seems Jackie is the only one she's ratted out.

'Tell Charlie about that,' the note says. 'Tell Charlie. Tell him.'

Farley closes the copybook again. Something catches his eye; the dip of a creamy bald head disappearing down the basement stairs.

'Gotchya,' he says and jumps out of the car.

By the time he gets back to the office, bangs off the reports to the solicitors and listens to everyone going on about what a great fella Slowey is for giving them a half-day from the comfort of his hotel terrace in Genoa while he waits for a tout to deliver two overpriced tickets for himself and young Tony. And by the time he drops Ma's copybook back up to the gaff and listens to Jackie moaning for half an hour about how hard it all is and about how he can't see why they don't just sell Ma's house, put her into a home where she'll get proper care.

'She gets proper care here,' Farley says

'Ah, come on now, just look at her,' Jackie says.

'What? She's an old woman asleep in the afternoon. What's wrong with that? Put her teeth in when she wakes, she'll look better then. And here, don't forget her tablets. I'll give you a ring.'

'I can't stick this much longer,' Jackie says, grabbing his hair and giving it a little tug, 'I'm telling you that now.'

'It's your turn, Jackie.'

'I'm not talking about now. *Today*. I'm talking about the foreseeable future.'

'Well, lucky for you she doesn't have that much of it left. Listen, we have the girl coming in Monday to Thursday, we can do the rest between us. What are you moaning for anyway? I'm the one has to live with her.'

'Suppose she starts, you know, shittin herself and that?'

'Jesus, what are you sayin that for?'

'I've been reading up on it. Intransient incontinence, it's called. That is, before it becomes established incontinence.'

'Fuck you and your whatever it is incontinence.'

'Why can't you just agree to sell her house? What the fuck are you holding onto it for?'

He can hardly tell him why and so he lashes the ball back. 'What's the matter, Jackie? Thrown all your money at the bookies again?'

And he's sorry he said it, the minute he says it, because when it comes down to it they both have their ulterior motives.

By the time he's done with all that, it's nearly four o'clock and he might be raging with Easton and Slowey and Jackie and the world and his wife but he's still fuckin starving and the match is starting in twenty minutes.

The car park of the West County Hotel is stuffed corner to corner and so he has to park on the kerbside outside. He takes a Thom's directory out of the cubbyhole and searches for the address he's been given for the maintenance dodger. The house registered to someone called Johnson; the dodger's landlord.

He calls directory enquiries, asks for the number for Johnson, jots it down on his hand and phones it. The new bird picks up. He can hear chattering voices behind her like there's a party going on in another room.

'Hello,' she says and a doorbell rings. 'O, hold on a sec please.' He listens as she greets someone. Her voice is excited, overly nice, trying that bit too hard, as the new bird tends to do; the party, her idea most probably, a chance to get his old mates on her side, to show off their life together in this upmarket, albeit rented house. 'O hiya. Mick, isn't it? Nice to see you again.'

'Ah howiye,' Mick says. 'Is Phelo not here yet?'

'Go on through, he's out the back. Lar? Larry? Mick is here. Sorry, Mick, just on the phone here.'

His mates call him Phelo.

'Sorry about that,' she says, coming back to the phone.

'Ah no bother. Just wanted to tell Phelo I've been held up and I'll be late getting there…'

'Do you want to speak to him?'

'Ah no, God don't disturb him and the match about to start. Sure I'll be there later.'

'Who is this?'

'Sorry, love, the line is very bad, what did you say?'

'I said, Who is this please? Who will I say?'

He gives her a name that sounds something like bllalaaargh and she says, '*What?*'

'I'm on one of those car phones, can hardly hear you. Look, just wanted to check you'll be there for the night – or will you be going on somewhere else?'

'No. We'll be here – there's food after. A party.'

'Great stuff. Looking forward to meeting you at last.'

'O.' She gives a small uncertain laugh. 'Yea, me too. Seeya then.'

He manages to get what has to be the last sliver of space out in the foyer. Jesus, the noise. That spiky, haphazard, nervy commotion of a herd collectively shitting itself. The double doors to the hotel bar have been removed, inside a cinema-style screen has been rigged up for the occasion; the backs of hundreds of heads turned towards it, and more spilling out to the foyer. A pair of lounge boys in cheap shitty waistcoats struggle down the stairs with a telly that's obviously been taken from one of the bedrooms and another pair, bearing another telly, waddle out of the lift. These tellys, along with two or three others, are plugged into different points around the foyer, attracting little breakaway groups from the glut at the doorway to the bar.

He's lucky to get the sandwich at all. The staff, if they're not arsing around with the tellys, are swaying through the crowd with overloaded drink trays and it's only because he helps one stick-armed youngfella who couldn't be more than thirteen years old to carry a tray of pints to a table down the end, that he's rewarded with what looks like the last ham sandwich on earth. 'Five minutes to kick-off,' he hears a woman squeal.

'Do you know what,' her husband groans, hugging his stomach, 'I think I'm gonna get sick.'

He'd prefer to watch the match on his own; not to have to listen to the innane little commentries going on all around him. To cry if he wants to cry, bite the hand off himself if it comes to it. He's not sure he can put up with all this: the push, the sweaty smell of fear, the false alarms, the tension. He's not sure he can't trust himself when he's surrounded by all this emotion. He decides to eat the sandwich, take a couple of slugs of the lukewarm coffee, go off then and listen to it in the privacy of his own car while making a slow way out to Rathfarnham.

He has his jaws poised around the sandwich when he feels a tip on his elbow. He turns, looks over the sandwich and sees her walking away from him, not looking left nor right, but straight ahead and up the stairs. He looks around; all eyes on all televisions. Farley lays the sandwich down and stands up. Fuck the sandwich, fuck the match, fuck Phelo or whatever he's called, and, as the sign in St Michael's Estate earlier said, fuck all the begrudgers. He's up the stairs like a light.

Before he turns onto the corridor he hears the sound of the key jigging into the lock. A clef of dark hair then, a sleeve of summer cloth and she disappears. Farley thinks of nothing beyond that door, all the things he will have to pass along the corridor in order to get there: pictures of kittens in ramshackle frames, a cigarette singe on the carpet, a splash of afterhours beer on the skirting board. A fire extinguisher.

'Hiya,' she says when he comes through the door and then she looks away.

A nod, a smile and he averts his own eyes.

It's always like this before they settle; hardly able to look at each other, hardly able to think of a thing to say. After all these years it's still that way.

'Sorry I couldn't make it on Friday.'

'That's OK.'

'Michael, you see. I'd no one.'

'And today?'

'Miriam brought him down to the mobile for a few days.'

Today's room – two beds; a small double and one single, quilted in shabby orange nylon. A plastic kettle stained brown at the spout, a short bare shelf up on the wall, where until moments ago a television would have been perched. He wonders if she's comparing this room to others. He knows she will be able to remember, off the top of her head, each and every one. Not just the room either but the reception desk, the attitude of the receptionist, the date, the amount of weeks that had passed since the previous room. He'd have to be reminded, his memory prompted and poked – apart from the few memorable ones like that chintzy place in Wicklow. Or Killiney Castle the time of the snowstorm. And the dives of course – plenty of those – for all the times she could only get away for an hour and hadn't wanted him wasting his money: Drumcondra, Parnell Street, the stadium end of the South Circular road. For the past year or so, since his mother moved in with him, it's every Friday afternoon in the abandoned house where he was reared. Apart from that one time, a few weeks ago at his own house, but that was a once-off, too risky and too upsetting for either of them to want to repeat.

'How did you know I was here?'

'Your car. I was passing and…' she gestures to a place outside this room, the world out there. 'I'm sorry, I know you want to see the match but—'

'No. No, I don't mind. Not at all. Were you not afraid anyone would? I mean, it's packed down there, you know? Anyone could.'

'Mandy, a friend, she works on reception. I didn't even have to go to the desk.'

'Can you – you know – trust her?'

'Ah yea, I know her this years, lived around the corner from us, we went to school together.'

He nods then scratches the back of his unitchy neck. 'So, that means she would have known—?'

'Martina? Yea, she knew Martina.' She gives an impatient sigh, a slight toss of her head. 'Jesus, Farley,' she says.

'What? What? Jaysus, I'm only asking.'

She sits on the edge of the double bed near the window, showing one red cheek. He's annoyed her now and that's the last thing he wants. The first thing he wants is to be over there beside her, pulling the clothes off her, making himself blind and deaf with the feel and smell of her.

'I'm only saying, if I'd have known, I could have got somewhere nicer for us, that's all.'

She nods but she's still not right.

He takes off his jacket, lays it on the back of the chair. 'Look, I can't have you paying, anyway,' he says, putting his hand down into his pocket.

'Stop it,' she snaps. 'Just...'

He sees now that she's been crying. He wants to ask why, to comfort her. He wants to cure whatever, or kill whoever it is that's upset her. But he just stands there. He can't stop looking at her hands. They are both staring at her hands. Clasped together on her lap, fingers pulling and twisting at each other like one live thing chewing another.

She says, 'I got you a present,' and her hands break apart and move away to pick up her bag from the floor.

He wants to touch her. Any sort of a touch, her elbow, her shoulder. He knows that sometimes the slightest touch is enough, to break it all down. To take him from here, into that blind, sweet silence. She shoves the present at him; small, square-shaped in a flimsy plastic bag. It strikes him that in all this time she's never bought him a present. He catches her eye and now he gets a sense of what may be coming.

'Farley?' she begins, then stops.

'Yea?'

'Farley?' she begins again, stops again.

107

He pulls the plastic bag away from the present and asks, 'So – what is it?'

'It's a CD,' she says. 'That fella you like, sings the football song. Pavarotti.'

For a minute he doesn't know what she means – see dee? Pav who? What fella is she talking about?

He sits on the end of the single bed by the door and looks at the CD box in his hands. And he can hear now, through the floorboards, the rumpus of the football match; an ocean of noise, lifting and falling, lifting again.

'It's bits from different operas,' she explains and he knows by the sound of her voice that while she speaks she is crying again, trying to form the words, to keep her breath, 'and the girl in the shop, she said… She said, the thing to do is to listen to them all first – get to know them and that, see which ones you like before you go buying the whole opera. I suppose it's a bit like a *Top of the Pops*, only posher.' She gives a long sniff then he hears her blowing her nose.

'Yea,' he says. 'Yea great, thanks. I haven't got a you know? A thing to play it on.'

'Ah, can't you buy one, Farley?'

'Course I can.'

Quieter now, she lifts herself from her corner of the bed, reaching out to the ashtray on the dressing table. Farley gets there first and hands it to her. She begins to search through her bag for cigarettes.

'Have you something you want to say to me?' he asks her when she has the cigarette going.

'Tony knows.'

'Tony? How could he know?'

'Well, maybe not for definite but he's suspicious. He won't be long putting it together.'

'Ah, you're imagining it. How like? *How?*'

'He's not a kid any more, Farley, he's a grown man.'

'I know he's a grown man, the world's full of grown men, that doesn't mean they all know.'

'They phoned from Italy this morning and I was talking to Frank and then Tony came on and I said something like, Ah God, it'll be lonely here on me ownsome watching the match what with Michael gone down to Wexford with Miriam and he said, just like that, and his da right beside him, "Can't you phone Farley if you're so lonely then?"'

'Ah, he probably just meant—'

'It was the *way* he said it.'

'Well, you know, he probably just meant like me being a friend of the family and that.'

'But you're not – are you, Farley?'

'Not what?

'A friend of the family. I mean, come on, for fuck sake, you're screwing his mother. His father's wife. You're no friend.'

The bitter way she says it. He opens his mouth to answer, but nothing comes out.

She's weeping now, big breathy sobs. And he hasn't seen her like this since the day of Martina's funeral. He gets up and crosses to her bed and sits down beside her, curving his arm round her shoulder.

'I was down with me ma last night,' she says, 'and you know she's not well at all and anyway she'd all the old photos out and was talkin about Martina, and I just. I can't. I just can't any more. The wedding photos – Jesus. You and Martina. My mother, your mother. Me in me little brides-maid's dress. O God.'

'Shh,' he says, 'shhh. It'll be alright.'

'I'm not taking the risk. The whole thing is all wrong. No matter what you say, Farley, it's wrong. It's not fair to anyone. Least of all you.'

'Me? What are you worried about me for? Jesus.'

'You should have married again by now. You're not a bad-looking fella, you know.'

'O, thanks very much.'

'Instead of wasting all these years on me.'

'Don't say that. It wasn't a waste. It isn't.'

She drops her head on his arm. 'They're me kids, Farley. I can't risk it. Neither of us is worth that.'

Farley takes the pillows from the bed, puts them behind his back and leans against the wall, still holding her. She smokes a couple of fags. He rubs her hand. Once she strokes his face and says, 'You need a shave.'

'I know,' he answers.

They stay like that for a long time listening to the distant roar of the match, heaving below them.

'I wonder how they're gettin on,' she says.

'Yea,' he says. 'I wonder.'

She looks at her watch and he knows the time has nearly come. He lets his head fall back for a moment, the edge of the window-cill slicing into his shoulder blades. He looks up at the flowery curtains and the plywood pelmet which, he notices, is about to come away from the wall.

He could always suggest they do it anyway, one last time, for old times' sake. When he was younger he might have chanced it. But he doesn't want to; not now.

He leans forward and kisses the top of her head. She slides off the bed, picks up her bag and goes to the door. There's a sudden, ominous hush from downstairs. In the silence he thinks of all the sex they've had over the years; the small, self-contained violence that sometimes existed between them, like they were punishing each other. Hers always physical, scratch, pull, bite, pinch. His, she once told him, was too emotional. He had and hadn't known what she meant.

Downstairs something erupts, like the spark of a huge furnace. Noise crashes through the hotel, a frenzy.

'We must have won,' she says.

The plastic kettle hops, the cups beside it rattle. The door at her back shudders. 'There you are,' she laughs through the tears, 'and we thought the earth wouldn't move today.' She looks at him for a moment, the slight stare in her eye more pronounced, as it always is when she's tired. Then she opens the door, and she's gone.

The noise continues, if anything it gets stronger. When he stands it seems to go right up through the soles of his feet. He is surprised to see how still the world outside is when he stands at the window. Still and deserted, except for her figure, crossing the car park. It happens, sometimes, when he sees her like this, at a remove, that he thinks he's looking at her older sister. He remembers now, another room; a room out in Bray somewhere. She'd whispered into his ear just as he was about to come, 'I know. I know you're pretending that I'm her.'

He'd been a bit shocked but came anyway, because it had been too late to do anything else.

'But guess what?' she said then.

'What?'

'That's OK because I'm pretending to be her too.'

He wonders if she's stopped crying.

Farley steps into the small square hall and stands at the parlour doorway. Ma, still on the sofa, but asleep. Jackie, conked out on the armchair by the fireplace, head flung back, mouth dropped to one side, looking a bit like Da after he'd had the stroke. A banana skin on the floor at his feet, a few stray Jelly Tots scattered on the chair beside him, the wrapper of the Club Milk on the fire grate. On the table a bottle of sherry that must have been in the press since God knows how many Christmases ago. Two cans of Guinness from the back of the fridge scrunched up in the fire grate. The room stinks.

Farley stays in the hall and tries to shake off the day. He puts his back to the wall, pressing it, stretching. Weary now, the turning points are slurring through his head. The fax man, the doctor, the woman with the black hair crossing over the car park of the West County Hotel. And the car, always the car, moving one minute through silent, deserted streets, the next through streets that are overrun by hysterical fans. Danger everywhere; fellas swinging out of lamp posts or hanging out of car windows. One of them, who had been standing on the roof of a moving van, had slipped off and landed on the road right in front of him. If he'd been going any bit faster...

He'd slammed on the brakes, got ready to call an ambulance. But the youngfella had bounced back up again: 'If you love Packie Bonner clap your hands. Clap your hands!' And he'd felt like getting out and knocking him down again with a punch.

Finally, the bloke in Rathfarnham, answering the door with a grin on his chops. A little gurrier with a Hitler moustache, full of himself with his three taxicabs on view through the open door of the garage and his little ponytail and his sovereign ring on his middle finger. The grin of course dropped the minute he copped what Farley was at. Cute little fucker, knew the drill right enough, throwing his hands up in the air, backing off – 'Here, you never touched me with that. It's not legal unless you touch me.' Then pouncing on the door and trying to close it in Farley's face.

But his foot got in first. He could have decked the little bollix there and then. To hell with the consequences, to hell with the fact that he could lose his licence or that some of the guests were beginning to notice and that in a few seconds' time he'd be making a run for the car. Farley reached in, grabbed him by the arm and through his teeth said, 'How about I stick it up your arse – it'll touch you then?' Then he'd shoved him away. 'They're your kids, for fuck sake. Your kids.'

There could be trouble over that. But if there is, Farley tells himself now, it'll be tomorrow's trouble.

Inside the parlour; a smell of cigarettes and drink, something else, vaguely floral. The early hours of the morning. On the telly a different world gently glimmers: green grass, slow legs in white trousers, the languid purr of a cricket commentator. Ma's eyes open.

'That fat bitch ate all the biscuits,' she says.

'She wasn't here, Ma.'

'And he gave me the wrong copybook,' she says, pointing to Jackie.

'Yea, Ma, I know.'

She goes quiet then for a minute, watching the cricket, pinching the edge of the duvet.

'Charlie?' she says. 'Charlie Grainger.'

'What, Ma?'

'Charlie?'

'Yea?'

'Charlie Barley Farley Grainger.'

Her hands go up, her arms stretch out. 'Weewee,' she says.

Farley sighs, takes off his jacket and helps her out of the nest, then lifts her, like a bride in his arms and carries her up the stairs.

She feels like nothing in his arms; her ribs through her nightdress; her lightness and lack of substance. She hums as she goes, laying her head on his shoulder. She does this sometimes, nestles up to him, becoming coy and even flirtatious, hinting at a former life that she may have had with Da. Once she even stuck her tongue in his ear and he nearly let her fall down the stairs he got such a fright. Of course he'd never tell Jackie that. There's that smell again. The floral smell. It makes him think of honey that's gone off. The smell of? He sniffs again, moves one hand slightly and feels the wet cloth of her nightdress. And so it's happened, just like Jackie said it would happen.

'We better get you a clean nightie,' he says.

Hunger

December 1980

HE OPENS THE BACK door to a mucous-grey morning; feels the damp coming up from the soil, the tired silence. Next door an old rubber glove hangs like a skinned hand off Mrs Carroll's clothes line. In his own hand, a bag of birdseed; on his mind, the half-written letter he's just left on the kitchen table. He can't remember how many starts he's made on this letter – at some point he'd taken to balling the rejects and bouncing them off the wall – but imagines when he goes back into the kitchen the floor will look like a yard of dead, white doves.

He brings the bag of birdseed outside and pours careful little mounds of it onto the feeder tray, then throws a few long scatters over the grass for the ground feeders. He steps back to allow the birds access and while he waits, reads the back of the bag. His eyes can't quite grasp the words and he wonders, not for the first time in recent weeks, if maybe he needs glasses. He lifts the seed bag closer to his face, then away from it and the list of ingredients comes into focus: black sunflower, white millet, naked oats, linseed. He likes that each of these smallest of things should have its own name, and he likes too the idea of people out there somewhere who actually work at picking and sorting the seeds, bagging and boxing them, just so birds can be fed and saps like him can take some small pleasure out of a dank Saint Stephen's morning.

Already a couple of robins are bouncing over the grass and a chaffinch is pooching under the feeder. The blackbirds next; one then two, then three of them. Farley turns and goes back into the kitchen. He looks down at his latest effort. From where he's standing he can't make it out. He lifts the page, passes it back and forward until he finds the right eyeline. It reads as nonsense now anyway, whereas five minutes ago, before he got the notion to go out and feed the birds, he had thought that maybe, finally he had hit the right tone. He puts the seed bag down and from his jacket hanging over the back of the chair, pulls an envelope out of the inside pocket, the slip of paper within.

For two weeks or more he's been carrying this bank draft around, since the day John Lennon was shot, in fact. Twenty-five grand. Until the moment the cashier's hand bashed the stamp down, Farley – when and if he did think of it – often had doubts about its existence. He had looked on it a bit like he looked on God – it might be there and then again it might not, but either way it wasn't going to make much odds to his life.

He has a memory of the cheque arriving a few months after Martina's death and of him going to the bank and shoving it into an account which he opened just for that purpose. The bank out in Donnybrook – a branch he'd never been to before, and he has no explanation for this choice unless he had picked it for pure inconvenience. And he can remember too declining first the offer of a chat with the bank manager, and next the offer of a spot of advice from a suit through an iron grille wearing a badge that said 'Victor'. The name had annoyed him; the suit; the colour, shape and length of the tie. He'd had to bite back the urge to tell Victor to go fuck off and mind his own business. That had all happened during a particularly angry phase in a long black winter that had lasted for maybe a year and a half; most of which he's forgotten. All he had wanted then was to get the cheque out of the house, out of sight and of mind. In any case he had always thought of it as Martina's money; her insurance, the price and worth that was put on her life. Besides, he had never really wanted to buy anything that couldn't be managed on his own weekly wage. He wasn't a smoker, didn't bother with gambling, not much of a drinker and as Jackie pointed out last time he put the hammer on him: 'A man with no family always has money.'

And so it might have stayed out there in Donnybrook, only for Lennon. He keeps coming back to Lennon, because if Lennon hadn't been shot then Farley would never have pulled into the spot down the quay from the Clarence Hotel to listen to the radio news. And if he hadn't pulled in he wouldn't have seen Slowey dip in through the hotel doors and by turn wouldn't have decided to dip in after him. And then the conversation, *that* conversation, could never have happened.

He had followed Slowey into the Clarence because he wanted to discuss the summons for that priest out in Sandycove. Or because he'd felt a bit shook after hearing the news about Lennon and wanted to talk to someone about it. Or because he wanted to ask about the Christmas holidays. Or maybe just because he fancied the idea of the Clarence on a winter's morning, hot coffee in a dainty cup, a fire bouncing in the grate. For whatever reason, he had followed him.

Inside the Clarence there'd been the usual hush. A priest in the corner behind the door, drinking brandy behind a spread of newspaper. He could hear the clink and fuss of table-setting coming from the dining room and from a pair of barristers hunched under the long churchy windows, whispers drifted into the echo. An elderly maid polishing the hood of the phone booth bobbed a 'good morning, sir' as he passed. And he had felt in good form and vaguely pleased with himself, as he tends to do whenever he goes through the foyer of the Clarence and remembers the way he used to be when he first started working for Slowey; embarrassed, guilty even, as if he'd had no right to be there and could find himself thrown out on his ear.

In the main bar, everything solid and contained; the fire, the wooden panels on the wall, the cranky porter wandering in and out pretending to be busy. At the bar, the bulky back of a man wearing a tweed coat and hat; behind it, a scarlet-faced barman. He hadn't seen Slowey at first, what with the dim light and the distraction of the voice coming out from the bank of tweed. Loud, lordly – possibly English – on the way to or from being drunk anyway.

'He means the *other* Lennon,' Slowey's voice said. '*John* Lennon from the Beatles.' And Farley saw him then, on the bend of the counter smoking a cigar. Slowey then turned to the barman, '… and *he* means the other Lenin, you know, the Russian revolutionary?'

The tweed coat drained his glass then lifted it out to the barman like a child looking for another sup of milk. The barman took a clean glass down and looked sideways at Slowey. Neither seemed to know what he was on about. Slowey rolled his eyes at Farley and said, 'Jaysus, blankety blank. Come on, we'll go inside.' As he moved away he raised his glass to the barman and tapped it with his fingernail, 'Another one of these and… coffee is it?'

'Coffee,' Farley said.

They had the small back bar to themselves. Early of course. He'd been surprised to find Slowey drinking whiskey at this hour of the morning but of course had made no remark. A peculiar mood, Farley could see that straight away. It made him feel he was intruding, like he'd better throw out an excuse for being there at all. The news about Lennon was already too old to use as an opener so he ventured instead, 'I saw you while I was driving on the quay and came in because see I wanted to ask you—'

'Yea?' Slowey shifting around in the seat, shoulders shrugging, smoking the cigar that bit too quickly, taking up enough space for three men on the seat while he was at it. Not really listening.

'O, I was just wondering if you decided about the Christmas break yet? That's all. See Jackie phoned last night and I said I'd ask.'

'You thinkin of going over there?'

'No. Well, I might after Christmas like. But I don't mind either if I don't.'

Slowey showed one eye over the cigar. The coffee arrived. The barman went back to the main bar.

'How long have you been workin for me, Farley?'

'Since I was mid-twenties. Twenty years so. Why?'

'You ever think of working anywhere else? I mean, I'm sure you must have had the odd offer – the wolves that are in this fuckin game.'

'You're not sacking me, are you?'

'No. Of course I'm not. I'm tippin you off, is all.'

'Tipping me off?'

Slowey gave the cigar a short round lollipop-suck.

'Look. Keep this to yourself right? The business – it's in trouble. And I don't know how and I don't know if – ah, it's this fuckin recession for a start or whatever they're calling it. And that bleedin National Understanding on top of it all. You know what the understanding is, don't you? It's that the employer goes out, grovels, gropes, begs for work, then the employee, instead of thanking him for a job grabs him by the nuts and squeeeeeezes.'

'Right.'

'Yea, right. If they're not fuckin whingeing, they're calling a strike. They'll dismantle this country, same as they dismantled England – know what I'm sayin?' A longer suck this time. Then he'd pulled out the cigar and frowned at it. 'I mean, grand, we might have some chance of gettin over all that but there's worse.'

'Worse?'

'Some prick has put a claim in against us. Don't worry, not on your patch – a Land Reg. job. Something that nine times out of ten wouldn't even be noticed but this little opportunistic bollix saw a chance to make a kill and in he goes like a light. A Spaniard. That size – yea, a Spanish midget. Drives a Mercedes, he can barely see over the wheel. Around my age, and he wears a leather jacket with a zip up the front. That's right, a fuckin zip up the front. One of those fuckers – know what I mean? Well, I either pay up or I can kiss me arse goodbye to insurance for next year. No indemnity insurance – no work. Or I could let it go to court and risk losing everything. Anyway, no point in going into all that now, mainly because I'll give myself a fuckin heart attack – you know? A fuckin heart attack. Do you want another coffee?'

'I haven't even begun this one.'

Slowey walloped back his whiskey and rapped it off the edge of the table. The barman peeped in, nodded and disappeared.

'What will you do?' Farley had asked then.

'Don't know. I'd sell up, but who's goin to buy a business in trouble? I could look for a partner but again, who the fuck wants to be a partner in a business that's going down the tubes? Not in this day and age. But I'll tell you what I won't be doing – and that's movin into the new house in spring, just a few weeks away from completion too. Jaysus, I've to tell Kathleen that yet. Happy fuckin Christmas, sweetheart – wha? I'll find a buyer for the house, wouldn't you think? Five bedrooms and a double garage – a double garage, fuck! When I think of it.'

They'd sat in silence then, Farley sipping the bitter end of the coffee, Slowey fidgeting beside him and suckling the cigar until Farley got up and went out to the jacks. And somewhere along the corridor or going up the speckled stone stairs, or having a slash or coming back down the stairs, he had somehow, without really realizing it, more or less made his decision.

'How much like would a partner have to put in?' he'd asked when he sat back down, 'just as a matter of interest.'

'Depends.'

'I mean, how much, how much would it take to get you out of trouble – to keep the business going?'

'Twenty-five grand. But I'd still have to sell the house. Why, do you know someone who's won the sweeps or something?'

'Ah, just wondering, that's all. It's a lot of money.'

'Who are you tellin?'

On the way out to Donnybrook he'd got stuck behind an H-block demonstration, the chant coming through the windows – 'WHAT DO WE WANT?' 'POLITICAL STATUS!' 'WHEN DO WE WANT IT?' 'NOW!'

Pictures of young men stuck on the end of wooden posts, who were starving themselves to death. And whereas before he'd felt sympathy for them, just at that moment he'd felt like plowing through the crowd in his rush to get to the bank, to get one step ahead of himself, before he got sense and changed his mind.

Farley sits down at the kitchen table, moulds the latest page into a ball and this time flips it over one shoulder, where it sounds like it may have landed in the sink. He pulls another page from the pad and flattens it out in front of him. Then he picks up the pen. 'Dear Frank,' he writes. Beneath that, 'I just wanted to say...' He sits back, thinks for a moment before saying aloud, 'I just wanted to say what? Come on, you fuckin thick – what did you just want to say?'

Outside the air is stippled with the hungry twitters of birds. He listens for a moment, then puts down the pen and picks up the bank draft. A paper slip with a few figures jotted on it and a round banker's stamp on the bottom. A promise – his own or the bank's, that he doesn't quite trust. Because somewhere between his childhood and his manhood, money seemed to turn into something else, something abstract; a notion that floats around in the air. You don't have to see it to have it – in fact the more you have, the less you probably see. He'd enjoyed being able to bring the draft around with him, just knowing it was there and that he was, for a while at least, comparatively rich, compared to most blokes he'd know anyway. It had put a little swagger to his walk, thrown a bit of light on his day, he'd even found himself playing up to the women. It had been good to know that even though he never would, he could, if he wanted, draw it out like a gun. He'd brought it into work each day, then home again each evening. Occasionally he had taken it out of one pocket and transferred it into another; his gardening trousers when he mulched the perennials, his corduroys when he dragged Ma's Christmas tree down from the attic and then spent an hour twiddling with light bulbs and wondering if he should tell her his plan, which of course he didn't. It was in his navy suit jacket when he went on the office drinks do, where he'd hoped to get a chance to talk with Slowey; chance after chance slipping away until Slowey got so pissed he couldn't talk at all. It was still with him on Christmas Eve when he stood for a half an hour in Kelty's butcher picking up Ma's Christmas turkey.

'New York dressed?' the butcher had said, laying the turkey out on the counter overarm like a garment while Farley prepared for the seasonal joke. 'Says you – if that's the way they dress in New York they can stuff it.'

And he had felt like saying, 'Is that supposed to be funny? Because it wasn't funny last year and what makes you think it'll be funny now and by the way, I'm carrying a bank draft for twenty-five thousand quid in me pocket, you stupid bollix.'

Until today he had only taken it out of the envelope once – that time he rang Jackie back to lie about how sorry he was he couldn't get the time off work to go over to see him. He had flapped it about a bit and tapped it off his nose while Jackie had lied back to him about what a shame that was because he'd really been looking forward to showing him around London.

'But listen, I sent that few quid over anyway.'

'O great,' Jackie had said, perking up because, let's face it, that's all he'd really wanted, the money. 'Eh, when did you say you sent it again?'

'Yesterday.'

'So it may not get here till after…?'

'O sorry, didn't think.'

'Ah no, you're grand. Eh, how much did you say it was for?'

'A hundred.'

'A hundred,' he'd repeated.

Was there a whiff of disappointment in his voice? Farley wonders now. Because that would be Jackie all over. No matter what you'd do for him he'd never be satisfied. Like you still owed him something. And why exactly? Because once upon a long time ago he'd had a book of poetry published, a book so skinny it wouldn't swat a fly and now he works as a teacher in some kip in the arsehole of London?

Farley had hung up the phone and said, 'If you're so fuckin clever how come you're always so skint? And how come you never copped that Martina, working in an insurance company, would have herself well insured?' And then he had slapped the phone with the bank draft, once, twice, three times, like it was Jackie's face. And the funny thing was, even though Jackie hadn't heard a word of it, he'd felt great after, not at all like he usually feels at the end of these telephone conversations with Jackie – off colour and slightly bereft.

Farley brings himself back to the letter, testing a few start-up sentences on the air. 'Dear Frank, if you are still. No. *If* you like I. No. I have this proposal to make. No, no, no fuck it – *no*.'

He takes the pen again and begins writing. 'Dear Frank, I'm enclosing a bank draft for twenty-five thousand and hope you will consider…' Consider what? Farley stares at the page a while then pushes it off the side of the table. He waits for it to flutter to the ground, then tears a new one off the thinning pad and holds it up to the light. 'Dear Frank, I'm enclosing a bank draft and hope you will consider taking me on as a partner in Slowey & Co. I meant to bring it up before now but thought you could do with the few days off to consider…' Consider? He's after using that word twice. Isn't that what Jackie said that time when he was advising him about writing letters – never use the same word more than once in a paragraph? And anyway, it's all too formal, too much like a letter looking for a job. Like he's begging Slowey to take twenty-five grand off him. 'What is wrong with you?' he says and whacks the heel of his hand off his forehead.

He stands up, goes out to the hall, then into the parlour, then back out to the hall where he sits on the third stair from the bottom, staring out at the glass bubbles of grey light through the front door. The day he was married his mother had given him a hundred-pound note. And he remembers this now for the first time in years. A beautiful olive-green thing. Lady Lavery on one side. A smirking river head on the other. It had a power and mystery that same note. He can't remember how or when they spent it in the end, but they'd held onto it as long as they could. It even came on the honeymoon. The note laid out on the bed between them and Martina giddy after the few Dubonnets and white with a towel pulled around her head, pointing at Lady Lavery and saying, 'That's me,' and then turning over to the river head, 'and that hairy randy-looking yoke – that's you!' And the clumsy overexcited sex they had then, the pair of them like chronic asthmatics, hardly able to breathe with a hunger for each other. And he had thought, Ah, this is fuckin great, this being married lark, able to do this anytime you like, no more groping and hoping in shop door-ways and up lanes, this is the business now.

He feels a knot in his stomach – could be hunger. Farley stands up, goes back into the kitchen, pours himself out a mug of milk, then looks at a not quite fresh slice of bread and wonders whether to toast it. He remem-bers then the leg of turkey Ma gave him yesterday to take home for the supper he didn't bother to have. He takes the foil package from the fridge and opens it out on the table, settling the salt and mustard around it. He eats from the foil with his fingers, dipping the shards of turkey flesh into the mustard and taking a bite now and then from the folded slice of bread, a slug from the milk. While he eats he thinks about yesterday, a different sort of a Christmas Day. For a start no Jackie and no Uncle Cal. Just him and Ma and the walls closing in. She'd sent him out to look for smokes, deciding that after all she may have been a bit hasty in giving up the fags before Christmas what with Mrs Kennedy, who smokes like a trooper, and her niece, God love her, with the gunner eye, coming in for her tea – it might look a bit mean if she'd none of her own to offer around.

He'd been glad to get out. Ma talking non-stop through her arse from the moment he put his foot through the door and the constant search party in between – O, where did I put this now? O, what am I after doin with that?

A sharp, bright day of shuttered shops and relentless church bells. In the end he'd had to bang on the door of that kip of an hotel in George's Street where a porter had grudgingly let him use the cigarette machine.

On the way home he had taken his time; not getting lost exactly, more enjoying the drive. The feel of the car only just serviced, the sound from the new radio that he'd had them install while they were at it; a string quartet on a BBC station. The sense that the music was sleighing him along through the deserted streets. An unnecessary turn here and there, a bridge there was no need to cross, a one-way sign defied, and he'd found himself somewhere at the back of Oliver Bond flats. Black narrow streets giving way to a sudden sunlit clearing. A derelict site. A halting site for travellers now that you'd never know was there unless you happened upon it. A large enclosure, maybe half an acre, fenced in green picket with a back-up lining of wire netting. A few caravans bunched to one side. He'd got out of the car. The sun spiked his eyes and he'd only then noticed the frost, a granulated coating of it all over the roof of the caravans, on the gas canisters lurking under the belly of each one, on the bank of tyres stashed to one side, the small red, windowless van. A piebald pony on a long rope had muck stuck to its coat and matted into the flare of its fetlock hair. This had puzzled him, because he couldn't see any muck, or any place for muck to be; only a big square of pebbles and cracked tar out of which grew a few hairs of grass. He'd been trying to remember what used to be there, because he had all these houses and warehouses in his mind and now that was something else gone for ever, when he saw the little girl coming out from behind a caravan. She was wearing a long dress or at least a dress that was too big for her; a boy's or a small man's jacket over it, and over that again, a manky Aran jumper. She was pushing a doll's pram; a new shiny thing with white wheels and hood. A present from Santy, no doubt. The pram wobbled over the uneven surface and the youngone pushed it on and on into the distance away from the caravans into the large open space at the other end of the site.

Farley pressed his hands on the wire, watching her. A child wandering around on her own, he had thought, anything could happen to her, anyone could get her. A child blue with the cold. He began to notice that she had a method of sorts, pushing the pram corner to corner, stopping at each one and adjusting the hood, bending to pick up things off the ground; pebbles, he supposed. He wanted to wait for her to make her way back down the site and pass him by, maybe give her a few quid for herself. But the door of one of the caravans had snapped open. A man came out and took a step down, staring at him like he was some sort of a pervert. Farley gave a half-salute and got back into the car.

'And that was Schubert's String Quintet in C Major on this bright and beautiful Christmas morning,' the announcer said when he'd turned the radio back on, each word delivered like a small carefully wrapped gift. He'd decided there and then what he'd do. He'd put it in a letter. Leave it into Slowey's house when he was at the races. That way he wouldn't have to see the reaction. Tomorrow. He'd told himself. He'd either do it tomorrow or the money was going back; half of it into the bank, the other half to a kids' charity.

Farley bundles the turkey bones and gristle into the foil and wipes the back of his hand across his greasy lips. The garden has grown quiet again; a shudder from the fridge or the sound of his heartbeat, that's all he hears. The afternoon already coming on. He feels shadows all around him; Slowey on one side, Jackie on the other, behind him stands his father, before him Uncle Cal. And it occurs to him then that all his life he's been surrounded by men more intelligent than he is. Even *in absentia* they continue to watch out for his mistakes. And he's never quite been sure if it's out of concern or if it's out of disdain. He pushes the plate away and pulls a new page to him. 'Frank – here's 25,000 quid. If you want a partner, you have one. If not, just send back the bank draft and we'll say no more. Best, Farley.'

He notes a small thumbprint of grease in the corner but doesn't really give a fuck now. Placing the bank draft back in the envelope he slips the folded page in beside it and draws a slow tongue over the flap.

She opens the door in her pyjamas, a talc-sweet smell like she's just out of the bath, hair in a bunch on top of her head. He tries to work out how old she'd be now – the years since Martina's death, the few years between the two sisters – and reckons on thirty-nine.

When he sees her – God, every time he sees her now. 'I thought you'd be at the races?' he says, looking and not looking at her face.

'Ah, didn't bother. Prefer to take advantage of the bit of peace.'

'I won't come in,' he says. 'In a hurry actually. Just wanted to leave this message for Frank. Well, maybe just for a minute then,' he says when she stands back and holds the door open.

He follows her into a lamplit sitting room; the telly, the galaxy of lights on the tree, the flames go-go dancing in the grate. There's a bottle of red wine shaped like a vase on the table, her glass, half full beside it. Newspapers spread on the floor, an ashtray and smokes.

'You're all nicely set up here,' he says.

'Will you have a glass?' she asks.

'Ah no. I won't bother.'

'Jesus, Farley, one glass is not going to set you mad.'

'Ah yea, I know but.'

'I felt like it today. Just one or two. No fun on your own, but. Don't worry I'm not locked.' She grins and he wonders if she's making a reference to that night last May.

'Yea, alright then, go on, I'll have one.'

He sits on the sofa and looks at the telly; Kirk Douglas talking through gritted teeth. 'Any good this?'

'Not bad. One of those Roman yarns, you know?' She turns the sound down and comes back with a glass, fills it and holds it out.

'Kids not here?'

'Miriam's taken Michael to Funderland and then to me ma's for their tea. Tony's at Leopardstown with his da. Jamesie's out somewhere, probably on one of his marches.'

'I thought the hunger strike was over?'

'Ah, you know Jamesie – South Africa, the hunger strike, workers' rights – there's always somethin.'

She lights a cigarette. And looks at him. 'So you heard the new house is off?'

'Are you disappointed?'

'Not much. Jaysus, Farley, what would I be doin out there anyway in the arsehole of nowhere? I mean to say. Between you and me I was just as pleased. You'd be all day cleaning a house that size. Anyway, there's enough room here since we got that last extension and the boys will be moving out soon enough. Jamesie is talkin about going away – did you know that?'

'I heard something alright.'

She shrugs. 'In anyway.'

He takes a sip of the wine and nods.

'See what I'm resorted to here?' she says, lifting a box off the fireside chair before she sits down; a flat rectangle with a picture of Santy on it. 'Eatin Michael's selection boxes. God, I'm so hungry. Couldn't be bothered making anything of course after half of yesterday spent in the kitchen.' She sits down. 'Unless you're...?'

'No. No, I'm grand.'

'Sure? Because I can make something now if you like.'

'I had a bit before I came out.'

'Right.'

He takes another sip; the bang of it wincing up his nostrils. 'How did the Christmas go?'

'Don't you mean – how did you get over the Christmas? Isn't that what all the oulfellas say?'

'Thanks very much.'

'We were expectin you to drop in.'

'I was over with the ma, you know yourself. First Christmas without Uncle Cal and what with Jackie away and...'

'We don't see much of you these days – thought you might have a woman stashed away somewhere?'

'No,' he says and looks down into his glass.

After a few seconds she speaks again. 'Did you go up to the grave yesterday?'

'I haven't been for a while to be honest.'

'No, neither have I,' she says and looks into the fire. 'I just – well, you know.'

'Yea, I know.'

He takes another sip and she curls one pyjama leg up under her arse on the seat, a slow drift of smoke coming towards him. And the thought comes into his head again, as it's done so many times since, of the night last May, after Michael's communion. They'd all gone to a do in the Terenure Inn and she'd asked him up for a dance. A fella in a two-tone suit bursting his boiler trying to sound like Rod Stewart, giving himself laryngitis. One of those slow, sleepy numbers. She'd felt a bit loose in his arms, a few jars on her. The shape and peculiar weight of a woman; the feel of the silk dress under his hand; the smell of her. And her voice softly singing, 'I don't wanna talk about it…' breath coming out with the words on his neck. It was like an electric jolt. He had panicked, almost walked off and left her standing there on her own but instead he'd started acting the eejit, swinging her around the place, pretending to be Lionel Blair or someone, trying to turn it all into a joke anyhow.

'Stop,' she had said, coming back into him on an underarm twirl. 'Stop, Farley. Just hold me.' Just hold me – fuck. And she'd looked into his eyes and said, 'You never look at me. Why don't you ever look at me?'

'I do. I do look at you, of course I do.'

'Well, I wish you'd look at me more. And I wish…'

'What?'

'I wish you could kiss me.'

'Ah Jaysus, Kathleen,' he'd said. 'Ah, come on now. Jaysus.'

Farley takes a bigger swig from the wine, lowering one eye against the whack of it.

'Do you not like it?' she asks.

'Yea, it's nice.'

'It's from California.'

'That right?'

'Yea.'

'Look, I better go. Let you get a rest.'

'Ah no, stay. Just for a little while.'

He nods and takes another sip.

'Do you know what I'd love now?' she says.

He clears his throat. 'What's that, Kathleen?'

'A few chips. Not ones I make meself, but chipper chips, you know.'

'Do you want me to go down to Filangi's for you?'

'Would they be open?'

'I could always try.'

'Alright, but only if you have some too.'

He nods and stands up. 'O, in case I forget I'll just leave this for Frank here behind the clock.'

He slides the envelope in and she looks at him. 'You sure now, you'll be back? Because I don't want to go to the trouble of making tea and all if—'

'What are you talking about? Of course I'll be back.'

He feels his face redden and turns it away towards the hall, because it had crossed his mind of course, that once he got out, he could stay out, worry about the excuses later. He just wanted to be away from her. Her in her pyjamas, with her pinky bath face and her talcumed skin, and her sleek black bun starting to loosen on top of her head.

'Won't be long,' he says over his shoulder.

He's only in the car when he wishes he was back inside with her. 'Fuck, fuck and fuck it anyway,' he says to the steering wheel. 'I mean, what the fuck am I supposed to do now?'

He drives to the end of the road, indicates to turn right towards his own house, then changes his mind and indicates left for the chipper. He'll leave it to chance, that's what he'll do. And the chances of the chipper being open are slim enough. If it is open he'll get the chips, bring them back to her, but won't stay. And if it's closed he'll drive straight by, go home, phone her from there and tell her he had something to do that he'd only just thought of.

He drives through a gauze of dusk, lights beginning to pop out from houses; windows, Christmas trees, porches and, when he turns for the shops, in one yellow blatant glare, from the window of Filangi's chipper.

Behind the counter, Filangi clatters and bangs.

'I didn't think you'd be open today,' Farley says, half hoping to hear that he's not, that this is just preparation for tomorrow, that in fact it's strictly against the law for a chipper to trade on Stephen's day.

'What else I do?' Filangi shrugs, turning just long enough to show a scowl. He lifts the basket out of the bubbling oil, gives it a shuffle and then an angry bang against the stainless steel sides.

Farley looks up at the menu, a childish arrangement of block letters, and orders whatever comes into his head – two singles, spice burgers. He remembers when she was a kid she used to love spice burgers.

'Would the cod be fresh?' he asks Filangi.

'What you fuckin think?'

'Right, just the chips and the spice burgers so.'

He sits on the window ledge and picks up a newspaper, a few days old. On the counter there's a collection box showing a picture of starving African children. In the paper an article on the hunger strikers which he reads or half reads; anything rather than think about Kathleen, sitting by the fire, waiting on him. The smell of the food begins to fill his head and even though he knows he can't be hungry, he is. Farley tries to imagine what it must be like, starving to death, watching your own flesh melt away, feeling your stomach shrink, your eyesight dulling, the bones shoving to get through your skin. And he wonders if it makes any difference if you do it by choice, or if you have no choice in the matter. Does it hurt any less? Does it hurt any more?

Filangi comes to the counter, dark circles all the way down to the middle of his cheekbones. 'Salanvinegar?' and seeing as how he has the plastic bottle already poised, Farley agrees.

A big fat brown bag sits on the counter, he pays, sticking the change down into the slit on top of the Africans' collection box and noting the hollow sound of the coins as they drop.

She laughs when she sees the size of the bag. 'Jesus, Farley, there's only the two of us.'

The two of us – O Christ. She has the fire built up, the coffee table all set out; two places side by side so they both have to sit on the sofa. Knives, forks, plates, bread buttered and cut into half-slices on the plate, like the way Martina used to do it. Salt and vinegar in glass bottles. In the dim light the fire-flames are long and vivid and he feels a sudden loneliness for all he's been missing; soft light, a good fire, the arrangement of bread slices on a big plate.

She opens the bag and picks out a chip, rolling it around in her mouth until its heat settles down. Then she takes a few more chips out, blows on them, puts her lips around them and mumbles something that he can't make out.

She sits down on the sofa, puts the bag on the coffee table and rips it up the middle. 'What else have we here – are they? Are they spice burgers?'

'I remembered you used like them when you were a youngone.'

She looks startled, as if he's said something to hurt her. She swallows and stands up. 'Farley,' she says, 'Farley, I—'

He puts up his hand to stop her. 'It's only a fuckin spice burger, Kathleen.'

'No, it's not that. It's—'

He doesn't want to hear anything. He doesn't want to know what's on her mind. He takes a step back, begins to turn away. 'Look, I better, you know – just go.'

'Ah Farley,' she says and this time he looks at her. Her hand reaches out, a jewel of a tear in one eye. 'Ah Farley.'

He takes a step back to her. 'Ahh, fuck it in anyway,' he says and grabs her.

Her lips are like food; warm, soft, vinegary, her face slick with tears. And in the long second of time that passes between clamping his mouth on hers and waiting to see how and if she responds, he is acutely aware of the room shifting and turning around him; the smell of the chips as they tumble to the floor, the shadows of firelight crawling up the wall, the lights from the tree bleeding into each other, her hands clawing at his shirt and pulling him down on top of her, and in the corner Kirk Douglas in a dress, miming.

Back in his own house he sits in the dark; too many photographs along the mantelpiece; too many eyes to catch his. He drags the Superser in from the kitchen, stares into its honeycomb heat for a while, inhales its gassy breath. He turns the telly on, then off again; opens and closes this book, that newspaper. He decides to try a bit of music instead; the Beethoven tape that he got in the library. But it's too much, Jesus, way too much and if he listens to any more of it his heart could explode. He makes tea. Then he eats all around him; sandwiches mostly, nearly a half a sliced pan's worth. He's ravenous but can't tell the difference between cheese and jam. All he can taste is salt and vinegar. In fact, that's what he'd love now: chips. But he can hardly go back down to Filangi's – supposing he started asking questions? Why you here again? Who you buy for now? Who you buy for last time? Since when you start eatin the spice burger – huh? He's like a murderer now, afraid of every move he makes, of getting caught out in lies he hasn't even told yet.

He wonders how she's feeling now; ashamed like he is? Exhilarated? One minute full of regret, the next skidding over the moon? Has she been telling herself, like he's been telling himself, that it's never going to happen again but at the same time knowing that when it does all the bad feeling will instantly melt, just while it lasts, just till the next time? Is she thinking already with the sly scheming mind of the adulteress?

He's on his way up to bed when the phone rings. Farley jumps. He thinks about ignoring it, but then supposing it's her? He looks at his watch, just before midnight. Hardly. He goes out to the hall, his hand darting towards and away from the phone as if it's on fire. In the end he just snatches it.

'Well, you bastard, what do you have to say for yourself?'

His heart bounces. 'Hello – eh, who's that?' he says.

'What do you mean who's that? Who the fuck do you think it is? Well, you're some dark horse – wha? You think you know someone – wha? You work alongside them for twenty year and you think—'

'O,' Farley says.

'Yea – O, you sly bastard. Did you rob a fuckin bank or what?'

Farley closes his eyes, feels his heart slow down; deeper on the drop, like a yoyo.

'Ah, you know,' he says, 'I thought you could do with it.'

'Me? Ah no, not me. No more me. It's *we* now, you and me, Farley. If you're sure about this – absolutely sure, then we'll go down to the solicitor's the day after tomorrow and… Seriously, Farley, seriously now. I can't begin to tell you what this means to me. We'll get it all down on paper and—'

'I don't know, Frank. Once you start involving solicitors they'll cream it off in fees and there could be tax issues on top of that. Best keep it between ourselves.'

'Well, I—'

'And one more thing.'

'What's that?'

'I'd prefer if we kept this quiet. I don't want Jackie and the Ma and that finding out.'

'Alright so. If that's what you want. You're sure now about the solicitor's?'

'Yea, I'm sure.'

'A gentlemen's agreement then?'

'A gentlemen's agreement.'

'Alright so, if you feel you can trust me.'

'Of course I trust you.'

'And I can, and always could, trust you.'

'Yea,' Farley says, 'yea great. That's great, Frank. So we're partners then?'

'Partners? Are you fuckin joking me now or wha? Listen, I'm divorcing this one beside me in the bed, I don't care how fuckin gorgeous she looks lyin there and I'm marrying you tomorrow. Ye budgie. You fuckin life-saving budgie. You know what? I never backed a winner all day, and I came home feeling like, well, I don't know what and then Kat gives me your letter and. And I'm hanging up now in case I make a fuckin show of meself here. But Farley, I won't forget this day. I'll never forget this day. Wenceslas wha?'

'What?'

'Good King Wenceslas. The feast of Stephen.'

'Goodnight, Frank,' Farley says, the words swelling up in his craw.

He waits for Slowey to hang up the phone, then comes back into the parlour and turns on the television. A late-night news report of a torch-light march through a night-time city that could be Dublin. Hundreds of people singing hymns and walking along with candles in their hands. And he stands watching for a while, the river of small wobbling lights move down a boulevard that could be O'Connell Street, and the occasional close-ups: a ruddy-faced child, a woman in a woolly hat, a priest wearing gloves. He can't make out what the banners say but has a mind that it's something to do with abortion. And he thinks to himself he'd better make an appointment to have his eyes tested because they really have been giving him trouble lately, words disappearing or tricking across the page. And if he can't see the banners properly and he can't work out for certain if the city is Dublin and if all he can see is Slowey lying in the bed beside Kathleen, and all he can do is wonder if she's wearing the same pyjamas, or maybe something else, or maybe nothing at all. Then yea, he probably needs glasses.

Father Rat

October 1970

IN HIS SLEEP FARLEY stirs, turns away from the noise, the darkness he senses around it. He's been dreaming about the child again, about carrying her in his arms through a series of connecting rooms. Showing her off. It reminds him of a swanky hotel, this place – say the Shelbourne. A foyer with sofas and chairs by a fireside, a small bar tucked off to one side, next a lounge leading into a conservatory; potted plants and well-dressed women sipping tea. Finally, glass doors to a terrace overlooking a lake. So no – not the Shelbourne.

He knows this dream well, knows the feel and shape of it, although he also knows that later he will only remember it in shadow. As if it's all gone on under black water, figures shifting about, river wrack and slithers of unidentifiable movement. Times when he's woken to a wet pillow and skin stinking of sweat. Times when he's pulled himself up out of bed and looked in the shaving mirror and found waiting for him there a stained face and red-veined eyes – he's known it was on account of that disremembered dream. Because it always leaves him that way, with a drained heart and the face of a drifter.

This time the dream is different. This time he can see it so vividly; every detail, every face, buttered in light. And the child of course. Always the child. The thing is, he feels so bloody happy. Not just content but over-the-moon sort of happy. Ecstatic, he'd nearly go as far as to say. He doesn't want to lose this feeling, to spend the rest of the day pining for a few watery shadows. He could stay here for ever, but for that noise on the far side of the dream, tugging and pulling at him; trying to reel him in.

Farley resists, keeps himself weighted, digs his heels down. He feels himself roll back into the dream. A moment of pure elation. The child – he just loves this child – is the centre of everything; the dream, this hotel, his body even. He hears himself say as much to the various faces he meets on the way: 'I can see now what all the fuss is about, this huge love for a child – but you know now, they might grow in their mothers' wombs but they crawl right out of their fathers' hearts.'

People smile, nod indulgently, a hand comes out here and there to touch the child's head as they pass by.

She's his little girl; four maybe five years old, gingham dress, two little bunches of hair over each ear. She lies on his shoulder, sucking her thumb, light and yet solid; a warm pillow in his arms. He comes into a long bar, a marble counter running down one side, the elbows of men in evening suits, scaffolded along it. He hoists her and stands her up on the middle of the counter where she makes a sort of a speech to the men, answering questions, throwing out witty asides. She can talk about anything this youngone – politics, philosophy, religion. This youngone is really some-thing else. And he's so proud of her; so proud that he has to stop himself from blubbering. Laughter and applause surge around her feet, the force of it all lifts her into the air. He opens his arms and she falls down into them, surprising him then with her sudden weight.

He moves to the next room. People sitting at tables grouped around a piano. 'Here – would you like my little girl to play something for you?' he asks, shifting her up into the crook of his arm. Again, there are silent smiles and slow nods. It's taken him a while to notice this – they only ever speak to the child, not to him. And here's something else he's beginning to notice – each time he leaves one room and passes onto the next one the child seems to be that bit younger. Younger and smaller. But the mad thing is, the thing he doesn't quite get: she has also, somehow, grown heavier. She plays the piano, the little hands milling up and down the keys, she graciously bows her head to the standing ovation. When he goes to take her from the piano stool she's shorter, chubbier in the knee, more like a two-year-old now although her mind is as clever as it was when she was the size of a five-year-old. She slips off the stool, glides under his legs and she's off at such speed that even at a sprint he has difficulty catching up with her. He scoops her up in his arms but finds himself stumbling because of the weight of her. Heavier again. They come into the conservatory; a dome of hatched light overhead, ahhhs and uuuuhs of admiration from the tea-sipping women, and this time when he looks at the child in his arms, he sees a baby of maybe six months old.

A baby who weighs a ton. A baby still talking and laughing and enthralling the crowd. The hair is gone, showing a tender skull, the pulsing bulge of a fontanelle, a few frail curls at the nape. The dress, miles too long for her now, hangs over her feet. The heft of her makes his arms burn. He asks if she'd like to sit down on a sofa, maybe stand on the table so all the ladies can see her. And she guffaws and says, 'Don't be so stupid – how can I sit or stand – I'm only a baby!' All around him people are laughing and this is beginning to distress him now, because it's not funny. Not in the least. Out on the terrace two nurses wander about and a man in a grey suit stands looking out at the lake, a stethoscope glinting on the end of a chain around his neck. He decides to take her out there, see if maybe they can throw any light on the matter. Because she can't get any smaller. Fuck – if she gets any smaller! But he can hardly move now, her weight dragging him down, right down until he's moving along on his knees. The knees give, he topples over and suddenly he's lying on his back on the floor, the baby beside him. He looks up and sees a ring of big faces looking down at him.

'Would one of you not help me? Can somebody not give me a hand here?' he asks. 'Just help me bring my little girl out to the doctor. There's something wrong, you see, she's too heavy and she's too small and I can't. I can't...'

He's crying, and the baby, a newborn infant with a squashed-up face and eyes like two pink-raw molluscs says, 'Ah stop that now, that's not helping anyone. Pull yourself together. Be a *man* for Christ's sake.'

'But I am a man,' he blubs, 'I *am*.'

Behind him the door to the terrace opens. He reaches down, grabs the baby and slowly drags her along the floor. He can see the doctor leaning on the balustrade, the dark gleam of the lake behind him, the two nurses. He waits to see will the doctor come over; but the doctor, beckoning him to come forward, has no intention of moving. He clenches his teeth and braces himself. A sound curdles in his lower throat, a deep unbroken grunt. He feels his head swell with exertion, his heart expand, his legs strain and ache. One last effort, one more heave, and at last. At last she lifts off the ground. But her weight is too much and he loses control of it, the dress rips in his hand. She swings away from him like a discus, over the balustrade, into the light, towards the black glass of the lake. No splash, no sound but he knows she's gone in. He covers his face with his hands and attempts to call out her name, but finds after all he can't remember it. He hears himself mutter into his hand, his teeth gnaw and scrape at his palm, they chew and suck on the torn cloth of her dress. The crowd closes in on him again. In the background someone calls out his name. 'Farley! Farley! You in there? I have someone here for you. Let me in, let me in.'

'I'm here, that's me. That's me. Have you found her? Is she alright?'

Somebody pulls his hands away from his face and he sees a man standing there, holding a matchbox in his hand. 'There you are now,' he beams. He slides the box open. A type of insect wriggling inside; a brittle, ugly, tiny thing with paper wings and a body made up of minute bones.

'O Jesus,' he says. 'O Jesus Christ, please help me.'

His eyes flick open, his neck and limbs jolt. He hears his breath catch.

Farley waits for his body to settle.

'I know you're dead, Martina,' he says then. 'I know that. I know that when I turn around you'll be lying there, dead.'

But when he turns his head there's only a blank blue wall. He can't understand it – he'd fully expected to see her there; cold and stiffening at the edges. Her skinned head on the pillow beside him; her closed, bald, lashless eyes; the hands, with their long bones and translucent flesh that were beginning to remind him of a long ray fish. His Belsen baby as she'd called herself. And it comes to him then, that was something that already happened; weeks, days, months ago. In another bed, in another room. Before he'd taken to sleeping in here; a single spare bed shoved against the wall.

He hears his name. 'Farley! Farley! You in there? Come on – will you open the bloody door?'

He identifies those sounds that had been trying to break through his dream: the clap of a door knocker, the buzz of a bell, a hollow voice through the letter box. He lies still, gropes around in his head for the details, the child. But all he can find is water and shadow.

Uncle Cal on the doorstep. Uncle Cal and some blondie bloke with hair like a girl; long and flicked at the shoulder. The bloke, otherwise burly, is frowning. In one hand he holds a black bag, in the other a contraption with a long nozzle attached to the top. It flits across Farley's mind that maybe he's come to take him away, that Uncle Cal's about to have him signed in somewhere and he wonders how and where the fuck that nozzle is going to come into play. But then he takes a second look at the white van parked out on the road – not an ambulance. A company van with a company logo glaring out: a large black rat with the words 'Pronto Pest Control' resting over the curve of its tail.

'You had to tell the whole neighbourhood, I suppose?' Farley asks as Uncle Cal steps in.

'Yea, well, the man has to advertise his business, you know. Make a living and that. Hint. Hint. This is Ronnie by the way. Ronnie the Ratcatcher.'

Ronnie tucks the nozzle contraption under his arm and offers his hand to Farley. The hand, taut in a surgical glove, comes as a bit of a shock. 'I prefer the term pest controller meself,' he says, 'but some people find that whole Ronnie the Ratcatcher thing funny.' He drops a glance at Cal and continues, 'So, what sort of evidence we lookin at here?'

'Evidence?'

'You know, droppings, torn bags, scuttlin, scratchin – whatever it was made you suspect there's rats in the house.'

'Could be mice either.'

'Could be,' the ratcatcher says but looks doubtful.

'Anyway, I didn't call you.'

'I did,' Uncle Cal says, 'after a neighbour phoned me about seeing one sniffing across the gutter.'

The ratcatcher nods. 'Kitchen?' he asks and Farley stands back to let him through.

He lays the bag on the floor, stoops into the press, showing over his trousers a crack in a plump, pink moon.

'Cup of tea, Cal?' Farley offers, reaching for the kettle.

'You must be fuckin jokin me,' Cal says, looking around, 'thanks all the same.'

He tries to see the kitchen through Cal's eyes: a sink that looks like a small car has crashed into it; an archipelago of solidified grease all over the cooker and worktop. Old food left out on the table, a black plastic sack stuffed with rubbish.

'Like is it any wonder,' Cal says with a sweep of one hand. He pulls out a chair as if to sit down on it, takes a look at it and puts it back into the table. 'I'm an old man, you know, I shouldn't have to be puttin up with this.'

'You can go if you want,' Farley says, lifting the sole of a bare foot to see it layered with crumbs and dust.

Cal takes off his hat and presses his forehead into his hand. 'Jesus, son. I just don't know what to say to you, I just— I mean, I feel bad enough, you know I do. But for fuck sake would you not just…'

The ratcatcher stands, two dainty bullets of shit balanced on the back of his middle finger. 'Rats alright,' he says, 'see – the shit is longer, tubular shaped. More robust, if you like. The mouse now is more of a pellet man.'

He brushes the shit off his hand and begins to outline his plan of campaign. Farley half listens. The rat's intelligence is mentioned a few times, his razor sharp memory is complimented. Something about the rat having picked out his travel route and how most likely he's set himself up in the attic. 'Would you have heard any sounds to that effect yourself?'

'I suppose. Thought it was cats or pigeons pecking at the tiles. Then I thought I might just be imagining it.'

'Sounds like our boys, alright.'

Farley looks over at Uncle Cal, notices he's wearing his good crombie carefully brushed, his scarf, his little pork-pie hat, his best suit showing through the chink of the opened coat. He vaguely wonders why he's all dressed up and why too he's wearing so many clothes.

'The rat, you see, will have worked out his area of transit. Food transit, that is.'

'O right, yea,' Farley says.

'And my guess is,' the ratcatcher pauses here and with the finger he had moments ago used to display the rat shit, lifts a long curl of blond hair behind his ears, 'he comes from the attic, down through the walls, in behind the sink there, along this wall and in the back way to *that* press.' He flicks the press open and Uncle Cal jumps. Then he puts his hand in and takes out a packet of rice, beans, barley – some sort of white stuff anyway.

'See these rips in the plastic? Only a rat'd have teeth that size.' He lets out a gentle sigh. Farley can't work out if it's respect or envy he hears in his voice.

'Ah-ha! Just as I thought,' the ratcatcher continues, 'run marks.'

'Run marks?' Cal asks.

'Yea, look here, on the walls of the press.' He steps back to clear a view although neither of them avail of it. 'Sort of oily stains that rub off his body as he brushes past the walls. I say he, but of course…'

'O Jaysus,' Cal groans.

He's at his hair again, back behind the ears, tossing it away from his shoulders. 'Now. What I'll do is this – lay a trap in the press there, another couple in the attic. I'm going to pull up a few floorboards there, lash down a bit of poison. And I'll be back in a few days.'

'A few days?' Uncle Cal says. 'What do you mean a few days?'

'If you just let me finish – I'll be back in a few days *unless* you hear anything, in which case you phone me and I'll be back pronto – as the card here says.' He reaches into his pocket and comes out with a card stuck between his two latexed fingers. 'It shouldn't take any more than three days. After which time they begin to stink,' he smugly adds.

'They?' Uncle Cal says.

'Could be a lone ranger, could be a whole colony. Who knows? Anyway, the attic?' He picks up his bag and his nozzle and makes for the door.

Farley says, 'There's a stepladder on the landing.'

'Won't be necessary,' he says with another flick of his yellow hair.

Uncle Cal and himself are left standing with the filthy kitchen table between them. 'You off somewhere?' Farley asks just to make conversation.

'Into town, to see Nixon, a few pints after.'

'Who's Nixon?'

'Who's...? The president of America, you fuckin moron.'

'O, I didn't know he was—'

'You don't know what's going on – do you? You have your mother up the wall. And only for that nice woman next door – what's her name?'

'Mrs Carroll.'

'Yea, only for her you'd probably be found dead, eaten be rats. Rats for fuck sake, Farley. I tell you, even in the worst days of the civil war, days when we were on the run like animals – we lived cleaner than this.'

'I know.'

'And Jackie says you told him fuck off when he called down the other week.'

'Did I?'

'Yea, not that I blame you. He should be told fuck off more often. Did you see his beard? What the fuck's he like?'

'A poet?' Farley suggests.

'A knacker more like. Anyway, I'm off.'

Farley follows him into the hall.

'Look, I have a message for you,' Cal says over his shoulder. 'From Slowey.'

'Why didn't he just ring me up?'

'Because your phone's been cut off – in case you didn't know. He says, you better get your arse in gear and back into work or you can kiss that same arse goodbye to your job.'

'I'm sick, I have a doctor's cert.'

'A cert from Halpin? Don't make me laugh. Listen, I could go down to that quack this minute and he'd put me on maternity leave if I asked him to. You're not sick, son, you're grieving, we all know that. But you have to get on with things. You just have to do it. Are you still drinking?'

'No. I stopped a couple of days ago.'

Uncle Cal lifts one eyebrow.

'Really, I just couldn't stomach any more. I'm finished with it now.'

'Take my advice, keep it that way. At least knock it on the head for a while. I know now what I'm talking about. It might seem like a solution, but it only makes matters worse. You have to go through what you have to go through – know what I'm saying? And nobody, I mean nobody, likes a drink more than me. But not at times like this. Now, I'll tell Slowey you'll be in next Monday, that'll give you time to get back on your feet, clean up this gaff, get rid of your pals in the attic.'

'Monday?'

'Yea, that's a week from today. Don't tell me you don't even know what fuckin day of the week it is?'

'Ah, I do.'

'Yea, of course you do.'

The ratcatcher comes slowly down the stairs, clearing his throat. 'Right, that's me done. That'll be twenty quid so.'

'Twenty?!' Cal says. 'Are you fuckin jokin or what?'

'Would you rather the rats?' he says.

'No, we wouldn't. Fix him up there, Farley.'

'And cash, if you don't mind,' the ratcatcher says. 'I'm not taking any more cheques till this strike's settled.'

'I haven't got twenty,' Farley says. 'What strike?'

The ratcatcher looks at him. 'You serious? The bank strike, it's been on weeks now.'

'You mean it's still not settled?'

'He's been away,' Cal says. 'Needs to catch up. Only just back in fact – and that's how come there's been rats.'

Uncle Cal puts his hand in his pocket and hands an envelope to Farley.

'What's that?'

'From Slowey. And if you had any idea the trouble he had getting that cash.'

Farley picks two tenners out and the ratcatcher reaches for them.

'Ahahah,' Cal says, swiping the money from Farley and laying it on the hall table. He points at the money and steps back. 'Don't go near him. Don't,' he warns. The ratcatcher gives him a sulky look and lifts the money.

'I'm not the one with rats in me house,' he pouts. 'O, and it mightn't be a bad idea either to give this place a good cleaning.'

The ratcatcher leaves and Cal buttons up his coat, settles his hat, plumps up the knot in his tie. 'Of course, everyone's drinking like fishes now – the pubs are the new banks, only place you can cash a cheque but only if you keep a full table – know what I'm sayin? Hungry fuckers. Hope half of them bounce when the banks open again.' He looks in the hall mirror. 'How old do I look?' he says.

'I don't know – how old are you?'

'Seventy-two.'

'You look great for that.'

'Yea, I know, I take care of myself, that's why. Nutrition, that's what

144

it's all about. Nutrition and takin it handy enough with the gargle. No smokin, that's another tip. Know what I could really do with though?'

'What's that?'

'A good ride.' He points his finger at Farley then hits him on the top of his arm. 'Careful – you nearly cracked a smile there.'

He's halfway down the path when Farley calls after him, 'Cal?'

'Yea.'

'Just wonderin – is Frank, you know, is he goin mad?'

'Nahh. He's just worried about you, that's all. We're all worried about you, son.' He opens the gate, closes it and points his nose towards town. 'Doesn't mean he won't sack you though.'

He watches Uncle Cal bustle down the road and then slowly makes his way up the stairs. Keeping one eye on the ceiling he listens out for something strange and alive. Behind the everyday household gurgles and creaks there is silence. He doesn't know how long he's been standing outside the bedroom door; the door of the room he shared with Martina. He's pushing it open now anyhow and even if the rat took up a cane and started to dance and sing Dixie, he wouldn't be able to hear it over the punch of his own heart.

A long time since he's been in this room – months maybe – the first time he's been in here sober since she died anyway. The wardrobe door is partly open; sleeves of her clothes peering out, one toppled tan leather boot beneath them. The bed is completely bare; the stark cloth of the mattress jars him. It was Mrs Carroll who stripped it. 'Let me know,' she had said, 'let me know when you're ready to sort through her things and I'll give you a hand.' He had nodded, turned away, unable to bear the sight of her kind brown eyes.

He sits on the end of the bed. Her side. He sits as he would have done on mornings when he'd time to bring her a cup of tea. Mornings before she was really sick, because from then on, even if she hurled the tea straight back up into the sick bucket, he always made sure to have time. He wasn't all bad.

He stares up the bed at the headrest, scanning it for the flimsiest piece of evidence that he once had a wife who once had black hair, who once had slept there. And that he had once slept beside, on top of, and spooned behind her. But Mrs Carroll has done such a good job of cleaning the place, not a trace, even of his Brylcreem-slicked head, his own little run mark, remains.

He lies back on the mattress, eyes closed, feet on the ground. He remembers the morning he woke in this bed and found her dead beside him. It was August and clammy, which is probably why, before he was fully awake, he noticed the cold patch on his arm where her hand had been resting. And a presence – which was odd, because surely it should have been an absence? A strange awkward presence, anyway, as if a thief had come into the room during the night and couldn't find a way out again. That was the morning after he'd gone on the piss with Uncle Cal. He was only supposed to be giving him a lift; one of those memorial service jobs they throw the odd time, for all the old codgers who'd fought in the Rising. And he hadn't liked to leave Cal to make his own way home, so had decided to hang around for a bit and wait. He had started to drink, one pint first, then another. About halfway down the third he felt this warmth coasting through him and it became a sort of joy to be there amongst all these old men who had seemed so alive and vibrant compared to the young death waiting at home. He was enjoying himself; it was as simple as that.

In the course of the evening he had phoned her – he wasn't all bad. And her voice – now that he thinks of it – the last time he would have properly heard it, told him to enjoy his few drinks. But not to drive the car if he got buckled. 'Is there someone sober there could drive it for you?' she had said.

'Course there is,' he'd answered, looking in at a crowd of scuttered oul lads, doddering on the edge of their seats.

She'd been asleep when he got home. Not dead, no, definitely not dead. Because he could remember rubbing her bare head with the palm of his hand, the strange, suede feel of it and her saying 'Shhh' to him. *Shhh.* She died in the night. The doctor said she would have felt no pain. But what did he know about the pain of her nights? All those empty hours she'd had to endure, sitting up holding her head in her hands from the pain of medication that just wasn't working? What did he know about her husband who had tried to stay awake with her, tried to share the parallel life she was leading. Usually falling back asleep soon enough, but at least he tried – he wasn't all... Bad. And he would start every day by asking, 'How did you sleep after?' and even if he knew she was lying, he'd call her a good girl when she said yes. Like sleep, any sleep was an achievement. Which of course it was, in the end.

Her cold hand on his arm. That's what kills him. The fact that she may have been frightened, have known this was it, this was the end now, and had been trying to wake him, trying to call his name. And him lying like a lump of meat beside her snoring his head off; the Guinness souring in his stomach, sweating and farting its way out.

Farley opens his eyes. He wants to tell someone how bad he feels, but there's no one to tell. If the phone was working he could go downstairs and pick it up and call a priest or a Samaritan or fuck it, the talking clock. And what would he say? 'The night my wife died I was too drunk to notice.'

He says these words now, out loud. 'The night my wife died I was too drunk to notice.' He shoots them up at the ceiling; twice, maybe three times and it makes him feel a bit better. An image comes into his head then, of the rat, on the other side of the ceiling. In black profile, an intelligent tilt to his head, a paw or a claw or whatever the fuck they have, resting on the side of his nose. Hearing his confession. The idea comforts him; the absurdity of it, along with the sound of his own voice, which seems the most absurd thing of all.

Farley turns to his side, pulls his knees up towards his chest and thinks about those few weeks just after the funeral. He had loved his wife completely. Completely. And yet after she'd died – a day or two after – every and any woman he'd come across he had wanted to knock the arse off her. Any shape or size, from twenty to ninety – it didn't really matter. His beautiful wife dead, warm in her grave, and him going around on a permanent horn.

He sits up again, puts his feet on the floor, stares into a stupid-looking picture on the wall of a tree in a field that someone gave them for a wedding present. It makes him think of the brasser. The brasser he picked up a couple of weeks after Martina died. Benburb Street, in the lashing of rain. He'd brought her up to the Phoenix Park in the car. Paid her the tenner in advance. And as she'd begun climbing all over his lap, trying to get him going and get his mickey out and up and have the whole thing over as quick as she could so she could move on to the next punter, he began to feel this rage take a hold of him, as if it was all her fault, that it was *she* who was disrespecting his wife. He'd pushed her off and out of his way. He'd called her a poxbottle and she'd called him a bollix and then he'd leaned over and opened the car and shoved her out in the rain. He had no doubt that he'd hurt her. Not intentionally but just the same. And he'd driven off up the road with the passenger door swinging open. The sight of her in the rear-view mirror with her dress up around her arse and her arms waving and her mouth wide open screaming like a witch down the road after him under the rain.

Farley looks at the photo standing on the dressing table; Martina holding her younger sister's baby in her arms. The sister not married five minutes when she was pregnant. 'What sort of a man am I?' he asks the little group.

He stands and his face is wet. He didn't even know he'd been crying. Pulling the end of his jumper up he gives his face a swipe. The things he'd forgotten, the things he'd rolled up into tight little balls and burrowed into the cracks in the walls. The next phase. Jesus, when he thinks of the next phase. Farley hears himself let out a small, tight laugh as he walks around to the far side of the bed. The wanking weeks. After the brasser he'd started coming in here to have a wank. Three, maybe four times a day. It was like being a youngfella again; red raw from pulling himself off. He'd usually go for one of Martina's pillows. Hold it in his arms and pull away. One night – Jesus, now that he thinks of it – he even put a nightdress over the pillow.

Farley stands with his back to the window and lets the minutes pass away. After a while he pulls a pair of his shoes out of the wardrobe. Socks still stuffed inside them. Socks he'd have worn when she was alive. He sits down, brushes the looser dirt off the soles of his feet and puts the socks and shoes on. Taking his time he leaves the bedroom and comes back down the stairs. In the hall he looks at the ceiling again. 'So, Father Rat, what do you think?' he says. 'What do you say? Am I absolved?' A noise in the kitchen. He feels himself stiffen. What sort of noise – he can't make it out. A thrashing sound, like a whip. The fucking rat, the half-poisoned rat, his tail lashing out against the walls of the press. O Jesus. O fuck. He reaches for the phone, remembers then that it's been cut off, drops it, opens the front door, closes it, then opens it again. Next door. He'll have to use the phone in the house next door.

He's either dreaming again, or else he's gone mad. Two midgets, dolled up to the nines, are standing in the doorway of Mrs Carroll's hall. Beehived hair on top of their heads, make-up all over their faces, big brassy earrings. They're wearing dresses cut away from their shoulders with wide spangled skirts on them and sparkly high-heeled shoes. The midgets squirm to stay in the frame of the doorway, the skirts of their dresses like umbrellas around them, wavering from side to side.

He just stands there looking at them.

'*Maaaaam-eeee*,' one of them then shouts into his face, 'it's Mist-er Grainger from next door.' He realizes then that it must be two of her kids he's looking at.

Mrs Carroll appears out of nowhere wiping her hands on a tea cloth. 'Ahh Mister Grainger. Come in, come in.'

The two girls, moving as one, waddle to one side to let him through then they push away up the narrow stairs like a two-headed glittery creature.

'I was wondering if I could I use your…?' he thumbs in the direction of a white phone on a polished table. 'Mine seems to be out of order.'

'Certainly, Mister Grainger. You go on right ahead there.' She twists her head to look up the stairs: 'Girls, have everything ready now – your lift will be here soon,' then lowers her voice to Farley like she's telling him something in confidence: 'They're going into the competition in the Claremont. Hence the, you know,' she lifts her finger and twirls it like a wand, all over her face, hair and body. He hasn't a clue what she's on about but nods and picks up the phone.

'Will you have a cup of tea, Mister Grainger?' she calls from the kitchen, 'while you're here?'

'Ah, no thanks, I won't.'

'A bite to eat then – something. A bit of apple tart? A – a sandwich maybe. I've a nice bit of ham here.' Her face round the door now, her worried, kindly gaze on him.

He must look as if he needs feeding, or maybe women just think all men without women do.

'How have you been keeping, Mister Grainger?'

'Great. Not a bother.'

'I do often mean to drop in but like, you know yourself, I don't like to intrude.'

Her face is all red, like she's embarrassed. He feels it too though he can't make out why. She could be worrying about ringing Uncle Cal of course and ratting on the rat. He could be ashamed of the rat. It could be a simple matter of that illogical awkwardness that the dead seem to leave behind them. Or it could be something to do with the pillows in his bedroom, Martina's nightdress – what if she'd found them, guessed what he'd been up to? He feels the burn on his own face now. They stand looking at each other for a moment, two red faces on opposite ends of the hall, beaming like traffic lights at a crossing.

'Well, I leave you to your call, Mister Grainger,' she says finally.

Farley nods, looks at the business card and begins to dial.

'O!' Her head pops out of the kitchen again. She stops when she sees him with the phone in his hand, puts the inside tips of her fingers over her mouth. 'Sorry.'

'No, go on – you were saying?'

'I've a parcel for you. The postman left it in a few weeks ago. Norman knocked in a couple of times but. Well, anyway, I'll leave it there for you.' She lays a bag against the wall nearby him. Farley looks at it, sees the logo.

'Is it from Clery's?' he asks.

'O God no, I just put it in there to keep it safe like.'

'Thanks.'

'No trouble, Mister Grainger. O and listen, if you want me to go in and help you sort through Martina's things.'

'O. It's done,' he says, 'all sorted.'

'O good. That's good.'

Farley goes back to his phone call; the dialling of numbers, the tone bleating down the line. She still calls him Mister. Probably knows more about his private life than he does; the little secrets women think nothing of telling each other across a garden wall or over an afternoon cup of tea. Martina she called Martina from the word go, but to the woman next door he's always been Mister Grainger.

He can hear the two youngones upstairs dancing and chanting over the landing, 'One and two, one and two, one to the left, one to the right, one in, one out. One *and* two, one *and* two.'

'Hello, is that Ronnie the R—' he says. 'I mean, is that Ronnie?'

The ratcatcher leans his arse on the corner of the kitchen table, a small sack bulging in one hand, a cigarette in the other. He's still wearing his surgical gloves. 'Right,' he says, 'we've your man from the kitchen press, your woman from the attic. That should be it now.'

'Your woman?'

'Honeymooners by the look of it. Put it this way, she was up the pole – about to pop any minute too. Lucky you called me when you did.'

'I didn't call.'

'O, that's right, you were away. Where were you anyway?'

'Well, I—'

'Thought so. Inside – weren't you?'

'What?'

'You know, prison. The Joy – was it?'

'No.'

'Don't tell me – Portlaoise? Limerick then? You look like a head that's been in Limerick. Ah now, you don't have to be ashamed with me,' he says, coyly fiddling a curl of hair between his rat-scented fingers. 'I do a lot of work in prisons – teeming with rats, most of them do be. You get to know – you know?'

'Right,' Farley says.

'And I tell you something else.'

'Yea?'

'Some of the nicest people you'd ever meet.'

Farley nods.

The ratcatcher straightens up, holding the butt of the cigarette high. 'Where will I put this? Does it make any difference says you?' He goes over to the sink and flicks it in on top of the dishes.

'I don't know who you had mindin the gaff while you were away, but tell you what, if it was my gaff I'd slit their fuckin throats for them. Good luck to you now.'

'Yea, good luck,' Farley says.

He turns on the radio and waits for a hint of the date. The bells of the angelus growl into the kitchen. He searches out a pen from the drawer by the sink, then on the back of an envelope pulled from a pile starts making a list. *Plastic sacks. Cleaning cloths. Disinfectant.* He can't think of what else he might need for a clean-up on this scale, nor does he fancy the idea of going into a shop and asking for advice: 'See, I haven't lifted a finger to clean the house since the wife died.' (O, you poor man, here sit down and I'll make you a sandwich.) *Scrubbing brush. Washing powder. Stuff for the dishes.*

Martina had looked after all that sort of thing; working and reworking the house and the garden like a woman with a compulsion. Or a woman with no kids, as his mother had often pointed out.

The angelus clangs off into the distance and is immediately replaced by the news in Irish: all gobbeldy-gook to him bar the occasional 'Nixon' popping out of the jumble.

Bleach for the jacks. A mop. Tea cloths.

He lifts his head from the list, his eye catching on the plastic sack of rubbish in the corner. Bumps through black-sheened skin. It makes him wonder about the mother rat, the babies inside her and if they all died when she died or if there were a few agonizing minutes, while the poison filtered through, of squirming and wriggling around in her belly. He feels sick now. Sick and childish and alone. Like a boy who finds himself locked into a dark school after all the other boys have gone home. A heave in the back alley of his throat; a long, dry retch: the drink pulling out of his system. He takes in a few deep, sour breaths – his own, or maybe the kitchen's – until the nausea passes away. His eye then falls on the Clery's bag. He goes to it, lifts it and looks inside. A brown paper package inside. Martina's – it would have to be. He never had a parcel sent to him in his life. Farley takes it out, his hand shaking slightly. An English postmark. He opens it up and finds another package inside bandaged in plastic. There's a covering letter but he can't bring himself to read it properly, darting through half-sentences and isolated words. *Dear Mrs Grainger... enclosed... catalogue... wish you... future... growth.*

He begins to unwind the plastic from the packet which turns out to be made up of more wrapping than content. Eventually he gets to the heart of it; several packets of seeds held in bunches by elastic bands. He flicks through. On the front of each sachet, a picture of a blooming confection in full and glorious technicolour. The names strange – even more so in English than Latin.

Farley goes to the kitchen window; through the smeared glass an un-recognizable garden, unruly and full of neglect. He stuffs the seed packets into his pockets and goes outside.

On the air, a perfume of impending decay. There's a slight chill running through it, like the end or the start of a season. The garden path is no longer visible. The grass almost knee-high. He wades through, feels the bite of a nettle sting on his hand, a prick of thistle on his opposite wrist. When he reaches the back wall he makes a parting in the long grass, then presses it down and stamps on it. Here he gets down on his knees. The flower beds by the wall are stuffed with bunches of growth bursting out of themselves. In between are straggles of sinewy foliage. He can't always tell the weeds from the flowers, the good from the bad; what should be killed off; what could be saved. In the end he picks on one area and gets stuck in. It's like pulling hair out of a head, he thinks, strand by strand, grooming away, until a beautiful patch of bald brown earth appears. He rips open a sachet of seeds, sprinkles a circle of yellow specks around this alopecia of soil. When the packet is empty he stands and comes back into the long grass. With his teeth he begins to open the rest of the sachets: African Bride, Honeywort, Love-in-a-Mist. He streels the seeds randomly over the garden – wherever they fall they fall. Farley turns in a circle, sees the sky, the top bedroom windows of the houses behind him, the crows on the crust of the rooftops before him. He sees the rough thick boundary wall between him and the street outside and the black apostrophe of a cat on Mrs Carroll's fence. He turns east, towards the city; west towards the sunset; north to the Park; south for the sea. He faces his own house, its windows and guttering. He turns away from it, then faces it again.

Rain

August 1960

FOR THE SECOND TIME in a fortnight he finds himself in one of these basement dives, surrounded by sweaty bastards. Last time there'd been jazz and women in slacks. Now it's just poems and blokes wearing beards. The poet, so-called, stands at the top in the spotlight of a dodgy-looking bulb that's strung up in one corner. The beam of light, slightly off-kilter, means his head stays out of sight and his voice full of eked-out emotion, is coming from the shadow. This may well be for effect but even if it's not, Farley isn't complaining – bad enough having to listen without having to look at him as well. The poem is called 'Rain' and seems to have something to do with the soul of Africa, or Africa in the soul of some down-at-heel under a bridge in London. It's a poem of few words and many pauses. He wonders if the rest of the punters, with their angled jaws and frowning foreheads, can really be as interested as they seem to be? Or is it a case of one half of them pretending to know what it's all about, while the other half is biding time till it's their turn to get into the spotlight and spout?

It could be of course that he just doesn't get it – because according to Jackie that's his problem with most things: politics, poetry, women, horses. 'You just don't get it – do you?' His brother's favourite dismissal.

One thing he definitely doesn't get is this – why Jackie asked him to come here in the first place, if he intended leaving him on his tod the minute they got through the door? Because he's been here at this table for at least twenty minutes, an upturned beer crate branding his arse, and still no sign of Jackie. He's clubbed in for the wine because two blokes sitting beside him had asked him to. But the smell of it now is enough. Last time there'd been bottles of Macardles and a piano. Conroy and Jacobs had been with him too, all in flying form after the cure from the previous night drinking at that party in Butlin's. The music had been alright too, once you got the hang of it and realized that those little outbursts of reverent applause didn't necessarily mean the song had come to an end. He'd liked the way the musicians had worked on a tune, running off with it, bending it into these peculiar shapes, then bringing it back completely changed, and yet somehow the same. And he'd liked too the girl with a voice like Kay Starr who'd got up out of the audience and sang 'Volare'. It had reminded him of the youngone in Butlin's; the redcoat with the black hair. The Kay Starr girl had sung a different version of course, slow and slightly sleazy. But the girl in Butlin's had sung it in Italian. He wonders again what happened to her after; how much trouble she got into and if maybe she got the sack.

His eyes are beginning to stream. He squints into a cave of mauve fag smoke and tries to swallow a chain of yawns. Last time – the jazz night – his eyes had been streaming too, but that was because he'd been laughing that much; mostly at the expense of Jackie's college pals. At least you *could* laugh. And talk too, between songs, or numbers – as Jackie's mates called them. He could talk about anything now after the few pints in Mooney's. The drink unscrewing his tongue. The Redcoat girl had said it to him; 'God, you don't wear yourself out talkin, do you?' But he'd talk to her now, if she was here, he'd have plenty to say alright. About the night in Butlin's. About thinking of her since, any time he hears that song that never seems to be off the radio. He'd tell her things too; about the driving lessons he's been taking from Uncle Cal – he could make that funny while at the same time let her know he's a go-ahead bloke. He could tell her about Conroy's bird being up the pole – although he'd have to think of a nicer way to put it. He could ask her all about herself, what it's like being a redcoat, what she does for the rest of the year and how come she knows the words of 'Volare' in Italian? He could tell her bits about himself then; his job, his brother, the jazz session last week. O, and of course, about Australia. He keeps forgetting about Australia.

The poem trudges on. Outside, somewhere overground, is a warm August evening and Conroy and Jacobs are out there in the middle of it. They should be at the ballroom by now; probably in the queue, sucking peppermints and eyeing up the talent. If they were here he'd be choking by now, trying to hold down the laughing. Conroy mightn't be the soundest skin, certainly not as reliable as Jacobs, but he's the funniest. Conroy would knock a laugh out of his own funeral.

He'd done his best to persuade them to come along. Earlier in Mooney's when Jackie had gone out to the bog, he'd even begged. But the boys wouldn't budge.

'Ah, go on,' he'd said, 'it'll be a laugh.'

'You must be bleedin joking me,' Conroy said, 'after stewing in that other pot last week – what was it called again?'

'The Cat's Tail.'

Conroy dipped his face into his pint and came back up with a comical tip of cream on the end of his nose. 'The cat's hole, more like,' he'd said and Jacobs' head nearly fell on the ground with the laughing.

'Ah, go on, just for an hour?'

'Listen, pal, this could be one of my last nights of freedom, so you know – no offence, but get stuffed.'

'I don't want to go on me own,' he'd said.

'You're not on your own, Jackie's with you.'

'Ah, you know what I mean.'

'I do know what you mean,' Conroy said, 'you'll be stuck with a load of snotty fuckers who think they're the only ones ever read a book, who believe, sincerely believe, they know more than you, me and him put together. And you'll probably have to listen to them prove that to you as well as to each other. All night. And I sympathize, really I do. But we're still not fuckin going.'

'I don't know why he wants me there anyway,' Farley said, 'it's not as if we didn't make a show of him last week.'

'What a bunch of saps!' Conroy said, throwing his head back. 'What a bunch of thoroughbred dopes.'

'It's because you're going away,' Jacobs said. 'He probably just wants to knock around with you a bit more, that's all. Look, why don't you go in for an hour and then make an excuse. Follow us down. You'll get in if you don't leave it too late.'

'Anyway,' Conroy continued, suddenly morose, 'I don't know what you're complaining about. You'll be in Australia soon enough. You both will – lucky bastards.'

'O yea, Australia.'

He'd forgotten all about Australia.

When they'd come out of the pub Jackie had hung back. At first Farley'd presumed he was lighting a fag, though a second glance had shown him turned to the wall, reading a letter. The air and the light had hit him, and he'd heard himself asking about the girl. 'That bird?' he'd said, 'that bird, you know that youngone we met in Butlin's last week – the redcoat?'

'Which one? Sure they all had red coats on them,' Conroy said, his eyes startled from the drink.

'Black hair, she sang that Italian song, you know? From Chapelizod, I think, she said. You know the one who came up to us in the lounge earlier.'

'O God now, let me see, let me see,' Conroy had said with a wink for Jacobs, 'can I remember – was she a hatchet-faced one with an arse the size of the back of a bus?'

'What?' Farley asked. 'No, not at all, she was—'

'O, hold on now, I have her – the dumpy little one that looked a bit like Jimmy Durante?'

'Ah, what are you being so smart about? I'm only asking do you think she got the sack after?'

'What do you fuckin care if she did? You're off to Australia.'

'I know. I just wondered.'

'Don't go complicating things now,' Jacobs said, taking a sidelong step in to him, 'remember, if my papers are already through, then yours won't be long after.'

'*What?* You don't think I'd… Jesus as if I'd—'

'Well, now, I'm just saying like, my uncle's gone to a lot of trouble getting you sorted and all and—'

'What do you think I am? As if I'd—'

'Just sayin now. You don't want to end up like Conroy here.'

'You shut up,' said Conroy.

'Amn't I learning to drive and everything? So I'll be all ready for action. I can't wait to go, I can't. Anyway, she's in Butlin's, isn't she? She'll be there till the end of September, won't she? I'll be gone by the time she's back in Dublin again.'

'Unless she was sacked,' Conroy said.

'Do you think she was sacked?'

'Forget about if she was sacked or not!' Jacobs said

'Ah, leave him, can't you?' Conroy said then. 'Can't he go out with the girl if he wants? It won't change anything, he's not going to give up his whole future for some dolly, you know.'

'I can't go out with her anyway, she's in Mosney. I don't even know where she lives. Jesus! And I'm not sure of her name, either.'

'Chapelizod – she'd be easy enough to find,' Conroy said.

'Will you stop encouraging him?' Jacobs said. 'I'm telling you now. My uncle.'

'What about your uncle?'

'My uncle now has—'

'Is it Marita – her name?' Conroy said. 'Or Marian, somethin like that?'

The group split in half at the corner of O'Connell Street: the boys heading south for the ballroom; him and Jackie northways to wherever the fuck he is now.

Crossing over the road into Cavendish Row, Jackie had said nothing. And heading up Parnell Square East, he'd said nothing again. He'd waited in fact till they were halfway down the basement steps of a house in Denmark Street before opening his cakehole at all. And then, 'She did get the sack by the way.'

'Who? What? Here – how do you know?'

'I know her pal's brother. Remember the little blondie one? She was sacked too.'

Jackie lifted his hand and rapped on the door. 'O, and another thing, she is in her arse from Chapelizod.'

'No?'

'Ballyer more like. The Avenue, so far as I'm aware.'

The door opened then and they'd stepped into the fug. Jackie, dispatching him over here, had said, 'I'll join you in a jiffy.'

A lot of jiffys have passed since then.

'Rain!' the poet's voice bleats out from the shadows. Farley waits for the rest of the line but nothing arrives until the word '*rain*' again, this time it trembles on a note.

He thinks now of Conroy and Jacobs disappearing down O'Connell Street, Jacobs leaning back on Conroy's scooter, hands clutching onto the sides of the seat, and the swerve of them under the trees; full of themselves and the dance ahead. And the trees full too with frocks of leaves. Trees, frocks and the smell of summer. If he was writing a poem, now that's what it would be about.

Another pause, longer than usual, and Farley feels his belly warm up with hope. A few seconds of unbearable hesitation while people glance at each other. At his table one of the blokes lifts his hands then pauses. And Farley feels like saying to him, 'Go on, clap for fuck sake, clap and he might stop because if Beardy claps, it means it's all over because he has a look about him of a leader of sheep. Then there'll be an interval. They hardly expect you to listen to any more than three of these on the trot, without some sort of respite. An interval, and he'll be out of here.' But the poet slips into another verse and Beardy's hands return to the table.

He can't see Jack anywhere. He's not at the wall, at none of the tables, even over his shoulder by the entrance – he's nowhere to be seen. Interval or no interval, after this poem he's off. Because otherwise he's going to have to put his own hands around his own throat and strangle himself out of his misery. He tries a sip of the plonk and feels his face wince all over. He notes the two beards are having no such problem and is worried now they're maybe going to put the hammer on him again for bottle of piss number two.

He feels a bit sick now; his throat thick and dry as if his gullet is lined with felt cloth. He wouldn't say no to a bottle of minerals. He'd give anything in fact to be standing on the balcony of the ballroom, guzzling it back, feeling it fizz into his nostrils and skulk down into his throat. The floor below packed with the twirl of girls, the smell of perfume and hair oil; a different kind of sweat than the musty bang that's in here. And the band belting it out; movement and brass and life, and above all people who know how to act their age.

Australia comes into his head – not the country but all the aggravation that's been leading up to it. Ma doing her nut. 'A *garage*?' she'd said when she found out. 'Do you mean to tell me you're going to leave your good job, go all the way out to the other end of the world to pour petrol into other people's cars – is that what you're telling me?'

She was sitting at the dining-room table, the contents of the large envelope he'd stashed under his bed spread out before her, every scrap of paper to do with his future; letters from the embassy; his post office book with the few quid he's been saving this past year; his resignation letter for Mr Caine. And the trade catalogue Jacobs' uncle had sent showing pictures of the town with its peculiar-shaped shops and tan-faced merchants and the page marked with the photograph of the garage where he and Jacobs would work; slanted rows of big cars on the forecourt, in this town called Wilcannia on a river named Darling. 'A *garage*?'

'It's not that kind of a garage, Ma, it sells cars. I'm going to train to be a car salesman.'

'But you can't even drive!'

'Uncle Cal is teaching me.'

'He never said.'

'I asked him not to until I'd a chance to tell you myself.'

'O, thanks very much and I wonder when that might have been!'

She sat pulling at her fingers like she was trying to unscrew them off her hand. Her face at once hurt and angry and her head loose on her neck, the way it tends to when she is building up to losing her temper. 'I had to find the envelope under your bed—'

'I was going to tell you.'

'Or were you just going to disappear?'

'I was waiting. And what were you doing rooting in my room anyway?'

'I wasn't rooting, I was coming up the stairs and happened to spot the envelope sticking out from under the bed and I thought it might have been more letters from Mr Caine that you'd forgotten to give me – not for the first time either.'

'Once, I forgot. Years ago.'

'All the money I forked out for your eduction. All the years I've sat at this bloody table typing letters for solicitors too cheap to pay for a secretary. Four pound a year your school cost me – do you have any idea what sort of money that is for a widow? Because let me tell you, your father didn't leave it for you, he had better things to be doing with his money.'

'What? What are you talking about?'

'And now you're just going to feck off as if – well, now. You're a revelation I must say. Well. Who do you remind us of, I wonder?'

'Look, Ma, I'll pay you back.'

'Ah, that's not what I mean and you know it.'

'I just want to—'

'When I think of the people who'd love your job, the opportunity.'

'Ma, I'll still be a clerk in twenty years' time.'

'O well, excuse me. It was good enough for your father.'

'Yea, and look how he was.'

It was brewing up for an almighty row and then suddenly she'd started to cry.

'Look, Ma, they mightn't even take me. I just want to try something, you know, I want to, I don't know, to—'

'Go on, say it. To get away from me.'

'Ma, what do you have to say that for?'

Jackie had come in then, swinging his duffel bag off his back and onto the couch. 'What's up?'

'He's going to Australia, that's what.'

'Yea? When's this?' Jack had asked as if she'd said he was going to Crumlin, then he'd sat on the edge of the sofa, pulled out a record and started to study the sleeve of it.

'Not for a while yet. That's if they let me in at all.'

'And what'll you do there?'

'Jacobs – you know – his uncle has a car showroom, in New South Wales and he's sponsoring me and Jacobs to go out there because, you see, the motor industry it's really taken off and—'

'Jacobs?' Ma muttered. 'What sort of a name is that?'

'Ah, it's not his real name, Ma, it's a joke.'

'A joke?'

'About a packet of biscuits, from years ago, it's nothing. Anyway, his uncle has this garage—'

'Well, what is his real name then – Arrowroot?'

Jack laughed. 'Very good, Ma,' he said, lifting the sleeve of his record like a communion host. 'Guess what this is? Benny Goodman. The double album. Carnegie Hall *Nineteen Thirty-Eight*. Got a loan of it from a chap in college. Gene Krupa's on it, Harry James – the lot. Talk about ace!' He was tapping his foot and nodding his head as if he could already hear the music.

'All the same, it can't be much of a place,' he said after a minute. 'I mean, if they can't even find salesmen of their own. Or maybe it's just not that much of a job.'

Farley had felt like planting him. 'No, no, it's not that. He prefers to work with his own. See he doesn't like Australians.'

'O yea, and why's that I wonder?'

'How would you know?'

'There's a few of them in college – they're a pain, nobody likes them. They don't even like each other, if you ask me.'

They were punching him from both sides, pointing their questions at him, pecking him with their doubts and their unspoken secret, superior knowledge, their ability to express their thoughts. And he couldn't seem to explain what he wanted to explain, to get the words to come out right. In the end he'd had to get out. He'd opened the front door and then changed his mind and decided to go upstairs instead. Obviously they'd thought he had gone out. At least, he'd heard Jackie say, 'You're worse, Ma, upsetting yourself – it'll never happen. You know what he's like. He hasn't got the moxie.'

'The what?'

'You know, the wherewithal. All cod that fella is. All cod and no chips.'

A few minutes later he'd heard the tick-tacking of her typewriter, and behind it the triumphant mayhem of Bennie Goodman's orchestra.

Farley hopes someone asks him about it tonight. He'd show them alright about wherewithal and moxie. He'd show them all cod. He hopes they ask right in front of Jackie too, because tonight he's more than prepared. He's read the catalogue, cover to cover; he's read all the embassy literature. Australia. Motors. Fellas are always interested in that kind of thing. He's even torn the page out with the picture of Jacobs' uncle on it. 'Actually,' he'll be able to say, 'I happen to have a picture with me – want to see? That man there, he'll be my employer and that car he's leaning on – well, that's the Holden, a bestseller in Australia you know – can't get them out of the factory quick enough.'

And he'd let them pass the page around, and watch as their eyes lingered on the car; the robust bonnet, the chrome bar across the front grinning out; the logo like a badge of importance beneath it. And they could stuff their poetry and their jazz and their coffee talk in their sissy Grafton Street cafes. And they could stuff too their Benny Goodmans and their Gene Krupas and all those other oulfellas they thought so great, they could stuff them along with their pissy wine. Because none of them, *none* would ever go as far as Australia and none of them would ever have a car as good as a Holden.

'Rain' has suddenly stopped; the poet himself confirms it, by tilting his ear into the spotlight and giving a tip of his head and Farley finds himself bashing his hands together; if not for the poem then for the magnificent Holden purring through the dusty streets of Western Australia, little sprays of sand in its wake. He lifts himself off the chair and tips the man beside him on the arm to indicate he wants to get out. An older man has stepped under the spotlight, a touch of the brigadier about him; ronnie overlip, cravat at throat, one hand half-slipped into the pocket of a checked blazer. The man beside Farley pulls himself up and leans back to make way. Farley moves to edge past them, already muttering his 'sorry now sorrys', when the brigadier speaks. 'The next poem is by a young man. This may very well be the first time you'll have heard his name, but I promise you it won't be the last. And we are looking forward to the publication of his first volume which will be coming out in the spring. So if you could please welcome John Grainger.'

John Grainger? Jackie? 'Fuck!' Farley hears himself say out loud, and sits down again.

He feels like laughing out loud when he sees his brother up there; like they were kids again and Jackie had got up for a dare. Reading out of his tepee of light; Adam's apple as big as a fist, pimples zinging out of his face. The page – not a letter after all – gently shakes in his hand and Farley feels nervous for him then, can barely look. The poem is called 'Death in Spring' and he's not sure what it's about, and he suspects Jackie may not be that sure either. But it sounds fuckin great. The words roll together, go off on waves, roll back again. And you can see what he's saying, even if you haven't a clue what that is. It's like the jazz last week, except more sullen.

Jack gets the biggest clap of the evening and Farley turns to Beardy number one. 'That's my kid brother, up there,' he says. Then he looks the other way, to a man and a woman. 'I was just saying there, that's my kid brother. Good – isn't he?'

The woman nods and smiles. The man says, yes.

By the time he gets up Harcourt Street the dance is almost over; early leavers already bailing out. Two plain-faced youngones linked to each other wander past giving out shite about everything; the music, the state of the fellas, the girls nothin but common tinkers squirting hairspray all over the Ladies'. A couple in the doorway of O'Hagan's solicitors are having a row. He gets to the ballroom – doors closed, just as expected. On the kerb outside a bloke astride a Lambretta scooter smokes a cigarette and absentmindely pats his quiff. Farley bends to the glass, sees the hands of the cashier through the half-moon window of her box office, fluttering with ticket receipts. He raps on the door, but if she hears him she doesn't let on. He takes a florin out of his pocket and ticks it off the glass; the bouncer looks up, shakes his head and looks away. Too late. He can imagine the boys inside; Conroy stuck into some youngone giving her the sugar and spice treatment. Jacobs' bony shoulders turning like a butterfly screw while he's doing the twist. Soon the last desperate dance; the smash and grab. Then the shuffle to the cloakroom for coats, or for the luckier ones, the shrugging for space in the jacks mirror before the walk home.

He sees the green slab of his last bus jostle around the corner at the top of the street and decides he might as well hang on and wait for the others – he can walk home with Jacobs because, unlike Conroy, he always goes home alone.

He steps over to the railings. He's not in the best; the drink gone dead in him, the waste of an entire evening, apart from Jackie's poems, the end-of-summer purple sky. Everything is annoying him. And Monday tomorrow, his day off, nothing to do only look at the face on Ma.

A middle-aged man in a beret comes down the steps of a house, ties a brown parcel to the back of his bicycle, then loops a cardboard suitcase over one handle and struggles off up the road. The lonely sight of the man drags him down even further. He turns and looks to the other end of the street; no one in sight as far as the eye can see; only himself and the quiff on his Lambretta. A sound cracks the silence; Farley jumps, then turns. The bouncer is holding the door at arm's length, allowing just enough space for a slim girl to slip through. The Lambretta clicks and growls. She perches herself dainty-sideways on the back seat. And now that space too is vacant. There's a muffle of music through the walls; the occasional blurt from Gene Pitney whenever the bouncer opens the door to let somebody else out. Across the road a nurse comes from the direction of the children's hospital and he stands to watch her, cloak stirring softly at her back. She has car keys in her hand and she's heading for a Ford Prefect parked under the street light. She opens the car, throws in her handbag, then pulls the nurse's hat off her head, fires that into the car as well. For a minute he thinks it's her, the girl from Butlin's, and he feels himself lift from the soles of his feet through to his stomach into his chest. But it's just a tired girl with black hair on her way home from work.

It was the hair he'd noticed first; a swatch of black satin on the back of her head. It was easier to notice things like hair and hands, when all the women were dressed the same – red blazers, white shoes, white skirts. There'd been other women around; holidaymakers or campers as they called themselves, but there was something about the redcoats, a sort of air hostess glamour that blew the rest of them out of the water. Redcoats or civilians, they all tended to have backcombed hair; blonde and mousey-browns, an occasional ball of orange. That stiff webbed stuff that he didn't care much for, scratching the side of his jaw on the dance floor or in a shop doorway where there was always the fear that if things got too heavy, he might knock it sideways off the top of her head. If the girl was much smaller, and she often was, when he looked down into her hair, he half expected to see some scrawny live thing inside, squawking for food.

Her hair, though, was real hair. Real and smooth and coiled like a thick glossy snake at the nape of her neck. He couldn't stop looking at that, wondering what it would be like to weigh it in the palm of his hand.

Jackie, even though it had been his idea and his college mate who had organized everything, never stopped moaning from the time they'd got off the train. 'A glorified concentration camp,' he'd called it, 'a bone to appease the lower classes while the big boys eat their dinner.'

'Do us a favour, Jack?' Conroy had said after a few such comments. 'Go fuck off somewhere and read a book.'

'I would if I had one,' he huffed.

As prearranged Jackie's redcoat mate gave them the recce over by the boathouse, holding a map open as if giving ordinary directions to respectable campers while talking out the side of his mouth. 'The trick,' he'd said, 'is to keep on the move. Don't stay at any one place too long, don't do anything to attract attention; no getting involved in slagging matches with the Northies, no whistling at the birds, no hogging the billiard table. You'll be alright till six, but after that you're illegal. So keep it clean – right? If one of the head honchos comes into the ballroom, ask a bird up to dance. If you notice anyone – other than a bird – looking at you for more than a few seconds, move on to the next spot. It's August and the place is jammers anyhow, but there's always the chance that someone not enjoying themselves is looking for someone else to blame – know what I mean? Once the campers are all tucked up, we'll get you into the staff quarters where there's a party tonight – boss away, cats will play. You can relax then. You'll be kipping in my chalet; the room-mate's old man has snuffed it; local bigwig – they're all gone to his funeral. Two beds and a floor, I'll leave it up you lot to fight it out between you. O, and in case you're worried about me – don't, I'm on a promise – winkedy wink. And if you're all good boys, tell you what – I'll sneak you in for first breakfast in the morning. After that you can fuck off home you and your ugly mugs.'

He backed off then, waving a cheery goodbye. 'Well, enjoy yourselves at Butlin's, chaps – anything else you need to know don't hesitate to ask any of our redcoats. So long now!'

Jackie decided to go for a swim. Conroy, Jacobs and himself had wandered around; Jacobs walking backwards looking at the women. They'd ended up in the coffee lounge sitting in front of these big glass windows that turned out to be the bottom of the indoor swimming pool. Disembodied legs wriggling about like big fat sea worms. Jacobs decided to look out for Jackie's legs and in the process nearly gave himself a heart attack. 'Jaysus,' he whispered, 'you can see the – you know, the hair on your woman's you know? Stickin out like, out the side of her togs.'

'You mean her pubic hair?' Conroy had said. 'For fuck sake, Jacobs, calm down, you think you'd never seen a fanny before.'

'I haven't!' Jacobs squealed and they all nearly died laughing.

That's when she came up to them.

'Well, gentlemen, I see you're enjoying yourselves anyway.'

'O yea, it's great yea,' Jacobs spluttered

'Mind if I ask to see your passes?'

Even Conroy had puced up to the roots, although he did manage to find his ticket.

'This is a day pass,' she'd said.

'That's right.'

'So we won't have the pleasure of your company this evening then?'

They just stood looking at her. She looked back at them. 'Because if I do see any of you boys still hanging about the place after six, well then, I'd have to inform security.'

'Right,' Conroy said.

She handed him back his day pass. Then she winked.

Jackie's mate had come strolling past them, grinning and wagging his finger. 'Ah-ha,' he said, 'caught youse out there.'

She lifted her eyebrows and then disappeared.

'She's a bit of alright – wha?' Conroy said.

'Yea,' Farley said, 'yea, she is.'

'Would you say she's his bird?'

'Whose bird?'

'Jackie's mate's bird.'

'What? O, don't know. Maybe.'

Later in the ballroom he saw her again. He'd been dancing with some butty little one from Finglas who'd asked him what chalet he was staying in, and when he said he couldn't remember she didn't seem to think it was odd that after nearly a week a grown man couldn't hold the number of a door in his head. The redcoat was foxtrotting an elderly man around the floor, soft blots of green and pink lights preceding them. The little one from Finglas kept rattling on about the great time she'd been having so far; fourth in the Miss something or other while her granny got fifth in the granny competition; her brother third in the table tennis. Meanwhile her ma and her baby sister won second prize in the Mother-and-Child Contest. Only her da didn't enter anything because he couldn't drink on account of his half of a stomach.

'Right,' Farley had said, steering her after the redcoat and the elderly man.

Then Conroy came along and tipped him on the elbow. 'Time to move on.'

He'd felt sorry for the poor girl all the same, having to leave her standing on the floor on her own with her family of runner-ups looking on from the shadows.

'A phone call,' he muttered. 'Have to go. Might see you later?'

'What time?' she said.

'Depends really.'

'Where then?' she said.

'In the bar.'

'Which bar?'

'Don't worry, I'll find you.'

He saw the redcoat again in the Pig and Whistle while a load of English people were swaying through an old Vera Lynn song.

'Look at them,' Jackie had said, 'don't know what to be doing without a war to fight, the dregs of the British army, redundant cannon fodder put out to grass. Jesus almighty!'

Then he spotted her again, outside the American Bar stopping to sign her autograph and have her picture taken.

'Fucking morons,' Jackie had said, 'pretending to be film stars. Pathetic self-delusional fools. God, the sooner I get out of this place.'

'Ah shut up, Jackie,' he'd said, 'do you have to be such a pain in the hole *all* the time?'

Jackie's mate was called Bob. He played the clarinet. He was a commerce student in real life, he said.

'Commerce?' Conroy said. 'Why did you pick that?'

'Because my oulfella is a prick.'

'O right, yea.'

They were in the staff area by then; she was sitting on top of a table, hand jiving to the music of 'El Paso' with a couple of other girls. Her hair was down over one shoulder, her blazer off, her white sleeves rolled up, her white shoes off. In a minute now, he'd decided, he was going ask her to dance.

He was half-drunk by then, all the moving around from bar to bar between trying to avoid the security men and the one from Finglas. More drink in here stacked under the table, the girl with the black hair swishing her legs to the side anytime anyone wanted to pull a bottle out of the crate.

'The thing about the sugar stick,' Jackie's mate was saying, cradling his clarinet like a baby.

'Can I ask you something?' Conroy interrupted.

'Shoot.'

'That bird, over there – is she your girlfriend?'

'Wastin your time there, but, my friend, you have my blessing. God loves a trier.'

A few seconds later she was standing on a chair singing 'Volare' and he could see Conroy getting ready to pounce, and he knew if he didn't move soon, he may as well forget the whole thing.

She'd insisted he borrowed some bloke's blazer before they went outside, in case security spotted him, then took his arm and brought him on a walk through the trees. He could hear the sea somewhere. Then smell it, then see it. The badges on his lapel rattled as they walked. She said, 'God, you don't wear yourself out talkin, do you?' and he couldn't think of how to answer that, so he just kissed her. And he didn't know what to do then so he just kissed her again, her long hair plush in his fingers.

When they got back to the party Conroy had disappeared and Jackie was asleep on the table. And his mate Bob, whose promise had obviously been revoked, had locked himself into his chalet. They could hear him snoring inside and when she'd shone a torch through the window, he was fully clothed on top of his bed, sugar stick lying across his chest. This left himself and Jacobs with nowhere to sleep. By then it had started to rain. Jacobs, with his hands dug deep into his pockets, was gently swaying from the drink. She'd taken pity on them and said they could stay in her chalet. She gave them her bed: he got in one end, Jacobs the other. She'd got into the end of the bed where her chalet mate was already asleep; small head deformed with layers of curlers. Jacobs fell asleep straight off, and they talked to each other across the few feet of darkness until Jacobs woke up again, giddy and full of jokes. He could see her stuff her face into the pillow to stop herself laughing out loud.

In the morning the rain had stopped, the sun pricked through the little boats on the blue and orange curtains, and her black hair, luscious and dangerous only an arm's stretch away from him. He noticed her mate had disappeared from the end of the other bed. She woke then and turned and sleepily looked at him and he hoped he hadn't too much of a gammy head on him. She stayed where she was while Jacobs and himself put themselves together. Nobody spoke but he could see by her face, now pale and a little strained, that she was worried in the light of day, away from her mates, away from the music. He touched the bed because it hadn't seemed right to touch her while she was in it. 'Thanks,' he'd whispered. 'Listen, could I see you again?'

She whispered back, 'Jesus, will you just get goin?'

When they got outside a security man was waiting.

As Jackie's mate had said – there's always someone.

They met Conroy and Jackie at the train station; Jackie sullen and silently smoking; Conroy grinning like a cat. And Farley had been shocked by the sight of his grin, knowing what it meant and knowing too that they'd probably have to hear all about it.

'I hope you were careful, anyhow,' Jacobs said, 'you've already got one pregnant, you can't marry two of them you know.'

'O yea? Well, at least I wasn't sharing her – not like you two perverts.'

When he said that Farley wanted to grab him, slap a loaf into his stupid head, smash his ribs with the heel of his boot and throw him down onto the tracks. And that's when he knew.

In the morning he wakes to a silent house. No tick-tacking from Ma's typewriter, no ill-humoured Jackie bashing around. Monday, his day off, the day after the poetry reading; that's right. He can hear the trees swishing across the wall of the Phoenix Park and from the army barracks down the road, a long disgruntled whinny from one of the horses. He lies for a while and stares at the ceiling, still in bad form although he can't figure out why. He says the word Australia. A short while ago, whenever he heard or even thought that word, it gave him such a lift. Now it hangs around his neck like a stone.

He gets up for a piss. As he crosses the landing he glances over the bannister. On the mat, a long envelope. Even from here he can tell where it's come from; the emblem in the corner, the length and shape of his full, formal name on the top line of the address.

He gets dressed and washes, then shaves; between razor swipes pauses to study the scowl on his face. Downstairs he lifts the envelope from the floor and drops it onto the kitchen table. A mug of tea and a cut of bread.

He takes a few sips, a couple of bites, looks at the envelope again, and decides to go out, leaving it unopened, behind him.

Just a short walk to clear out his head; get the paper, come back and read it over a fresh cup of tea. Maybe open the letter then, and see what the verdict is. He gets to the end of the road and turns the opposite way to the shops. A quick stroll in the Park first. Nowhere in particular, just a ramble. He comes in through Ashtown Gate and follows the bridle path towards White Fields Gate, stopping when he gets to Butcher's Wood. The smell of rain on the air, the deep moist green of the trees, the clasped shadow. He looks over the paling, at the greasy still lake, trying to recall a story his granda once told him about the lake and a secret that was stuck to the bottom of it. Then he turns and makes his way down alongside the wall of the school where his granda used to be caretaker, keeping to the narrow pathway they often walked together when he was a boy. His stride feels looser now, he's beginning to enjoy the walk, the feel of the ground underneath his feet, the overcast sky blotting all thoughts from his head. He decides to keep going, down through the Furry Glen, into the silence.

Nobody crosses his path and anyone he does see he sees from a distance; across the acres, the insignia of two racehorses pressed against the sky; in the direction of the Cheshire Home, a nurse pushing an old soldier in a wheelchair. A woman in a black raincoat, cycling. He comes out at the turnstile gate, down Park Lane to Chapelizod village. People suddenly. Two men talking outside the shop, women at the bus stop; boys playing cards on the steps of a house. The sound of a butcher, chopping. He means to stop here, maybe go in and have something: coffee, a pint, a read of that newspaper he's been wanting to buy. But he's through Chapelizod before he knows it, and halfway up Ballyfermot hill.

He comes onto the Avenue. An endless cram of houses behind iron-rod fences; farty gardens, door after door, number after number, must be running to well over a hundred. He follows the road in its shape of a crescent; nobody about, except a girl in a van-shop, peering out through the hatch at him, and a woman inside a house cleaning the windows. The squeak of newspaper against glass as he approaches; the pause just after he passes. He crosses the road and comes back the other side. Turning the corner he can't work out now if this is the same road or if he's wandered onto another because the place has suddenly filled up with kids that weren't there a minute ago. He sees the van-shop again, the girl outside it now, swiping rain off the front of it. It's only now that it registers that somewhere along the way it had started to drizzle and now it has stopped; that sly sort of drizzle that you hardly feel at all and yet leaves you saturated.

A youngone is drawing chalk boxes on the pavement. Two boys are nailing hammers into a misshapen go-cart. He watches for a few seconds and then crosses over to them. The girl is about twelve; she wears pink specs with a patch over one eye. She's standing on one leg now and in her hand holds a tin of polish that she seems about to throw, except she doesn't. She stays, balanced on one foot, barely wavering, and stares at him out of her uncovered eye. He only has to mention the word Butlin's.

When he knocks at the door, he's holding the polish tin in his hand. The sleeve of his jumper is drenched and his hair when he tips it back off his forehead releases a dribble. Behind him he hears the bicker of kids queue-ing at the van to buy sweets with the coppers he gave them. A woman with thick grey hair answers the door and even though he can't quite remem-ber what the girl looks like, he recognizes her face in the woman's. He opens his mouth to speak but then sees her legs coming down the stairs. 'It's alright, Ma,' she says.

She stands in the doorway, arms folded to her chest, a hip jutted to one side, a furry slipper. Behind her the door is pulled over. Her hair is tur-baned into a towel and he gets a fright at its absence, because it's the hair he remembers, above all else.

'What are you doin walkin up and down the road?' she says.

'I wasn't walkin up and down the road.'

175

'I seen you; walkin up and down like you're not right in the head. Well? What do you want?'

He nearly says, 'You.' But instead he starts stumbling and stuttering: 'I heard, you know, what happened and that and well, I just wanted... well you know I'm sorry for... For that.'

'Yea, well so you should be, me ma is going mad, thinks I'm some sort of a tramp; two fellas in me room all night.'

'I – I could tell her – you know, explain.'

'Ah, don't bother, that'd only make her worse. Anyway, it doesn't matter now. I was sick of the place. And there's only a couple of weeks left.'

'What'll you do now?'

'A commercial course. Get a job as a typist,' she says and then shrugs.

He looks up the road, and then back at her. Even without the hair she's still gorgeous.

'Anyway,' he says and takes a step back.

'Is that it?'

He steps forward again. 'I'm supposed to be going to Australia,'

Her eyes flicker. 'Yea, well, don't let me keep you,' she says.

'No. I didn't mean... What I mean is... I don't know. Here – I thought you said you lived in Chapelizod?'

'Had to say that, to get the job. People are snobs, you know? Maybe you are, for all I know?'

'No.'

'Where are you from then?'

'The other side of the Park.'

'Where?'

'Blackhorse Avenue.'

'Are you a poshy?'

'No.'

'You sound like one. Carmel Waters says your brother goes to university.'

'Who's she?'

'Her brother knows your brother. She got the sack too in case you're interested. Though if you ask me she deserved it. She was with your mate, that bloke you know?'

'Conroy.'

'Yea, him. Now she's after hearin he's gettin married. A bastard, he is. A liar. I suppose you're the same?'

'*No*. Look, you know when I said about Australia. See, I applied ages ago now and—'

'And wha?'

'Nothing.'

'Ah go, if you're goin. I couldn't care less.'

Behind him the gate creaks open and the youngone with the specs comes in licking an ice pop.

'Look, Martina—' he begins.

'O, he knows me name!'

The little girl walks right up to him and for a minute he thinks she's going to let it out that he only knows her name because she told him. But she plucks the polish tin out of his hand and says, 'Thanks for mindin it for me.'

'You're welcome.'

'Bye now.'

'Bye.'

She steps past Martina into the hall.

'Martina?' he tries again.

'Ah what? Look, will you say whatever it is you're tryin to say – will you?'

'I just wanted to ask you if you were doing anything on Wednesday, that's all.'

She's annoyed, her face full and flushed, her eyes glint. 'Why would I want to go out with you? You're going away. Of course, you're probably just like your mate, lookin for a bit of fun before you head off. Well, you can look somewhere else.'

'No, it's not like that.'

'Calling here to tell me you're going to Australia, what business of mine is it? I'm going with someone anyway, hope you know. He's mad about me, he is.'

'Yea, well I wouldn't blame him.'

She turns her head away. He waits but she says nothing then, glaring down the road like she's watching out for someone.

'Alright,' he says, 'sorry.'

He walks to the gate. He's stepped out onto the path when she calls out to him, 'I could meet you at the Corinthian, there's a picture I wouldn't mind seeing.'

'Would you meet me after work?' he says. 'Six o'clock.'

She nods, biting her lip, then closes the door.

A flutter at an upstairs window. He thinks it might be her, but when he looks up he sees the little girl standing with the curtain veiled around her head, sucking sideways on the end of her ice pop, peeping out from her one good eye. He waves but she doesn't wave back.

When he gets home Jackie and Ma are in the kitchen; the air thick with the talk they've obviously been having about him.

'There's a letter for you,' Ma says after a few seconds' silence.

'Yea, I know. Saw it there earlier.'

'Well, why didn't you open it then?'

'Because I don't want to know.'

'How do you mean?'

He pulls up a chair and settles it into the table. 'I don't want to know if I got in or not.'

He sees Ma and Jackie swap looks.

'I've met a girl,' he says. 'I'm not going to Australia.'

'What girl?' Jackie asks. 'Not your one from Butlin's? You don't even know her, for Christ's sake that's just ridiculous.'

'I know what I want.'

'Rubbish,' Jackie says, 'you don't know your arse from your elbow, you.'

'I've made my decision. That's it,' Farley says,

Ma's face is all lit up. He knows that in the normal course of events Ma wouldn't approve of her; a girl from Ballyer who says I seen and I done. But he also knows Ma already loves this girl; this girl who is keeping him from going away and by turn, keeping the few quid coming into the house as well as postponing the time when she'll be left on her own. Because Jackie might be her favourite, but if there's one thing they all know, it's this – Jackie is always going to put himself first.

'I can't believe you'd hang your hat on a one-night stand,' Jackie says, 'I mean to say, I thought even *you* had more sense than that.'

'I'm not interested in your opinion.'

'What are you sayin then? That you're going to marry her?'

'I don't know, maybe I will. Eventually. But if I do, it'll be nothing to do with you.'

There's a knock on the door. Farley lays his hands out flat on the table, 'So can we leave it at that? Ma, will you throw out that envelope?'

Ma nods, Jackie rolls his eyes and looks away.

A bloke standing there, maybe a couple years older than himself. At first he thinks it's a pal of Jackie's but then the bloke says, 'I'm here about the ad in the Four Courts – a Mrs Grainger, takes in typing and that?'

'That's right,' Farley says, 'hold on I'll get her.'

'Any chance you'd give a hand with some stuff in the car first?'

Farley nods and follows him out.

The bloke opens the boot; inside there's boxes full of papers: envelopes, letters, receipts.

'Hope she does a bit of bookkeeping as well,' he says.

'Are you a solicitor?' Farley asks him.

'Do I look like a bollix? No, I do work for them, you know, like an agent. Not that long out on me own actually.'

'O? I work for a solicitor.'

'Yea, which one?'

'Caine's on the quays.'

'Caine – tried to get a bit of business off him but not a budge.'

'Ah, he's like that.'

'Maybe you'll put a word in for me?'

'Maybe I will.'

He dips into the car, pulls out a box and lays it on the cradle of Farley's arms.

'Do you do much court work?' he asks.

'Nearly all court work.'

'Yea?'

'What about serving summonses – you do that?'

'No. We send them out to an agent.'

'Could you ever see yourself doing them?'

'Don't know. Is it hard?'

'No, just a pain in the arse.'

The man looks at him for a minute like he's studying his face.

'Ever feel like a change of jobs – let me know. I'd give you a business card but they're not ready till next week. What's your name?'

'Farley. Well, Charlie.'

'Charlie or Farley?'

'Farley's a nickname but it's what most people call me.'

'Like the film star – Grainger – O yea, I get it.'

'Well, I don't like to say that really.'

'Why not?'

'People might think I'm full of meself.'

'Let them think what they like,' he says, pulling out a box and settling it into his arms. 'By the way, my name's Frank.'

'Frank?'

'Frank or Hank.'

'Really?'

'Nah. Just Frank. Frank Slowey.'

A Night of Perfect Seeing

September 1950

GRANDA BILL ALWAYS CALLS him Charles. Char-less, is what he says. For the past few mornings he's been waking to his feeble whisper: '*Char-less, Char-less*, wake up now, come on, son, it's time we were off.' And he always thinks the same thing just before he opens his eyes, that he's at home in his own bed, that the voice belongs to Da, the hand is his hand. Even though Da never called him for school in his life, nor did he ever address him as son, and in anyway, Da's been dead for over six weeks.

He opens his eyes; darkness all around him like a black cloth fraying. He can hear Jackie breathing beside him and knows he must have sneaked into his bed again in the middle of the night. It's been the same every night since they came to stay in Gran's house, although Jackie usually manages to get back to his own bed before it's time to get up, before he has to admit that at thirteen years old he's afraid to sleep on his own. Jackie is afraid of ghosts but Farley knows, one way or another, Da is never coming back.

He goes out to the kitchen and his breakfast is waiting; tea in a big blue-striped mug, a back rasher buckled across a slice of bread. 'Remind me now to mooch a couple of eggs from Wiggy this morning,' Granda says. Then he takes a mug of tea in to Gran. When he comes back he sits staring into the empty fire grate while he waits for the tea to darken. After a couple more minutes he holds his mug out to Farley to pour – his hands, he says, are not the best this morning, must be all the rain. Farley pours him a sample drop, waits for Granda to check its colour, then continues to pour.

Granda Bill reaches into his back pocket; a silver flask twists into his hand. He pours a tawny slug of it into the tea and goes at it in short swift sips. 'I suppose I better shave in case any of the girls are around,' he says, 'we'll be indoors today – luggage day. Don't forget.'

By girls he means nuns and Farley knows this is a sort of a joke not meant in any way to be disrespectful, but it thrills through him like a greedy sin; the thought of all that flesh under cover. Bellies, backsides, diddies, whatever that contraption is they have down below. He feels himself blush, his Adam's apple swells up in his throat. He's afraid Granda Bill will guess what he's just been thinking or what he's so often thinking these days. But Granda is already on his feet, face turned to the shaving mirror perched on the mantel. One bloodshot eye peeping out, he begins to foam up and the skin on his face, crushed with wrinkles, disappears under curls of lather. His nose, when he pulls it up, gives him the face of a garden gnome. Beside him, facing out, is a photograph of a young Granda Bill in full uniform, bar and badged, a Sam Browne belt across his chest. And there isn't a whole lot of difference between the old and the new, apart from the ronnie over the younger lip, the clearer expression in the eyes. He is not alone in the photograph; another soldier is standing beside him. The other soldier is a more handsome man, a good four inches taller. He's looking straight into the camera, whereas Granda Bill is looking away. The other man is Gran's first husband; Granda Grainger. The other man is Da's real da.

Gran once said they didn't have film stars as such in the days before the Great War, but if they did, Granda Grainger could have been one. He was easily the best-looking man she'd ever seen, on or off the screen. She told them that one day when Granda Bill was at work, taking the photograph down and holding it low in both hands. 'But of course,' she had said then, 'looks aren't everything.'

In the mirror Granda Bill pats his old face dry, then carries the bowl outside. Farley looks around for yesterday's paper, spots it there, folded on the armchair, racing page facing out. He promised to bring Concilia another newspaper today, but he knows it can't be this one; not with Granda's equations like a secret code in the margin and Jackie's selections and his own wild guesses marked there for today's race meetings. Granda says there's nothing better for taking your mind off your troubles than picking out a few horses over a cup of bedtime cocoa. As soon as they'd finish work today, he promised, they'd come home for a quick wash and then they'd all go down to the pub to listen to the racing on the radio. They could eat their sandwiches there; they could even have a long glass of lemonade. Farley likes the names of the racecourses: Lanark, Manchester, Folkestone, Baldoyle; the names of the horses too: Soubrette, Devil's Dance, Dancing Flame – the way the names are pulled out of the names of the mother and father, a little something from each. When they were younger, Jackie and himself used to play this game of what their names would be if they were horses. Cranky Clatter and Face of Boiled Shite were the only two he can remember now. He gets bored with the arithmetic end of things; the talk of handicaps and draws, the form and forecast. And anyway, since he got the holiday job helping out in the race-course stables, he can't bring himself to believe that any amount of thinking and totting could make a racehorse do something he doesn't want to do.

Granda comes back with a shirt collar in his hand; ducks his head and begins to fumble. 'Do you want me to do that for you?' Farley asks.

Granda Bill nods and sits down. Farley stands at the back of the chair.

'You see—' Granda begins to explain and Farley stops him.

'It's alright, I have it.'

He knows it hurts Granda to talk these days or that at least he only seems to cry whenever he stops keeping busy and begins to speak at length. It's as if the sound of his own voice fills him with sadness. In a way it puzzles him why Granda should cry so much, not because Da wasn't his real son, but because hardly anyone else in the family seems to have shed any tears. Apart from himself, but he wasn't really crying for Da. Ma might cry for all he knows, because he hasn't seen her since she went off for her rest a couple of weeks ago. And before he went back to Birmingham Uncle Cal gave himself and Jackie permission to cry. 'It's alright to cry when somebody dies, cry all you like, boys.' But even though Uncle Cal said that, for the whole week he was home during and after the funeral, they didn't see him cry one tear for his dead half-brother.

Farley cried though. Farley cried on and off for over a week and men patted his arm and women gave him powdery hugs. He cried when they told him, 'It's not looking good, son,' and he knew he'd have to cancel his trip with the cycling club. And he cried when they put the pennies on Da's eyelids because he knew the miracle he'd been praying for wasn't going to happen. He cried the next day when people were dropping in and out of the house and he thought of all the lads crowding the platform of Westland Row station. And a few hours later when Ma sent him out to make yet another cup of tea, and he thought of them all bobbing across the Irish Sea. When they took the coffin out and when they slid it into the hearse; when they took it out again and carried it into the church. When they carried it out of the church and put it back in the hearse. And every time he consulted the map he kept in his brain and wondered what are they doing and where are they now – Newhaven, Dieppe, Rouen? As they lowered the coffin into the ground he reckoned on Paris, and sobbed.

Granda Bill has gone quiet in himself these past weeks. Farley misses talking to him because when you get him on good form nobody tells a story like Granda Bill. Stories about the Great War. Stories about other things. In school teachers often warn them not to go pestering old soldiers. 'They don't like to discuss these things,' was what Master Rowe used to say, 'and it's not up to us to open old wounds.' But with Granda Bill there was never that problem; he'd talk about the war till his head fell off, about the rats and the hunger and boots rotting off his feet. About the noise and the death and the smell of guts. He'd tell stories about Granda Grainger too, his old friend, that Farley used to believe, until Jackie said he had to be making half of them up because nobody could be that much of a hero, or that funny, or that clever. But Farley can't think of Granda Bill as telling lies. He just borrowed the best bits from all his comrades and gave them to Granda Grainger to make him look better; the man whose door he would knock on one day to break the bad news to his widow, the widow he would later snare for himself.

He settles the collar down and helps Granda put on his jacket. The suit is too heavy for summer, but it's as well to look respectable, Granda says, in case Mother Battleaxe is about the place, and in anyway it's an old enough suit so it doesn't really matter if there's a bit of damage done. He takes his Fusilier pin off the lapel and puts it into his pocket.

'Some of them oul nuns,' he says, 'do be fierce nationalistic.'

He has names for all the nuns; Mother Bernadette is Mother Battleaxe, Sister Ukaria is Sister Eureka, Sister Eugene is Sister Egghead, Jarleth is Garlic. He goes on about the suit for a few more minutes while he winds his watch and locates his snuffbox and checks the keys on a bunch hanging by the door. He's talking so much that Farley is afraid he might start crying again.

It's still dark enough when they get outside and because for once it's not raining Granda Bill says they might as well walk the short cut, because driving all the way round by the North Road would nearly take you as long. In a way Farley's sorry they won't be in the car because it would keep Granda distracted while he weaselled in a few of the questions that are stacked inside his head.

The first thing he'd ask is if Granda had a word with Ma yet, about his leaving school and getting a job. The next thing he'd ask about is the funeral – if Granda Bill had known any of those people who had shuffled across the front row, offering hand after hand, under a long blur of faces.

185

Or back in the house, the man who had called for silence and said he'd been asked to say a few words – just who had asked him? And who was he in anyway? And what about the woman at the back of the chapel with the feathery grey hat like a dead pigeon on her head – who was she? And what was she crying for and why hadn't she come back to the house?

Farley senses the frailty of the old man beside him, the grief that would crack like a shell if you touched it, and decides today is not the day to go asking questions.

They walk on. He can see Venus twitching in the still black sky and it makes him think of Concilia, the story she'd told him about borrowing the telescope from the science lab and smuggling it up to the music cells. And how every night when the convent is in darkness she sneaks up to watch Jupiter. Jupiter in the southern sky. The light around it delicate and flecked. 'Like a jellyfish,' she said, 'if you know what I mean?' He nodded even though he didn't know anything except the sound of her voice, the hard whiteness of her teeth, the blue-grey marble of her eyes. That was the first time he'd met her and it had all happened so quickly he hadn't had time to wonder.

He'd just come out of the second-floor dormitory where he'd been sent to fetch Granda's tools. And there she was, waiting on the flight of stairs above. She didn't say hello or show any surprise at a youngfella wandering around the dormitory on his own. She just started straight off about Jupiter and the telescope. Her face encased in its wimple had seemed like some sort of a moon. She said her name was Concilia, then she asked him if he could bring her a newspaper. It wouldn't have to be an up-to-date paper, any newspaper would do. Although not too old either, not months old anyhow – and she only wanted it at all if he could promise to keep it a secret.

He'd agreed on both counts. In return she offered to show him Jupiter. A sky, lightly clouded was best, she said. That was what was known as 'a night of perfect seeing'. She could leave the side gate open for him, sneak him in. A little before eleven o'clock would be the right time for him to come.

He hadn't known where to look, what to say when she came up with this suggestion. She didn't seem old enough to be a figure of authority and she wasn't young enough to be a friend. She was a woman. A nun. At the same time something about her was all wrong. She'd been clutching the bannister as she spoke to him, turning her hands back and forwards over the lip of it. He had felt sure the palms of her hands must be burning. Her eyes too wide and bright, yet her voice was steady and soft; a posh voice, slightly purred, maybe Scottish.

He had begun to mutter excuses, 'Well, I don't… I mean, see, I'm not sure if—'

Then she'd let a sudden gasp. Amplified on the echo it had made him jump along with her. 'Shhhh, shhh someone is coming. O Jesus of mercy help me. O Jeee-sus.'

Her whisper was louder than her speaking voice, the way she'd said the second Jesus more like a curse than a prayer. She'd lifted the skirt of her habit and belted off up the stairs; black stockings and black granny shoes spinning like a rudder behind her. Farley was left standing on the return, mouth hanging open. He'd looked down the two flights of stairs leading to the big entrance hall and then craned upwards to the two flights above him leading past the top dormitory to the fifth narrow staircase for the music cells. He listened intently. He stayed there for moments. But there wasn't a sound in the house.

The dark eases and second by second falls away. The trees become trees instead of hovering black angels. The ground feels weak underfoot; a damp smell of soil and stone, the menthol tang of Granda's snuff. He can hear Granda breathe and grunt beside him. He wonders if he should tell him about the nun. But he knows Granda Bill, for all his little jokes and secret nicknames, worries about keeping in favour and doesn't want to add to the burden. 'Who was the woman in the back of the church with the grey feathery hat, Granda?' he hears himself ask instead and wonders why a nun and a woman with a funny hat should be tangled up in the same thought in his head. Granda stalls for a second, pulls out his hanky and blows his nose, then he walks on, breathing and lightly grunting again.

Farley imagines Concilia creeping through the dark house up all those flights of stairs. He doubts he would have the nerve to do that, certainly not at that hour of the night, not on his own. Even in daylight, after years of helping Granda, he still feels sometimes spooked; the empty beds, the hollow presses, the skeleton in the science lab, a forgotten hockey boot under a bench. Or that stand-up trunk in the luggage room still unclaimed after all this time; the girl's name on it – Sylvia Ridgeway. She must have died in the school and the trunk, no longer needed, had just been forgotten.

Concilia had said he would tell. Three days ago she said it, when he had slipped her the night before's paper. 'Of course, you will tell.'

'No I won't. I promise I won't.'

'You're a man, aren't you? You'll tell.'

They come into the farmyard and Granda stops for a chat with the farm manager. They talk about Korea and Indo-China. The chances of another war. The manager says if it comes to it, Truman won't let them down, they could rely on the Yanks before, they can rely on them again.

The manager is known as a 'clever man' and Farley sees Granda is listening carefully to every word he says. He mentions places like Suwon and Formosa. The People's Republic of China. The names sound like gold dust to Farley and he wonders exactly where they are.

'If there's another war,' he hears himself blurt, 'I could join up, I could be a soldier.' The words sound stupid and childish bouncing around the farmyard and the sideways glances he gets from both men confirm this.

'It'll hardly come to that,' the manager mutters, folding himself into his van. Then he closes the door and drives away.

Wiggy comes out of the barn, cigarette poked from the corner of his mouth. He's dragging a milk churn behind him, the sound of it scraping onto the yardstone. 'I thought that fucker'd never go,' he says, the cigarette jumping up and down as he speaks. It's almost bright now in the yard and there's a smell of multi-flavoured shite; milky cows' plop, the gusty honk from the stables, the sweet-musty smell of the hens' poo. They step into Wiggy's office; a disused stable with an old teacher's desk for a table, a few bockety milk stools and bits of things hanging out of rusty nails. Granda takes a page of paper from his inside pocket and flattens it out on the desk, the names of the horses are all there. He puts his money on top of it.

'The boys picked out a few,' Granda says, 'if you wouldn't mind?'

Wiggy squints down at the paper and blinks. 'Jaysus, who picked that treble?' he says. 'Throwing good money away – is that yours?' he asks Farley.

Granda says, 'No, that's the younger lad, he gets a bit carried away.'

'I was thinkin you'd have more sense,' Wiggy says to him, and Farley nods although the truth is he can't even remember which horses he picked in the end.

Wiggy tells him to go into the barn and bring out a couple of eggs.

'How many?'

'Just the two.'

And Farley knows he's going to make Granda ask for the eggs again, because he always does that, makes people ask. It drives Farley mad and he wishes Granda would just buy his eggs in the local shop. Whenever he suggests this, Granda always says, 'Ah, that's just the way Wiggy is.'

When he comes back in Granda and Wiggy are still discussing the racing. Wiggy is holding a blowtorch under the base of a kettle with no lid on it. The torch squirts fire up through the kettle. Wiggy turns a blank face to Farley as if he doesn't recognize him or know what he's doing with two eggs nesting on his palms. He has a fat, bare face, a pinkish head with just a few curls in the centre of it. His gummy mouth finishes off the look of a big fat baby. 'Pop them in there,' he says, 'slow like, I don't want them crackin.'

'Into the kettle you mean?' Farley says.

'That's right, two birds one stone, lower them in nice and aisy daisy.'

Farley tries not to look pleased when the eggs slip out of his hand into the water without any mishap. Granda tips a small hill of snuff onto the back of his hand. 'Right, Char-less, I want you to go over to the convent, see if the luggage has arrived, then knock on Sister Marble's office and ask for the dormitory list so we can see which piece of luggage goes where – right?'

Farley nods. He watches the eggs bob around in the kettle while he waits for Granda Bill to snort up his snuff, give his nose a good rub, then pull out his hanky and barp. 'After that you better check on the light bulbs in the classrooms.'

Farley is about to go when Wiggy realizes that he's forgotten a spoon for the eggs. He sends him down to the farm manager's wife.

But the manager's wife takes her time coming to the door, peeping around it, one hand clutching her dressing gown to her throat. Then there's another long wait while she shuffles back and the spoon comes around the door on its own.

When he comes back, he gives Wiggy the spoon and watches him chase the eggs with it round the water. He lifts the first one and settles it onto the top of an empty milk bottle. The other he leaves resting beside a stack of buttered bread on wax paper. He takes a packet of tea then and pours from it straight into the water the eggs have just left, then gives it a stir with the spoon before closing the lid on it. He brings the spoon over to the egg and clips off the top of it. 'Ah fuck it in anyway,' he says, his face all puce, 'it's hard now, so it is. If there's anythin I can't stand it's a fucken hard egg!'

But he turns it inside out and eats it anyway, taking a bite from the bread to follow. 'Pour us out a sup of tea there will you?' he says to Granda through a mouth stuffed sideways with bread.

Farley gets to the kettle of tea before Granda, to save his stiff hands. Then he pours for the two men. Wiggy gets stuck into the next egg, takes a few gulps of tea in between, before stretching his mug out to Granda. 'Here, give us another peg of that whiskey there.'

The flask glints into Granda's hand; the last dribble of whiskey clings to the neck of it. Farley knows then Granda's been tipping away at it because earlier at breakfast it had been full. Wiggy sips and swallows and says, 'Ah, that's grand.'

Farley is about to leave when he notices a jacket hanging on a nail; a newspaper rolled into the pocket. He notices too that Wiggy is wearing a different jacket with another newspaper rolled into its pocket. Wiggy seems content now, a baby again, smacking his lips and licking his gums and so Farley decides to chance it. 'Would you have a newspaper you're finished with, Wiggy? An old one will do.'

Wiggy frowns and says, 'God now, I don't know did I throw them out?'

'What about that one there, sticking out of the pocket? See, that jacket there,' Farley says.

'O right. I'd forgot about that. What date is on it? Have a look there.'

'Thursday.'

Wiggy takes the eggshell from the bottle and squeezes it in his hand, then he takes another sup of tea. Making him ask.

'Would it be alright if I took it?'

'What?'

'The paper?'

'Of course it would, youngfella. Take it away.'

'He's getting very interested in world affairs,' Granda says and Wiggy nods and says it's as well to keep informed.

Sunlight gushes down on the yard; the sudden burst of it, tiring his eyes so that all he really wants to do is lie down and go to sleep. But the thought of Concilia pushes him on. He walks past the manager's house where he notices the curtains are still drawn, then through the yard round by the back of the convent. He scans everywhere for Concilia; the lawns, the kitchen garden, the armada of bulging sheets outside the laundry, the windows all the way up to the crenellated rooftop where he reckons the music cells would be. He comes round by the front, keeping enough distance from the house itself, so that even if he can't see her, she might happen to look down and see him. In his head he hears Frank Sinatra singing 'Autumn Leaves' – 'But I miss you most of all, my darling, when autumn leeeeaves start to fall,' and he imagines himself, as he is in this moment, appearing in a later conversation. She will say: 'It was when I looked down from the window and saw you walking through leaves, I knew then I could never be a nun, that from then on my heart could only go in the one direction.' She would take off her wimple, her long blonde – no, black hair would collapse onto her shoulders, he would lean down to her and find her lips and— He turns the corner of the house but all he finds is Jimmy Ball's black bicycle, empty basket frame tilted into a pot of geraniums, and there at the front steps Jimmy himself with a basket hooked onto his arms.

'What the fuck you doin here?' Jimmy asks.

'Helping me granda.'

'Where's he then?'

'Talkin to Wiggy.'

'That fuckin thickhead.'

'I've to check the light bulbs in the classrooms.'

'Left school have you? About time too. Don't know how the fuck you stuck it that long. Tell you what – they like their breakfast, this lot.' He hoists the basket to show. 'Drippin, rashers, the two puddins – O, and plenty of sausages. I'd say they're fond of a sausage in here.' Jimmy winks and sticks out a pink sloppy tongue.

Farley looks into the basket at the shapes of butcher's parcels stacked inside. He feels likes saying, 'What do you expect them to eat – grass?' But he nods and says nothing. He's always been afraid of big fat Jimmy Ball.

'So, what are you goin to do with your life then? Just fuckin work here for the nuns?'

'No. No, I always help out before term begins.'

'Doin what? Checkin the fuckin light bulbs? Sure that's not a job.'

'During the summer I was working in the stables when the races were on. Mucking out and that.'

'Sure that's only now and then. That's fuck all use. And what'll you do when the flat season is over? The smell of horse shite – disgustin. Don't know how you put up with it. No. What you want is a real job. I can ask if they need an apprentice in my place. I'm well in there, me. Boss thinks I can do no wrong, fuckin thickhead he is. One fella's missing the tops of three fingers – would you credit that? Two from the right, one from the left. You'd want to see him slaughter a pig.' Jimmy lets out a long pig squeal and then beams with admiration.

Farley looks down at Jimmy's stained apron, the dried blood under his fingernails, the offside stare in one eye that makes it impossible to look him straight in the face.

'I'm going to write to me da's old boss. He probably won't give me a job in his office but he might refer me on to a colleague. Well, anyway, that's what he said at the funeral.'

'Right,' Jimmy says, 'suit your fuckin self so. By the way. Sorry to hear about your da.'

'Thanks.'

'No bother.'

The convent door opens then and Jimmy turns towards it. 'Ah, good morning, sister,' he says, in a careful grown-up voice. 'I have your delivery here, sorry to disturb you now but I tried round the back and there was no reply.'

Concilia stands aside, pulling the door with her into the entrance hall. They step in and she closes it, then the skirt of her habit swings around and glides away. They follow until they get to the kitchen then stand for a moment and watch her disappear up a long straight corridor. The dull polished sheen to its floor makes him think of a street after rain and he imagines the two of them walking along, her linking his arm, the collar of her trench coat pulled up to protect her black – no, blonde hair, the lights from the shops dribbing onto the street and her purring into his ear, 'The age difference doesn't matter to me; why you're more mature than most men *twice* your age.'

From the side of his mouth Jimmy Ball drops a comment – 'An awful waste that – know what I mean?' Farley doesn't know where to look. To say such a thing. About a nun. About Concilia. He feels shocked, outraged, and utterly thrilled.

Granda lifts the back of his hand and pats his eyes dry. Farley doesn't know if this is because his eyes are sore on account of the mustard gas during the war, or if maybe he's crying again. Da's death seems to have made Granda old. He takes longer to haul the trunks up the stairs than he did last term, with more heaving sighs than usual and more rests needed, not just on the landings either but now mid-stairs as well. Every time he stops he gasps out a few words.

'You have to concentrate, son,' he says.

'I am concentrating.'

'No, I don't mean in carrying this thing. I mean generally, you have to get yourself *interested* in something. Know what I mean?'

A smell of whiskey wanders from Granda's breath all the way down the slope of the trunk. And this annoys Farley, because too much whiskey makes Granda stupid, repeating himself and generally talking through his arse telling him what he hasn't and has to be.

'You have to be a soldier now, Char-less, for your mother. A soldier like your granda. Your *two* grandas used to be.'

'I'm not a kid any more, Granda. You don't have to talk to me that way.'

'Exactly,' Granda Bill says and groans up another step. He stops again. 'I treated the two boys the same you know. Your da and your uncle Cal. I never favoured Cal though many expected me to.'

'I know that, Granda.'

Granda Bill nods. 'Where did you say this one is going again?'

'Middle dorm. Fourth bed down on the right.'

'Right. How do you think young Jackie is – would you say? Would you say now, he's alright?'

'I think so.'

'A bit quiet, would you not think now? Spends a lot of time on his own.'

'He's just playing with his collections and that.'

'His collections?'

'You know, the way he collects things – stamps, cards, now it's information on racehorses – he's making his own form book, you know?'

'O right. But he still seems too quiet. Surly like.'

Farley doesn't want to say his brother is always that way, that he's just like his da was, surly by nature.

The trunk bashes upwards stair by stair, the sound of it banging through the empty school like gunshot. 'We have to start thinkin about getting you boys home,' Granda says.

'Is Ma home then?'

'She will be on Monday.'

'Is she better?'

'Ah, better enough, I suppose. She'll be a while yet. And you pair will have to behave. How many stairs left behind me?'

Farley looks over his head. 'Four to the landing.'

'When you were a little fella you were in hospital – do you remember that?'

'Of course I do.'

'That was when your da was working down the country – do you remember that?'

'Yea.'

'And your poor ma was that worried about you, that when you were discharged she moved back to Dublin to nurse you better because, you see, you had to go for check-ups every week and the house in the country was too cold. Do you remember *that* now?'

'Ah Granda, yes, I remember. I remember it all. Come on, we better get a move on.'

'Well, now it's your turn to nurse her.'

'O great.'

Granda scoops up a long breath of air. 'You see, son, if you get your-self interested in things then you can you start working out the plan of your life – know what I mean?'

'I am interested in things.'

'Like what?'

Farley looks down at the trunk, the labels at their haphazard angles. Singapore. Hong Kong. Malaya. 'Travel,' he says, 'I'm interested in seeing places.'

'Good. Now *that's* good. But you have to find the *wherewithal* to travel, you know. You can't just take off like a bird. You have to work towards finding the means and the ways – hope you know.'

Granda sniffles up the last three steps. Bash. Bash. Bash. They stop on the landing and he puts his hands down on his thighs and hangs his head for a minute. Snuff-brown snot falls from his nose and Farley pre-tends not to notice. He looks through the window over Granda's bent back; the leaves on the red beech jiggling on the branches. The big wall behind it. Then he looks at the trunk again. It's been sent from Hong Kong ahead of the girl. The girl's name: Vida Singleton. And he wonders what a girl with such a name could look like and how come she was born so lucky.

Granda takes out a hanky and ruffles it over his nose. 'Fourth bed on the right did you say?'

They drag the trunk through. Along the rows of beds other trunks stand like headstones. They reach the fourth bed and Granda sits on the end of it. He seems a bit shook.

'It's a sad time, son,' he says. 'A sad time for us all.' And he begins to cry again.

'Would you like a rest, Granda?'

Granda nods.

'Will I go on so?' Farley says.

Granda nods.

'Will I give you half an hour say? Will I see you outside Sister Martha's office then, after you have a little rest?'

Granda nods again, then lays his head down on the striped ticking of Vida Singleton's naked pillow.

He finds her weeding plots in the little graveyard on the hillock. He stays at the entrance and looks at her for a while. She seems so calm, kneeling on a cushion, stooped over a grave. Her skirt is clipped Bo-Peep style at the side and two puff sleeves sit high on her arms so he can see her wrists and the shape of her bare arms as far as her elbows. She keeps flicking her veil back over her shoulder as if it's hair. He stays still, barely breathes in fact, but she knows he's there anyway, because without turning around she asks if he would be kind enough to pass her a trowel from the box by the gate. She takes it from him without looking at his face, then just holds it in her right hand while her left hand plucks and fingers the soil. She asks if he likes school and he says no, not at all.

'We all have to do things we don't like,' she says serenely.

She has a mole, he notices, on the side of her face, dark like a beauty spot. And something about the mole makes him afraid of her. His stomach feels queasy, sweat greases his palms.

'Now you ask *me* something,' she says

'Like what?'

'You know, a question. I asked you if you like school. And you answered. Now your turn. You ask, I answer. And what with all the questions and answers threading between us, we can make a conversation in no time.'

The way she said *threading*. Her tongue plotting the word through her teeth.

Farley says, 'Alright then, where are you from?'

'Ayrshire. That's Scotland in case you don't know. Where are you from?'

He looks back over his shoulder and says, 'Down the road.'

She gives a small laugh. 'Down the road? How old are you?' she asks him.

'Fifteen. How old are you?'

'You should never ask a lady her age,' she says with a soft upward glance.

'You're not a lady, you're a nun,' he says.

'That's not a question. You're supposed to ask me a question.'

'What's your name?'

'They call me Concilia. And I'm not a nun. I'm a postulant.'

'What's that?'

'It's not your turn,' she scowls. 'You're supposed to wait your turn. You look a lot older than fifteen.'

'Do I?' he asks.

'Yes. I had a brother who died in the war but nobody cares a *jot* about him.' She smiles again. 'I suppose you shave and everything?'

He feels his face flare up. 'It's not your turn,' he says stiffly and the smile slips off her face. He looks away, mortified. After a moment he returns with an answer to her question: 'Sometimes. Sometimes I shave.'

'*What?* I can't understand what you're saying, all this mumbling and muttering and—'

'Sometimes.' His face is so hot now that his skin is ready to crack.

'Sometimes,' she repeats with a quiet, cruel sneer that makes him dislike her. She begins stabbing the soil of the grave with the trowel.

'Did you bring my newspaper?'

He takes it out of his pocket and lays it down beside her.

'Did you tell anyone you were bringing it?'

'No,' he says.

'Good. I read all sorts of things in your papers. Horrific things, you know. No wonder they don't let us read them in here. Do you know what I read in the last paper? I read about this wee baby who burned to death in his pram. Did you read about that?'

'No. No I didn't.'

'A candle left on the shelf above, dropped into the pram in the middle of the night. Can you credit that? Not the mother's fault, the judge said. Well, who's fault was it then, that's what I'd like to know?' Her voice is lifting. Anger.

'I don't know,' Farley says.

'That wasn't a question. I know you don't know. Honestly!'

Farley waits a few seconds and says, 'Anyway, I have to—'

'Aye, away you go, wee boy.'

'So long then.'

She speaks so quietly now. 'If you tell anyone we've been speaking or that I asked you to bring me a newspaper, I'll say you tried to rape me.'

'*What?*'

'I'll say you tore my clothes off and tried to kiss me and then you tried to put your thing into me. That's what I'll say. They will easily believe me. Because even if it's *not* true it's what you really want to do. So in the eyes of God you are in fact a rapist.'

He stares at the back of her head trying to come to terms with her words. Then he turns and begins to run.

He runs back down the slope of the field but before he gets to the boundary fence, has to stop because he can't breathe. He's crying now; the tears, hard and angry and sore as if he's crying hailstones. It feels as if they're ramming up against him before pushing through his skin. He stands under the trees and waits for it to pass. After a while he feels able to pull himself together and begins to briskly walk. He has to get off the convent grounds, the thoughts of running into one of the nuns. Or Wiggy. Or Jimmy Ball. Or anyone at all. And the thoughts of walking down Knockmaroon Hill with Granda half-buckled beside him. Or sitting amongst old men for the afternoon, choking on their smoke and their stupid horse talk. If he hurries back to Gran's he can tell Jackie he's not feeling well and send him back to meet Granda on his own. If he hurries back to Gran's she might still be out buying her Saturday messages and he can sneak into the bedroom for a lie-down, no questions asked. He will not think about the woman in the graveyard, the walk on the rain-coated street, the colour of her hair. He will not think about anyone or anything, just how to get back to Gran's and hide there and never think about or come near this place again.

Farley leaves by the side gate and stays by the wall where the ground is still slippy and there's less chance of bumping into anyone. He's stopped crying now and feels he may never cry again, but he doesn't want to see anyone because he's afraid they will guess, the way people always seem to recognize shame. He stays by the wall until it stops shielding the convent and becomes part of the Guinness estate. The ground here is flooded, small impassable lakes of old rain and the only way past them is to veer away from the trees. The light broadens. A racehorse springs into view coming from the direction of Castleknock Gate; the horse's legs bunching and unbunching in a slow, tight canter. Farley stops and lowers his head, in case the rider is one of the lads from the stables. He thinks about taking cover, but it's all open space here, bar a few scrawny sapling trees, tottering like cripples in iron braces. He feels like running back, or diving into a ditch. But in the end it doesn't matter, because the horse points itself towards the Fifteen Acres and the rider, hands pushed down, head lowered, is preoccupied with staying on his mount.

They have left an archway of daylight behind them. Farley sees another shape there. A figure. This time he doesn't try to hide but moves towards the figure, recognizing more and more of it, as they come closer to each other.

By White Gate's Lodge they both stop.

'Sandwiches for the racing,' Jackie says, lifting his elbow to show the package under his arm, 'chocolate and all.' For once he seems cheerful.

'What are you doin here?' Farley asks him. 'You were supposed to wait for us to collect you.'

'Gran had a visitor. The woman from the funeral – with the pigeon hat? Except she wasn't wearing it. The hat, I mean. She's a culchie by the way. And Gran doesn't like her.'

'How do you know?'

'I heard her talking. She talks like Master Barry.'

'No – I mean, how do you know Gran doesn't like her?'

'Don't know, just do.'

'I'm going home,' Farley says.

'Home, home or home to Gran's?'

'Gran's.'

'You can't go. You'll just get sent back out again.'

'Why?'

'Because of the visitor.'

'I won't go near them.'

'I'm telling you, you'll only be sent back out. Here – do you think I look like Da?'

'A bit. Why?'

'Nothing. I came into the kitchen while they were talking and the woman said, That's his son isn't it? And Gran says yes and your woman goes, My God, he's the image of him and then she pulls a hanky out of her bag and starts sniffing.'

Jackie waits for a minute. 'So? Are you comin or what?'

'I don't know.'

'Well, I'm not standing here all day, anyway. I'm off,' Jackie says, passing him by. 'I'm going to win today – I just know I am.'

For a few seconds Farley watches his brother move away. When he reaches the start of the Guinness estate he calls out after him, then breaking into a trot, follows him on the bridle path back towards the convent wall.

The Fly-fisher

December 1940

HE KNOWS IT'S A visiting day. Everyone gets clean pyjamas, even the boys who never get visitors, and one nurse goes round tightening all the beds and another goes round combing all the boys' hair to one side. He knows it's nearly three o'clock. The ginger boy has turned the other way letting on to be asleep because he says he hates stupid visiting hour and once in the toilets he told Buddy that he even wrote a letter to his ma down the country telling her if she ever came up to see him he'd give her such a punch in the stomach.

'To his own ma? Did he say that, *really*?' he asked when Buddy told him, whispering in the dark across their two beds. '*His own ma?*'

'That's what he said.'

'His own ma.'

He knows it's three o' clock on the dot. All the boys' heads are turned to the door to see who's first in and it's usually Buddy's ma unless she has to go to work selling fruit outside the races. But today it can't be her because Buddy's not even here.

'Nurse, excuse me, nurse, hey, nurse, comere – where did you say Buddy is gone again?'

'I told you, he's gone for an X-ray and then to see the doctor – do you not remember me telling you that?'

'No. I mean I don't know.'

'Are you feeling a bit tired again?'

'No. Will he not be back in time for the visitors?'

'Tea time I'd say now before we see him again.'

'Tea time? Ah nurse, that's *ages.*'

Buddy's his best pal and his ma is the best visitor ever. She comes into the ward speaking in her sore throat voice and whicking her scarf off her head with her big purple hands. She has lemon-coloured hair and her eyes are grassy green, same as Buddy's. She wears a spotty pinny under her two coats and one jacket, with big pockets low on the front and you can hear the coins jigging inside when she walks along. For the first few minutes she's always freezing then she starts taking off her coats and jacket, pulling sneaky bars of chocolate out of all the pockets on the way and throwing them at the boys to catch or leaving one under the ginger boy's pillow and not caring a bit if it's against the rules. 'Ah, bugger them oul nurses and ask me big brown barney,' is what she always says and then everyone shouts out laughing.

Buddy is always first to laugh with his mouth wide open. But you can see his eyes are looking all around to make sure everyone else thinks she's funny too.

Things keep going *fizzzz* in his head. They come in, they go *fizzz* and then they melt away again. Gran says it's on account of his tablets.

She's sitting on one corner of the bed now, looking at him with her head to one side. Granda Bill is sitting on a chair on the opposite side. And he's not sure how long they've been there because it feels like only a minute ago since he saw them coming through the door, but it feels too like he might have fallen asleep again.

'Take your time,' she says.

'What, Gran? Take my what time – what, Gran?'

'Answering the question. Take your time.'

She pulls the pin out of her hat, puts it on her lap and sticks the pin back in again.

'Ouch,' Granda Bill says, letting on to be the voice of the hat and then he knows that visiting time is only starting because the first thing Granda Bill always does is pretend to be the hat going *ouch*.

'What did you ask me again?' he says.

'What's your number? Your hospital number. Think now, there's a good boy.'

'Em.'

'What's the first number then?'

'Five,' he says. 'Five, like my age.'

'Good. Now what's after that?'

'Three like my little brother's age. Then...' he puts his hands in the air and shouts, 'Ten like all the fingers I have!'

'Shhh, shhh, good boy,' Gran laughs, 'you'll waken that little ginger chap.' Then she goes, 'Five, three – and what's another way to say ten?'

'Don't know.'

'One O. You can say – my hospital number is five, three, ten. Or you can say, it's five, three, one, O. Have you got that now?'

'Here – what age is our baby?'

'There's no baby,' Gran says. Granda Bill turns around on his seat and folds his coat over the back of it.

'Gran?'

'Yes lovey?'

'Em, what was I goin to say, eh, comere. I just... O yea, the bed is too tight, it's choking me stomach. I can't move, I can't *move*.'

Gran comes to the top of the bed, tugs up the clothes and he feels it loosen. 'Better?'

He nods and pulls the blankets down past his hips. 'Buddy's not here, he's gone for an X. An X-ray.'

'Is he now?'

'What's that mean? Granda Bill, what's that mean – gone for an X-ray?'

'Well, what happens is this – they put you behind this machine and what it does now is it takes a photograph of your insides. And you can see your skeleton.'

'Skeleton?'

'O yes, all your bones and behind them your heart, your guts – the works. They can see everything that's going on in there.'

'Wait till I show you,' Gran says and she leans down to her shopping bag and for a minute he thinks she's going to take out a picture of her skeleton but it's only a newspaper that comes out of her bag. She sits back on the end of the bed and starts turning the pages, licking her finger. He wriggles his way out of the bedclothes, kneels up and crawls to her, putting his hand up to trap a whisper into her ear.

'You're not allowed have newspapers in here. Or comics. Buddy's ma brought in a comic and the boss nurse went mental. But Buddy's ma didn't care. See, Gran, paper brings all the Germans in and they make us sick.'

Gran laughs. 'Not *Germans* – *germs*. Did you hear that?' she asks Granda, 'he says you're not allowed bring papers in because the Germans will make you sick. Instead of the *germs*.'

'Same difference, some might say,' Granda Bill says and winks at him.

Gran turns him so that now he's sitting with his back to her. Her arm comes over his shoulder and he feels like a big soft chair behind him. 'See, that's your hospital number there. Five, three, one, O,' she says. He follows her fingertip and looks at the number. 'And that's your hospital up there.' Gran brings her finger up to the top of the page. 'Cork Street Fever Hospital – see? That's where we are now.'

He nods at all the rows of letters and numbers.

'And far away, way down the country your mammy and daddy are—'

'Where down the country?'

'A place called Cork.'

'Cork?'

'That's right. Anyway, they're sitting in their kitchen—'

'What colour is their kitchen?'

'I don't know, I've never seen it. Anyway, this very minute they're sitting down, looking at a page just like this and they're reading these words here: "5310 – continues to improve." And they're delighted because do you know what that means?'

He shakes his head.

'It means you're nearly better.'

'It means you could be home before Christmas,' Granda Bill says.

'Well, now we don't know that for certain,' Gran says, lifting a finger. 'We don't want to be getting our hopes up.'

'Is my da not gone fishing?'

'Fishing?' Gran says.

Granda Bill says, 'That's one way of putting it.'

Behind his back he feels Gran stiffen.

'Gran?' he begins but the curly nurse comes in before he has a chance to think of a question and Gran hooshes him up and back into bed. Then she folds the paper and puts it back in her basket. Gran takes a bottle of lemonade and a little bundle wrapped up in a cloth out of her bag. She pulls the cloth away and shows him a currant cake.

'Nice?' she says, and puts them into his locker and he nods his head yes.

'Nurse?' he calls out to the curly nurse. 'What time will Buddy be back?'

'After tea, I told you.'

'Don't be shouting at the nurse you,' Gran says, 'manners, please!'

He lies back on the pillows. 'Where's Cork?' he says to Gran.

'It's a county down the country, where your mammy and daddy are.'

'Why?'

'Well, your daddy has to work there for a while, so they're living there.'

'Why can't he just work here?'

'You see, son,' Granda Bill says, 'because of the war there's not as much work up here for your da as there used to be, and so that's why he had to move to Cork. Now your poor ma was too lonely up here all on her ownio so she followed him down because you see—'

'Ah, there's no point explaining all that to him,' Gran says, 'he's only a child.' Then she gives a big tut and tosses her eyes.

'Buddy's ma comes every visiting day. And on the other days she stands on the street and you hear this big whistle and then when you look out there she is waving up.'

'Lovely carry-on,' Gran says.

Granda Bill laughs. Then he puts three fingers up in the air. 'See, son, when you think about it, there's three reasons why your ma and da can't come up to see you. One – your da has to work. Two – there's no petrol for travel. And three – if your mammy came in here she could bring the germs back to little Jackie and then he'd be sick too.' Granda puts his fingers back into his hand.

'O. Three reasons. O.' He thinks about that for a minute then says, 'When I'm all better will I have to live down the country?'

'Not for a while. You'll stay with your gran and me, till you're ready and back in fighting form. Nearer the summertime.'

'But your mammy will probably come up and see you. And she might stay for a few weeks even. Once you get the all-clear,' Gran says.

'With my da?'

'No. He'll have to work.'

'And my brother?'

'Ye-es. Yes, he'll have to come too because who's going to mind him while your daddy's at work?'

'And fishing. Because he's too small to bring fishing.'

'Yes.'

'And the baby because the baby's—'

'There's no baby, I told you,' Gran says. Granda Bill stands up, takes a breath through his teeth then slowly walks up the ward. When he gets to the top he stops at the long window looking out.

He wonders why Granda Bill wants to look out that window because there's nothing to see there, only a tin roof below. The other window would be better to look out because it's on the far side of the ward and when you look down you can see a big piece of Cork Street and all the things going by; carts and horses, wheels of the bikes, people with all their different hats on their heads. Or Buddy's ma. The first time he ever saw Buddy's ma she was down on the street waving up. He'd only just been moved into the ward from another ward that he can't even remember now and when they heard the big whistle Buddy said that was his ma and if he liked he could look down with him and pretend she was his ma too. But when he looked down he knew there was no point in letting on really because, even though he couldn't remember his own ma that well, he knew she was too different to that big woman down there with a big man's coat on her and a scarf instead of a hat and a pram stuffed with apples and sweets instead of a baby.

'Gran?'

'Are you tired, love?' Gran says. 'Here – stop picking your nose, making a show of me.'

Gran takes out a hanky and wraps a bit of it around her finger and starts picking his nose instead.

'Are you sure there's no baby? See I remember, ow, Gran, that's hurtin me – ow – nose.'

'Sorry, love.'

'And I thought the name was something beginning with Bar, bar, bee. Something like that. A girl baby, Gran.'

Gran turns the hanky inside out and puts it back in her pocket.

'What did you have for your dinner?'

'I don't know, brown stuff.'

'Brown stuff? Don't like the sound of that – did you eat it?'

'Some. Anyway, I can't go home before Christmas because then see, Buddy will be on his own and anyway Santy thinks I'm here because I already sent him a letter.'

'We can send Santy another letter. And what happens if your mammy comes all the way up from the country to see you for Christmas and you're not there. Sure that'd break her heart.'

208

'Well. Well, she can't come. She'll have to stay down the country and mind my little brother and the—'

Gran sniffs her nose. 'Why don't you go for a little sleep, lovey?'

'I'm not tired, Gran,' he says, 'I'm not. And I'm fed up of everyone saying I'm tired. And I'm *not*.'

But his eyes keep trying to close on their own, even when he pops them out wide.

'Why don't you close your eyes then for a little minute? You're very whingey, that means you're tired.'

'Ah no, I'm not whingey, I'm not. You'll only go home if I close my eyes. You'll only leave me.' He bashes his fists off the downturn of the sheet.

'I won't. I'll stay.'

'Do you promise but? Do you promise?'

'I said I'll stay. I promise I'll stay.'

'Till Buddy comes back?'

'We'll see.'

'Ah, don't say we'll see. I hate when you say we'll see.'

Gran puts her hands under his pillow on both sides of his head and pulls the pillow around his ears and makes it rock side to side. 'Isn't that nice and sleepy now?' she says. 'Isn't that nice and cosy?'

'Till the bell rings then, Gran?'

'Till the bell rings.'

He lets his eyes close. Orange and pink curtains. He can hear all the sounds in the ward; the different voices at the different beds. A coughing boy on the end of the row, another boy crying because his ma never came up. He can even hear the soft footsteps of the curly nurse coming up to his bed and asking Gran how things are.

'He keeps asking about the baby,' he hears Gran say.

'Just ignore him, pass no remark and he'll forget about it sooner or later.'

He wants to say he doesn't forget. He saw it, he smelled it and once he even held it in his arms and touched its little pink bootee. Bar bar bar. Ba.

209

But his eyes won't move at all now and his tongue feels fat and lazy in his mouth. Everything inside his head is gone fizzy again.

He thinks about County Cork far down the country. He thinks about Cork Street out the window. And how come you need petrol for one and not for the other and what's far away and what's not.

The boss nurse slapped him because they were playing Jumpthebeds. There were four of them playing; him, Buddy, a boy called Harry who went home the next day and the ginger boy who'd only just arrived but wouldn't tell them his name yet. There was no one in the little glass room and no sign of a nurse up and down the corridor and that's why they thought they were safe to play. He was on Buddy's team and halfway down their row of beds jumping on and off, bed after bed fast as they could go, trying not to wake the boys that were sleeping and trying to get the biggest jump out of the four empty beds because the bigger you jump the faster you go and Buddy standing at the end of the row saying, 'Come on, come on, we're winnin we're winnin!' And then suddenly she came flying into the ward out of nowhere and Harry said after you'd think she was on a broomstick she came in that quick and that quiet.

She caught him first, pulling him down off the bed and swinging him around and then giving him a wallop on first the bum and then another smack on the back of his head. Then she leapt over to the side and trapped Buddy in the corner and for a while they were skidding this way and that, her with her arms out wide and her feet making little hops. Buddy trying to scuttle under and around her and then he got fed up with that and anyway he'd started coughing again so he just said, 'You touch me and I'm tellin me ma the next time she comes up.' And that was the end of the slapping. Harry and the ginger boy got off free.

She shouted instead, 'Ye get back in that bed this minute, ye shower of little gurriers or I'll schalp the lot of ya.'

After the smack he dived into bed and covered his head and first he thought he was just going to laugh like everyone else was under the covers, but then he started to cry. And he didn't know why because the smacks didn't hurt him all that much, unless it was the fright of her long bony hands and her big angry face and unless it was because it wasn't fair that he was the only one who got slapped when it wasn't even his idea to play Jumpthebeds. And unless it was because he wished he had something to say, like Buddy had to say, about telling his ma on the next visiting day.

The curly nurse says they're too giddy. 'You pair are too giddy by far,' she says. 'Now, I'm warning, if you don't pipe down I'm calling the doctor to give the pair of you a big needle in the bum.'

He likes the curly nurse. She makes funny faces and sometimes when she's on night duty she tells them a story. Once in the middle of the night her and another nurse taught him and Buddy how to dance. The nurses were whispering and laughing in the glass room and he could hear the radio music and they couldn't sleep so Buddy shouted out, 'Nurse, I'm burstin!'

And then he shouted out, 'Nurse, I'm burstin too!'

And the two nurses came out and said they were a right pair of chancers. They'd left the glass door open behind them and the music was louder and Buddy started wriggling his arms and he said, 'Hey what's that music, nurse? What's that music?'

The curly nurse said, 'That's only the great Glen Miller.' And then the other nurse started dancing around wagging her hands and the two boys copied her and then they stood up on their beds and now they were tall enough to dance with the nurses, twirling them under their arms. After a few minutes the curly nurse lifted him off the bed and they danced all around, all the way down the ward. Then they danced out the door. And they danced down the corridor and she dipped him and lifted him and swang his legs around one side of her body and then back the other and she da da dahed into his ear and he couldn't stop laughing for a while and then he did stop laughing and just felt the walls going round and round and up and down with the music, and the biscuity smell of her black curly hair bursting out from under her white hat and the sound of his breathing and her voice in his ear, singing.

The clatter of rain on the tin roof wakes him up and the first thing he notices is that Buddy is gone. It's night-time but he can still see through the dark by the small blobs of red from the nightlights and the yellow light coming out from the glass room, that Buddy is gone. He sits up in the bed and peeps down towards the door of the ward; the shape of the bent head in the glass room means that tonight the boss nurse is in charge. He tries to see the locker on the far side of Buddy's bed. Buddy keeps all sorts of things in his locker; tin boxes mostly – of marbles, of pencil butts, of soldiers, and there's more than a dozen Dinky cars in there and a red London bus as well.

He lies for a minute and tries to remember if Buddy came back from his X-ray. He was supposed to come back for his tea. But he can't remember now what day it is – if it was a boiled egg tea or a square cheese tea or a Sunday bun tea. He slides out of bed, the soles of his feet make a slap on the floor and he waits to see if the boss nurse has heard him. But she's still writing stuff in her book. He looks around the ward at the shapes of the sleeping bodies. He looks at all the Christmas things hanging up; tinsel twirled through the bars on the beds and the picture of Santy on the wall and the paper chains that him and Buddy made to go between their two beds. And now he's standing at Buddy's bed. The locker is open and there's a smell of cleaning stuff off it and all the tins are gone and the cars and the red bus too. All that's left is the mattress rolled up at the top.

'Where's Buddy?' he asks the boy on the other side, shaking him awake.

'What?'

'Where's Buddy gone?'

'How do I know? Lemealone.'

'Where's Buddy?' he asks the boy across the ward, shoving his shoulder to wake him up.

The boy pulls himself up on his elbow, rubs one of his sticky-out ears and shakes his head slowly.

He goes to the window at the end of the ward and looks up at the big blackout curtain. He gives a jump and tries to grab onto a corner but he's too small to reach it. So he gets a chair and staggers with it across the room. Then he climbs up on the chair and pulls a gap in the side of the curtain and pulls and tugs until thumbtacks start to pop out. He climbs again and now he's on the window cill. It's the wrong window; he knows that. But the window for Cork is on the other side of the ward and it's too near the nurse in her glass room. This is the window where you see nothing only the tin roof and you can't even see it that well now because all the other windows of the hospital are blacked out. The rain has stopped and he looks for the night sky. But he can't see it either. He can't see the street and he can't see Buddy. He can't see anything. The dark is too dark.

'Buddy's gone,' he says to Gran.

'Well, he must have gone home so,' Gran says.

But he knows by her face that's not true.

'He went in the middle of the night.'

'Are you sure? Maybe you were asleep.'

'He went in the middle of the night and his things are gone except for his cars and his red London bus that are all washed and clean out in the playroom.'

'But sure he might have left them for the other kids to play with.'

He knows by her face.

'Buddy's gone,' he says and starts crying.

He wakes up in a different bed. A bed as big as a field. It has a thick quilt with all different green shapes that makes a funny noise when he moves. It's Gran's bed. There's a pair of Granda Bill's trousers over the chair, and Gran's net for her hair is on the dressing table.

'What's he doing that with his eyes for?' somebody says and he sees a little boy standing at the end of the bed.

'Who are you?' he asks the boy.

'Who are you?' the little boy asks back.

And now there's a woman standing behind the little boy. The woman is wearing a blue coat. Gran comes in behind them and says, 'Ah, there he is, awake at last. Well – look who's come all the way up to see you.'

'All the way up from down the country?' he asks.

'That's right,' the woman in the blue coat says and then starts to cry.

'What's wrong with her?' he asks Gran and Gran gives him a look.

He turns in the bed, the way the ginger boy used to do, and presses his face into Gran's long sausage pillow.

'Ah, he's a bit shy,' Gran says, 'he's bound to make a bit strange at first.'

He presses his face harder into the pillow and he can get Gran's flowery smell now and Granda Bill's snuffy smell and even though his eyes are shut and squashed into the pillow, he can still see the shape of the people at the end of the bed. He counts the shapes, then he lifts his face and looks at them for a second just to be sure; the woman in her blue coat, the little boy in his cap.

'Where's the man?' he says, 'is he gone fishing?'

The woman stops crying. 'He has to work,' she says.

He puts his face back in the pillow again. And he can't work it out because when he closes his eyes into the pillow the woman is holding something up in her arms. But when he looks back into the room, her arms are just folded.

He feels himself shrink into the pillow. He opens his mouth and sounds come out but they don't shape into words. His face is lying against something white and smooth and for a minute he thinks it might be the pillow or it might be the woman's skin but it's too cold and too hard to be either. And the smell. The smell of dust and piss. The sound. The gentle sound of water.

*

214

The sound of gentle water. He sees now that he's on a river; a basket at one side of him, a cloth spread out on the bank. Coloured jewels and feathery knick-knacks across it. He holds a long bendy stick in one hand. A rod. That's what it is. A rod in one hand, a wire in the other like the string of a bow. He's wearing rubber boots that come up to his thigh; boots that he recognizes from a box in an attic: his father's boots. He takes a step down and the water, cool through the rubber, licks around his ankles, over his shins. He feels himself sway, yet his feet are held firm. He knows nothing of where he is or why he is here. In a river. Fishing. Yet his mind seems to know what to do. His mind is sharp. He can follow the course of each thought; strong, swift, all encompassing. Out over a glittering river he watches it loop, flick and cut. The precise glint of it, against an audience of thick dark river trees. He can feel his body sway again; side to side, back, forward. A dizziness spreads through his legs, arms, chest and throat. His heart burns and swells. Yet his feet remain solid and wedged into the bed of the river. It is sunset or maybe sunrise but either way he notices a soft reddish hue is beginning to spill into the sky, fall over the trees, along the bank, down into the river. He is alone. Alone on the river bank. A man, a boy, a child, a baby, a man again, all at once.

He sends his command like a fly to the target. He sends it again, and again it returns. Each time it comes back to him he feels a moment of futile joy.

Christine Dwyer Hickey is an award-winning novelist and short story writer. Twice winner of the Listowel Writers' Week short story competition, she was also a prize-winner in the prestigious *Observer*/Penguin short story competition. Her bestselling novel *Tatty* was chosen as one of the 50 Irish Books of the Decade, longlisted for the Orange Prize and shortlisted for the Hughes & Hughes Irish Novel of the Year Award, for which her novel *The Dancer* was also shortlisted. Her most recent bestseller, *Last Train from Liguria*, was nominated for the Prix Européen de Littérature. She lives in Dublin.

Acknowledgements

The author would like to acknowledge the assistance of the Irish Arts Council in the writing of this book.